CANDLELIGHT
Supreme

"JAMES THREATENED ME AGAIN TODAY," BRENDA SAID IN A SHAKY VOICE.

"He keeps holding this stupid thing over my head. Why would he do that if he had nothing to hide?"

"Maybe he wanted to protect me from finding out that the woman I've been sleeping with has also been putting the moves on my brother!" Zack replied, a sardonic expression darkening his face.

"No! I didn't! I wasn't!"

"Oh no? Sounds like you were milking both of us for your own pleasure."

"Zack! Surely you trust me more than that! I'm telling you . . ."

"I know what you're telling me. You've enticed both of us. And now you want to get rid of one of us."

"Oh God, that's not true! I love you, Zack!"

"And I love my brother. You're a fool for trying to come between us." He walked out, leaving her staring, too shocked to cry, too stunned to move.

CANDLELIGHT SUPREMES

QUANTITY SALES

Most Dell Books are available at special quantity discounts when purchased in bulk by corporations, organizations, and special-interest groups. Custom imprinting or excerpting can also be done to fit special needs. For details write: Dell Publishing Co., Inc., 1 Dag Hammarskjold Plaza, New York, NY 10017, Attn.: Special Sales Dept., or phone: (212) 605-3319.

INDIVIDUAL SALES

Are there any Dell Books you want but cannot find in your local stores? If so, you can order them directly from us. You can get any Dell book in print. Simply include the book's title, author, and ISBN number, if you have it, along with a check or money order (no cash can be accepted) for the full retail price plus 75¢ per copy to cover shipping and handling. Mail to: Dell Readers Service, Dept. FM, 6 Regent Street, Livingston, N.J. 07039.

ISLAND OF SECRETS

Tate McKenna

A CANDLELIGHT ECSTASY SUPREME

Published by
Dell Publishing Co., Inc.
1 Dag Hammarskjold Plaza
New York, New York 10017

Dell ® TM 681510, Dell Publishing Co., Inc.

Candlelight Supreme is a trademark
of Dell Publishing Co., Inc.

Candlelight Ecstasy Romance®, 1,203,540, is a registered trademark of Dell Publishing Co., Inc., New York, New York.

ISBN: 0-440-14141-9

Printed in the United States of America

August 1987

10 9 8 7 6 5 4 3 2 1

WFH

To Gen & Gil Ruston and Dee & Gus Harris,
sweethearts and lovers for over fifty years.

As always, to Rog who brings me the most
beautiful roses in Tucson.

To Our Readers:

We are pleased and excited by your overwhelmingly positive response to our Candlelight Supremes. Unlike all the other series, the Supremes are filled with more passion, adventure, and intrigue, and are obviously the stories you like best.

In months to come we will continue to publish books by many of your favorite authors as well as the very finest work from new authors of romantic fiction. As always, we are striving to present unique, absorbing love stories —the very best love has to offer.

Breathtaking and unforgettable, Supremes follow in the great romantic tradition you've come to expect *only* from Candlelight Romances.

Your suggestions and comments are always welcome. Please let us hear from you.

Sincerely,

The Editors
Candlelight Romances
1 Dag Hammarskjold Plaza
New York, New York 10017

ISLAND OF SECRETS

A steel screen separated the two faces. Impenetrable steel. But the two men ignored the barrier and spoke intently, as if it didn't even exist.

"You okay in there, James? Anything you need?"

"Yeah, sure. What's to need? They provide everything. That's part of the service here."

"How about some different tapes? Special food? Your TV's working okay?"

James Ehrens chuckled and his brown eyes crinkled as he forced a smile. "A woman. Send me a good-looking broad, Zack."

"I'm afraid that isn't on the list. Anyway, I'm not so good at picking them. Look what happened to my choice."

"Hell, Zack, Charmaine is one good-looking woman. Give her credit for that, at least. She's just a little spoiled."

"Yeah. She's a beauty, all right." There was a degree of bitterness in Zack's low, rumbling voice. "She couldn't take the rough times, though."

"Hell man, it was too much to expect of any woman." James leaned toward the wire mesh dividing their space. "You sure it's over for good?"

11

Zack nodded briefly. "Yep. Our divorce is final. She's gone back to Sacramento. It's a relief."

"And you?"

"I'm packing for Ireland. We're going to make it work there, James. You and me together. I swear it. By the time you arrive, Ehrens Enterprises will be humming again. Sometimes it's best to pick up the scattered pieces of your life and start all over somewhere else. I think this is one of those times."

James folded his arms on the cold metal desk between them and sighed. "Well, I sure as hell have made a mess of mine. But I don't know if another new start will do it for me."

"Course it will," Zack insisted. "As soon as you're out of here, you'll fly to Dublin. We'll work it out together. This time, we'll make sure it works, James. You'll see."

"You really take that saying about being your brother's keeper seriously, don't you, Zack ol' buddy?"

"I mean it this time. We'll do it. I'll give it all I have. But you have to make up your mind and give one hundred percent, too."

"Oh hell, Zack, of course I will. I've learned my lesson. Too many times. This is the last stretch I'm going to do in the slammer. But, I hadn't planned on skipping out of the country. Thought about going to Mexico once, but not this far away."

"You won't be skipping anything. I've already worked it out with your lawyer and the parole board. If you serve the maximum time, they'll let you leave on a six-month visa. If the first trial period goes okay, they'll extend it. You'll be under my custody, helping me—working for—our business. New start for both of us."

James shook his head and ran a hand raggedly over his darkly handsome face. "God knows I need it. I don't think I could have made it this time without you, Zack. It's been hell. Now you're arranging to get me out and head for a foreign country . . . hell, I couldn't ask for more."

"Ah, what're brothers for? We weren't able to do as much as we wanted, which was to keep you out of here."

"This one isn't too bad." James motioned to his surroundings. "The lawyer you got was okay. And with my good time, I'll be out in three or four months."

"Good time? You sound as though you're having a party in there. You mean time off for good behavior?"

"Yeah. It's no party."

There was an uneasy moment as the two brothers' eyes met and exchanged glances that revealed years of pain and frustration and disappointment. This wasn't the first time James had spent time in prison, nor the only time Zack had tried unsuccessfully to help his brother. This scene was all too familiar—the two handsome, similarly chiseled faces huddled together, separated by a wire screen.

"Ireland isn't going to be like a foreign country," Zack said after a moment. "There's no language barrier, unless you get into the Gaelic areas."

"But they all have accents."

"Yes, but you get used to it quickly. And we'll have help with this. Through a government program, I contracted with an Irish law firm to help us make this transition. They'll assist us in picking the plant location, placing bids for the building contracts, even hiring the first employees. Believe me, with their economy, they want this to work as much as we do."

James watched his brother's enthusiasm grow as they talked about Ireland and the possibilities in store for them. Maybe it would provide what he needed, if he could get away from those who influenced him and tempted him with promises. He leaned forward. "What's it like over there?"

Zack recalled the place he'd just visited briefly. "It's a pretty country with rolling green hills. The people are warm and friendly; business opportunities are excellent. Lots of tax breaks. Support from the local government. Best of all, because of such high unemployment, there's a guarantee of a full plant of employees as soon as the building is completed."

"Hell, it sounds too good to be true."

"This is the break we needed, James. It's going to be better than we ever dreamed. These people want us there. They need the jobs we can provide."

"Us?" James laughed with a rueful chuckle and motioned around him. "I doubt that they really want me."

Zack shook his head. "They don't have to know about your past. You can start with a clean slate the minute you leave here."

James nodded slowly. "I can't believe you'd do all that for me."

"I'll do whatever is necessary."

"When do you leave?"

"Next week. Now you keep your nose clean in here.

14

You'll be joining me in Ireland for a new life before you know it."

"Hell, you spend an hour in this place and you know it. The bars are always there. I'll be counting the days, hell the hours!" James responded.

"Me too." Zack shifted uncomfortably. He hated the thoughts of having his brother in prison and leaving him there while he took off across the ocean.

"Maybe you're right, Zack. You always are. Sure could use a glass of Irish whiskey and a freckled-faced Irish girl about now."

"In due time." Zack chuckled. "But remember, moderation with both."

James eyed his older brother sheepishly. "You know I never went in for moderation."

"Some people wouldn't consider it a fault, James. For you, though, it just hasn't been right."

"But this time it will. I'm coming to Ireland a new man."

Zack thrust forward a strong thumbs-up fist since they couldn't shake hands. "See you in three months." He wheeled around and, long legs striding rapidly, disappeared down the hall.

James watched his older brother leave, then with a resigned sigh followed the uniformed guard back to the lock-up area. Maybe this time would be different. In Ireland. But he knew there were no guarantees in life. Especially in his. Oh, he'd try. But no guarantees. Life itself was too risky.

Zack Ehrens left the prison without looking back. Several of the guards eyed him suspiciously and the check-out man made sure of his identity before he opened the locked door leading to the outside. But

Zack was used to being mistaken for James. The two brothers who grew up on the streets of Philadelphia had always looked alike. But that was as far as the resemblance went. Inside, they were as different as night and day.

Right now, Zack felt as if he carried the weight of the world on his shoulders. And that world had fallen apart in the last six months. His business was bankrupt. His marriage down the drain. His brother imprisoned. His life was a damned wreck.

Would he be able to salvage anything with this new beginning in Ireland? He shoved the heavy metal door open and squinted in the California sun. Yes, by God, it had to get better.

CHAPTER ONE

He was a big man, she noticed on entering the pub. Raw-boned, angular, and lean. His shoulders were broad and stretched the tweed jacket to its limits. He laced and unlaced his large hands, as if he were uptight about this meeting. He shouldn't be. It was a simple arrangement. As she walked closer Brenda noted the slight graying in his dark brown hair and figured him to be thirty-four or five. And handsome.

"Hi. You must be Zack Ehrens. I'm Brenda O'Shea from McGuinness and Sons. We'll be working together."

They shook hands, and she slid into the booth opposite him.

His unsmiling response was puzzled and, she suspected, disapproving. "You're American?"

"Yes. Born in the U.S.A.," she quipped.

He didn't laugh.

A green-vested waiter approached and she ordered a pint of dark Guinness, Ireland's most popular stout. "You too, Mr. Ehrens?"

He nodded shortly. "Sure."

She folded her fair-skinned hands on the table.

"Now with your type of business, what will you need first, Mr. Ehrens?"

"Need, Ms. O'Shea?" *Everything,* he thought sarcastically. "Interesting question. Do you want the truth, or what's going through my mind at this moment?"

"Let me rephrase that," she said, smiling indulgently. "How can I help you? My job is to make yours easier."

"I liked the original question better," Zack said candidly. "You're the liaison?"

Brenda O'Shea met his gaze steadily. There was definite disappointment in his tone. "I've been assigned to you, Mr. Ehrens."

"An American woman? I hate to be discouraging, Ms. O'Shea, but I need someone who knows the ropes over here with a determination like steel to help me get my business off the ground."

"I think you'll find my determination measures up satisfactorily. And as for ropes, I won't leave you floundering. We need your business here in Ireland, and I intend to make it viable. I'm going to stick to you like glue for as long as you need me."

"Look, Ms. O'Shea, this is going to take lots of hard work, and I'm not sure you're the one to do it." His sharply chiseled face grew tight and his brown eyes seemed to darken as his voice took on a more serious tone.

There were tiny lines etched from the corners, but Brenda suspected they didn't get there because of smiling. The man was deadly serious, and Brenda was curious about why.

"If you're up to it, I am," she said simply.

"You're certainly stubborn, if nothing else." He glared at her, considering how he would approach her boss and ask for another liaison without making her look bad. She just seemed too softly feminine for the job he knew they faced. And he'd feel better working with a man, not this red-haired, blue-eyed beauty across the table. How the hell could he concentrate on business when she turned those fantastic blue eyes on him, anyway?

"Let's start by getting to know each other and dropping the formalities. First, call me Brenda." She paused to smile tightly. "I've been working in Ireland for two years. Yours isn't the first American business I've launched here. And I certainly hope it won't be the last. I ran my own business in Baltimore before coming here, so I do have business experience and some idea of your needs."

"You're right on top of the situation, then."

She amended her claim with a clearing of her throat. "Your, uh, business needs, that is. Of course, we'll have to work together on the unique elements of Ehrens Enterprises. I'll be glad to help you understand Ireland and its culture. That's very important for someone like you moving into another country with plans to hire the locals." Brenda stopped for a sip of her stout.

Zack pressed his lips together in a shrug. "Okay, so you have credentials."

Her eyes narrowed slightly. This one was going to be tough to convince. "According to my file, you're Zack Ehrens, President of Ehrens Enterprises," she continued. "And you're here to build a platinum processing plant in Ireland. Now, I'll admit, I know very little about platinum. Just how does your business work?"

"That's what I mean. You know nothing about this business."

"Not many people do, Mr. Ehrens. I'm assuming that's what's going to make your business unique and successful. Not every Tom, Dick, or Harry knows how to process platinum, for Pete's sake. I don't have to know how to shear sheep in order to sell a wool sweater. So, tell me how you do whatever you do in platinum." She ended, glaring at him.

He set his jaw and eyed the blue-eyed spitfire across the table. "To put it simply, we buy the rough ore in a pretty messy form and clean it up or process it into a refined or pure form of platinum. It rolls out of our plant, ready to sell in sheets a thousandth of an inch thick."

"Thank you for putting it so simply, for a simple mind," she said testily.

Her eyes flashed indignantly at him as she worked to control her temper with this temperamental man. He was, after all, a client. And she couldn't very well go back to Padraig and say, "We clashed and I lost the client."

But her spunk affected Zack, much to his own surprise. "Well, I uh, didn't mean to sound so condescending. It's just such a complicated process, it's hard to put it into layman's terms. Uh, laywoman's terms."

"You certainly wormed your way out of that one," she said with a tiny smile. She still wasn't convinced he had confidence in her ability, but felt she had to find out more about his business. "Where do you buy this rough ore?"

"Mostly from mines in Canada. Also, Colombia and South Africa."

"None from the United States?"

"The mines haven't proven profitable yet. There is one in Montana that shows promise."

"And who buys your finished product?"

"We're negotiating accounts in England and Sweden. But when the plant is closer to producing, we'll be able to sell to any number of places."

"What's platinum used for?"

"It has thousands of uses," he said enthusiastically. "It's an excellent catalyst with a very high melting point. It's used in cars, spacecraft, missiles, electronic pacemakers, glass, jewelry, dentistry—"

Brenda held up her hand. "Catalyst?"

"A catalyst starts a chemical reaction while remaining unchanged," he offered readily. "So when it's added to other metals, it becomes an alloy that improves the properties."

"I see." She grinned. "Thanks for keeping it so simple. Do you feel as though you've been teaching Chemistry 101?"

"Look, Ms. O'Shea, it's nice to meet a fellow American, especially one who's so pretty," Zack said, his expression softening. "But even with your impressive credentials, I can't imagine you doing the kind of job I'm going to need."

"Why? Because I'm a woman?"

He shook his head and tried to deny the obvious.

"Imagine it," she said crisply. "Admittedly, I'm not a chemist. But I do know my job. Why don't you give me a chance?"

"Well, I—" He paused and shrugged.

"Don't let the atmosphere fool you, Zack. This is how we do business in Ireland. Easy and casual, not pushy and fast. That's why I had you meet me here in this pub. It's where business is conducted. Drink up." She motioned to his full pint and he obediently lifted the drink to his lips. "Leave your tight jaws and ulcers in the States. Things are going to be different here."

"I don't have forever to get this plant in operation, Ms. O'Shea."

"Brenda."

"Brenda, I need to get it going as soon as possible. It's a matter of economics."

"I understand."

"I don't think you do," he said, countering her seemingly agreeable response. "My company went bankrupt in America. Do you know what that means? Funds are very limited right now. I'm in a hurry."

"If you want to work here in Ireland, you'll do it our way, Zack. Or you won't do it at all. Now, I'll do my best to push it through quickly, but we're not on California rush time here." She leaned back on the high-backed, wooden bench that had probably seated hundreds of drinkers conducting thousands of dollars' worth of business through the years. That thought was comforting to Brenda because she liked to mingle the new with the old. Maybe that's why she liked Ireland so much.

"Okay, I'll give it a try."

"You mean you'll give me a try? I don't see where you have much choice, Zack. Incidentally, you've got a good-sized chip on your shoulder, and I don't think I'm the cause of it."

He sighed and looked away, giving her a view of his

straight-lined, assertive profile. Had he really been such a jerk with her? "No, you aren't. I suppose I did bring my uptight jaw and a pile of problems with me. But I've had it rough the last few months and I really want this to work."

"So do I, Zack," she said gently. "Let's start from today and go forward. No looking back. Everybody has a past. So yours wasn't great. Let's leave it at that and proceed. We have a plant to build, and together, we're going to do it."

He looked at her curiously for a moment before speaking. Something in her urgent expression convinced him it would work. "I like your attitude, Brenda."

She smiled at him and relaxed somewhat. Round one, a draw, she thought. Although an American, Brenda O'Shea looked Irish with auburn hair and ice-blue eyes and a line of faint freckles across her nose. When she smiled, white teeth gleamed behind naturally red, heart-shaped lips. "First thing we need to do is to find you a comfortable place to live. Where are you staying now?"

"The hotel across the street."

Brenda opened her notebook. "The first order of business is to get you into something that feels like home. Now, how big a house do you need? When is your family coming over? And how many are there?" She noted that he didn't wear a wedding ring, but many married men didn't wear one, especially when they went abroad. Even if he wasn't married, he might have kids. Or—

He shrugged broad shoulders. "Just me. And I only need a couple of rooms and a kitchen. That's all."

She looked up and her blue eyes met his brown ones for a flickering moment. The brown in his eyes had marvelous flecks of gold, reminding her of a tiger's coat. And those eyes were captivating, hiding emotions that he wasn't willing to reveal. Not with her. Not now. Even with his doubtful attitude toward her, he was appealing. He had a commanding presence and the way he lifted his chin told her he had a tremendous amount of pride. She liked that in a man.

"But it says here you're married."

"We've divorced since I filled out that application."

"Oh. Just an apartment, then?" she managed to mumble, trying not to show any response. "Or do you prefer a house with more privacy?"

"I don't plan on doing much entertaining here," he said succinctly. "Anything will do, as long as it's clean and cheap."

She smiled warmly. "Everything in Ireland is clean. We take pride in it."

"And cheap? Funds are low, remember?"

"By American standards, yes." She made a few notes on the paper. "Do you need it furnished?"

"Of course. I came here to start a business, not set up housekeeping."

"Let me see . . . there are a couple of apartments for lease in my neighborhood. It's a nice, quiet area where several Americans live. Shall we start there?"

"Why not? Let's hurry and get this part finished." He started to push away from the booth but she placed her hand gently on his.

"Slow and easy, remember, Zack? Not too fast. Don't bring your ulcer to Ireland. This is a good place for healing."

He paused and glanced down at their hands. Her touch was cool and commanding. Maybe it was just what he needed. "That's why I'm here. I need some healing."

"Then we'll start now. Please, take your time finishing your Guinness, Zack," she encouraged softly.

He sighed and leaned back. Her gaze was as soothing as her cool touch. Strangely, as they sat there, the tenseness in his neck and shoulders began to slip away and he smiled. "Brenda O'Shea, you have your work cut out for you."

"My pleasure, Zack Ehrens."

"Are you married, Brenda?"

"No. Like you, I'm divorced."

"Good." He gazed steadily at her. "Maybe this won't be such a bad arrangement, after all."

"This isn't an arrangement, Zack. It's strictly business. We have lots of work ahead."

"I like you, Brenda. Like your spunk."

"And I like you too, Zack. Like your eyes."

They laughed and finished their pints. It took them another half an hour, but by then the conversation was gentler and much friendlier. During the time they sat there, Zack completely forgot his plan to talk to her boss and ask for a different liaison. Time slipped by quickly, and he forgot about his hurry to get the apartment hunting finished.

He was captivated by Brenda O'Shea's laughing blue eyes and the delicate way she sipped the dark, foamy stout. And he relaxed for the first time in weeks. Perhaps for the first time in months . . . since everything began to fall apart for him.

When she took him to her neighborhood, it wasn't

surprising to Zack that he liked her apartment building best. The flat directly above hers was empty, and he turned to her after they walked through it once. "This is good enough for me."

"This one?" Brenda looked around the modestly furnished rooms again. "But Zack, it's so small. There's no outside patio, only this little balcony." She leaned over the railing and looked directly down onto her own tiny garden with its two rose bushes and single lounge chair.

He stood beside her. "I don't care about a garden. If I want to see one, I'll hang over the rail and look at yours."

Suddenly, she wheeled around to face him. "Don't think that because I live down below, we'll—"

"Hold it! I'm not thinking anything because you live down below. I like this place. It's comfortable, clean, and close. We have lots of work to do and this'll make it much more convenient. Won't it?"

"Yes," she mumbled reluctantly. He was right. It would be easier to have Zack living above her. And fun. Now what made her think that? She didn't even know the man. But she liked him and was undeniably glad Padraig had assigned her to work with Ehrens Enterprises.

Barrister Padraig McGuinness gazed intently across his broad desk. His blue eyes stood out like diamonds and his thick shock of white hair ruffled around his ruddy face. "So how did it go, lass?"

Brenda smiled and opened her notebook officiously. She didn't really need to refer to her notes; she remembered every detail about Mr. Zack Ehrens. But, for her boss, she'd feign a businesslike attitude. "Good. We discussed what needed to be done first. Even found an apartment for him, and he should be moving in this weekend."

Padraig raised bushy gray eyebrows. "Found a place already? Pretty fast, eh?"

"Well, we looked at several and he made a quick choice." She wouldn't tell Padraig that the apartment Zack chose was directly above hers. "He, uh, has no family to move over here. It's just him. And he insisted that he didn't need anything very special."

"No family, huh? Divorced, I presume? Most Americans are," Padraig observed grittily.

"Including me, Padraig."

"I didn't mean that to sound offensive, Brenda. It's just that sometimes these Americans seem to take their marriage vows so lightly. So many of them move in and out of marriage like it was a new job. Look at Kate and myself, married thirty-two years and still going!"

Brenda looked at the handsome, white-haired man in admiration. He spoke in lilting phrases that sounded almost like poetry, and she loved to listen to him. "That's something to be proud of, Padraig. But all of us aren't as lucky."

"Ah, yes. I understand." His white hair contrasted with his bright complexion, and his striking blue eyes were like bright, shiny gemstones. "I know you had your reasons, Brenda, and good ones, too, according to your aunt Brigid."

Brenda smiled indulgently. "Don't forget she's my aunt and is going to sweeten my tale considerably."

"I've known you two years now," Padraig said,

27

leaning forward on the rich, mahogany desk. "You're a hard worker and an honest soul. I believe what she says, and I'm glad you're working for McGuinness and Sons. Now, tell me more about this Zack Ehrens and his business."

Brenda glanced down at her notes before answering. "He's very intent on making a go of this business in Ireland. He seems a bit, uh, frustrated and anxious to do it, and do it now. Typically American, I suppose. Always in a hurry."

Padraig nodded. "Bankruptcy does that to a man. Wounds his pride; knocks the pins out from him. All he can do is come back fighting. But that's good. Makes him a better candidate for business. Our business, and Ireland's. Think he's got the guts to make it, Brenda?"

"Oh yes, I certainly do. He can hardly wait to start looking at property. That's why he settled so quickly on a place to live. I think he just took whatever was satisfactory, so he could get on with his work." She paused and bit her lip. Did she really believe that? Or did she suspect that Zack took the apartment chiefly because it was near hers? Well, whatever the reason, that part of her job was done.

Padraig handed her a folder full of papers and property maps. "Here's some possible sites for the plant. Several along the river as he requested. Others with good access to the waterway for transportation."

"Okay. Zack should be moved in and settled by the weekend. We'll visit these sites next week. I'll let you know if any of them are good enough prospects to meet with the owners."

Padraig stood up and Brenda folded her notes and

followed his motion. "Good, lass. I'll notify you if we come up with anything else that looks promising."

She nodded and tucked her papers into a briefcase. "I'll be in touch later next week, Padraig."

"Aye. How's your aunt Brigid?"

"She's fine. I'm going to see her Sunday."

"Ah, good. Tell her I said hello. And . . ." He leaned closer as if to share a secret. "You might check to see if she's made any extra pans of her Guinness cake. My, my that woman can cook!"

"Yes, she can," Brenda agreed with a laugh and turned to leave the austere mahogany and book-filled law office. "I'll see what I can do."

"Thank you. Uh, Brenda—"

"Yes?"

"Watch out for that new client, Mr. Ehrens. Divorced men are . . . you know."

"Padraig, I'm a big girl. I can take care of myself."

"I know. But I'd have your aunt Brigid to answer to if anything happened to you. And you know how feisty she can be sometimes."

"Don't worry. Mr. Ehrens and I will keep everything strictly business." Even as she said it, Brenda wondered if she could gaze into those brown eyes of Zack's day after day and keep everything on a business level. She, too, was divorced and lonely. And very human.

"If he's a smart man, he already has designs on a pretty girl like yourself."

She paused and smiled at Padraig. "I'm sure he's a smart man, but I think his only designs are to make his business work this time."

"I hope so." Padraig waved a burly hand as she left.

Brenda's footsteps echoed through the high-ceil-inged hallway and she thought of Zack Ehrens and his "designs." Smiling to herself, she remembered his jut-ting, tight-jawed face with the straight nose and reflec-tive brown eyes. Those eyes . . . hinting of a mysteri-ous past. She couldn't help being curious about him. The few things she knew about the man were that he was serious—maybe too serious. And honest. And worried. And . . . what had Padraig said? Wounded. Yes, that was it. Zack Ehrens had been wounded and now he was determined to make it back. And damned intent about it.

Even though she knew he was taboo, she was in-trigued by Zack. All evening she couldn't get him out of her mind, even that night as she lay in bed, listening to the silence around her. There were no sounds up-stairs. Zack hadn't moved in yet.

By noon on Saturday Brenda could hear thumping and scraping above her. Her heart quickened. Zack was in the process of settling into his apartment. She tried to keep busy and not think about him and what he was doing. And how brown his eyes were and the masculine breadth of his shoulders. But she didn't have much success.

At dusk her phone rang. "Hello?"

Zack's voice was low and very masculine. "Brenda? This is Zack. Would you like to come up for a drink to toast my new apartment?"

How could she refuse? After all, he was her new client. Her heart pounded unreasonably. Calm down, she told herself. This is silly. "Sure, Zack. Give me a few minutes to change into something decent." Then another thought struck her. "You can't have your phone in this soon."

"You're right. I'm calling from the corner pay phone."

"Why didn't you just . . . oh never mind. I'll meet you upstairs in a few minutes." She hung up the phone chuckling and immediately wondered what to wear.

CHAPTER TWO

Zack replaced the receiver with a youthful whoop and sprinted all the way from the corner phone booth to their apartment building. Brenda had sounded surprised to hear from him, and her lyrical voice sent his senses soaring. He'd debated whether to call her or just drop in, then decided calling was better. When he could no longer resist the urge to see her again, he'd searched for a phone, by then doubting that she would even be home on a Saturday night. But she had been there, as if fate had detained her until he called.

Hell, he didn't really believe in fate. And there was no such thing as luck. You had to make your own luck in this world, good or bad. And his had been damned bad for too long now. Time to change that.

Zack paused on the stairs and glared at her silent door as if willing her to open it. But she didn't, and he went on up to his new apartment. He walked around, trying to get accustomed to the unfamiliar surroundings. The only belongings he brought to this new life were his clothes. And his problems.

His dark eyes fell moodily on the long white envelope on the dresser and his thoughts raced unavoidably back to his brother, James, still in prison.

James. How did I let you get in this fix? Why wasn't I watching more carefully? Why did you get involved . . . why . . . why . . . a thousand why's. I let you down. Zack clenched his large, square hand into a determined fist. *But no more. It won't happen again. I won't let it.*

He walked to the window and looked down on the darkening street. A woman's odd-sounding Irish brogue drifted up and away. "Oh God, can I make it happen here?" he muttered, half aloud. "Can I make our lives so good that he won't stray outside the law again? Can we make it this time?"

Zack folded his arms firmly across his broad chest. *Yes, damn it!* he vowed silently. *This is a new start. This fresh, green country is where it will happen. I swear it!*

He stared unseeingly at the small park across the street. It reminded him of a park near their walk-up apartment in Philly when he was a kid. Zack had stood on the corner selling papers in a cold, dreary job. But James had other ideas about how to make money. Oh, how their mother had cried the first time James was caught stealing at age twelve.

He remembered her screaming, "Why did you do such a thing? Why?"

"But Mom, it was for us, don't you see?" James had claimed, and they let him off that first time.

Unfortunately, James was right. They were raggedly poor and desperately needed the money. But it never occurred to Zack to steal it. Not at age fourteen. Yet even at twelve, James was more street wise, more sophisticated in some ways, than Zack.

Their poverty only made Zack more determined to

33

make it, to prove to the world—or at least to the people on the block—that the Ehrens kid could make something of himself. And he had, too, until last year when everything fell apart. The business. His marriage of five years. And on top of everything else, James's arrest and imprisonment. But that debt would soon be paid, and James would be here in Ireland within a few months. Then things would improve for both of them.

A knock at the door jolted Zack back to the present. Brenda! His heart thudded as he swung the door open for her.

She gazed up at Zack for a moment, anticipation filling her ocean-blue eyes. He wore a gray and white striped shirt with the sleeves rolled up to reveal muscled, hairy forearms and gray cords that hugged his thighs tightly. He looked very casual and handsome. Brenda knew he'd been working on the place this afternoon, yet he appeared clean and fresh and extremely masculine. And somewhat relaxed even though his face held a tight expression. He was still quite serious. Crazily she wanted to change that and bring a smile to his chiseled lips.

She'd forgotten how tall he was as she lifted her head and thrust a single crimson rose bud toward him with a tentative smile. "Welcome to your new home, Zack."

"Thank you." He seemed to inhale her beauty for the moment they stood there, then looked hesitantly at the rose. "Thanks," he mumbled again, taking the rose and brushing her hand in the process.

"Do you have a bud vase for it?"

"I don't know." He stepped back for her to enter and shrugged. "Sounds strange, but I'm not sure what's here." He felt clumsy receiving the flower. It was a simple, friendly gesture, and yet he thought it was an incredibly nice thing for her to do. This woman was gracious and generous, and it had been a long time since anyone had been so affectionate to him.

"Then let's see if we can find one," she said, heading for the tiny, windowed kitchen. "If not, a glass will do. We just need to get it in water."

As if the place was hers, she began an earnest search of the cabinets, opening and closing doors and rapidly scanning the shelves. "Nope. Nothing. Well, this glass will be fine." She filled the glass with tap water and handed it to him.

He sniffed the delicate petals before sticking the rose into the glass. "Nice. Adds a much-needed feminine touch around here."

Brenda smiled up at him, glad he appreciated the simple beauty of a rose. It spoke well of a man, that he could take the time for little pleasures. Then the moment became awkward, and she motioned around her. "I like your kitchen, Zack. I didn't notice earlier how many windows you have in here, but it's nice and light. Has a good view of the park, too. Of course the windows cut down on cabinets. But then I guess you don't care about that."

"No. I won't be doing much cooking."

She turned around and faced him. "Why are you looking at me like that? Am I jabbering too much?"

"Not at all. It's just that the flower is such a nice gesture and . . . it's beautiful. Like you, Brenda."

She took a deep breath and tried to shake off the constant vibes she had when she was around him. *That's* why she had been jabbering so much, to try to take both their minds off the electric currents running between them. She could see that his expression had changed when he looked at her. There was a small light in his dark eyes and it made her slightly nervous about being alone in his apartment with him. She wanted to appear busy, to continue talking and keep him talking. But he just stood there looking at her. So seriously.

"I have a couple of rose bushes on my patio, and they produce an occasional flower. That's all I could find on such short notice to bring for your house-warming."

"You didn't have to bring anything."

"A single bud isn't much."

"To me it is. I've never received flowers from a lady before."

"Never?" She laughed nervously. "That's a shame, Zack. Everyone should get flowers once in a while. So, where shall we put this one? Can we have some lights in this place? Let me see what you've done to it." She took the glass from him and marched into the shadowed living room.

He followed her, pausing to switch on a table lamp. "Well, what do you think about the decor? Is it me?"

She placed the rose in the center of the coffee table and her blue eyes danced around the room. "Actually, it looks more like something the building super threw together—early conglomeration."

He nodded grimly and let his eyes follow hers. "When you rent it furnished, you have to take what they offer, I guess. And this is it. I did remove the lace doilies from the sofa and the plastic covers from the lampshades."

Brenda plopped down in the middle of a run-down Victorian sofa and stretched her arms out both ways. "Nice, in an oldish sort of way. You must admit, it's clean. But what you really need, Zack, is something more modern. I imagine your place in California was sleek and uncluttered."

His gaze clouded at her mention of his former life. "You're wrong, Brenda. I never decorated our place in California. Wouldn't know where to start. That was my ex-wife's department and she chose some damned fancy French stuff. Now it's all gone over to her as property settlement in the divorce."

"She got the house?"

"She got whatever was left, including the house and the Mercedes."

"And you, Zack? What did you get?"

"I got out. Shirt on my back plus a few extras."

"Enough money to start a new business in Ireland."

"Barely. Hey, would you like a brandy? I bought some especially for tonight."

"I'd love it." Brenda watched him move to the kitchen, admiring his broad shoulders and the trim fit of his waist. She admired the way his lean body moved across the room. She watched his large hands grip the brandy decanter as if he were completely in charge of the world. She was mesmerized by those blunt-fingered hands. His long fingers wrapped around the glasses and he sloshed the amber liquid as he approached her. Quickly she reminded herself again that he was a client and she had to keep this strictly business.

She steered the conversation to their mutual business. "There are several good properties for sale that might suit your needs. We can start looking on Monday."

"The sooner the better. How about tomorrow?"

She gave him a scolding look. "Tomorrow's Sunday, Zack. There are certain things that are not conducted on Sunday here. Business is one of them. Unless, of course, it accompanies a jaunt in the country or a horse race or a ride with the hounds."

He leaned forward. "Ride with the hounds?"

"A fox hunt."

"They still do that?"

"You bet. It's great sport. You should use tomorrow to relax, maybe get familiar with Dublin. Take a walk in the park and learn to slow down, Zack."

"I'm not sure I know how. It's been a long time since I felt secure enough to slow down. I have a lot of pressures and the main one is to get the plant going." He slumped back in the chair and sipped his brandy absently.

"Let me carry some of that responsibility for the plant now, Zack. That's my job, so share it with me. You take care of learning to relax."

He squinted his dark eyes wickedly. "Why don't you teach me, Brenda? You seem to have conquered the art."

"Don't forget I've had two years to lose my American tendency to rush. But, if I took on the project," she paused to assess him with teasing blue eyes, "I'd start with smile lessons. You're too serious, Zack. Don't you ever smile?"

"There hasn't been much to smile about in the past few years, Brenda. Sorry if I seem like a dour old bear. That's just my nature, I guess."

"It doesn't have to be, Zack. I'd like to see a smile. I'll bet you'd even like it."

He drained the brandy and jiggled the empty glass in one big hand. "More brandy? Or should we find a place to eat supper? Either would bring a smile to my lips, Brenda."

"If I have more brandy, I'll be giggling into my glass. I'm afraid you'd find me terribly embarrassing."

"Then let's go eat before we have more to drink. Do you know any place special?"

She shrugged. "Well there's a little pub a couple of blocks away that serves great soda bread and Irish stew. How does that sound?"

"Terrific! Let's go." He rose and, taking her hand, ushered her quickly down the stairs and outside to the street. Feeling very much at ease, they walked the two blocks to the restaurant, talking the whole time. Zack even managed a chuckle or two, and Brenda noted how nice his eyes looked when he smiled.

"Here it is," Brenda directed, pointing to a golden-lit window.

"Smells great, even out here." Zack's arm circled her back in the process of reaching to open the door.

Brenda paused, holding on to the moment of strength he exuded. She looked up into his dark eyes and spontaneously reached up to touch the corner of his mouth. "Why Zack, I do believe I see a smile there. And your face didn't crack or anything."

He inclined his head toward her and murmured, "See how good you are for me? I never could have mustered this smile sitting up there in my apartment all alone tonight."

She felt unnerved by his frank remark and his closeness. What could she say? *You're good for me, too, Zack Ehrens.* She didn't say it, but she felt it. Averting her eyes from his intense gaze, she pushed on the door. He followed her into the warm, smoky pub.

They sat across from each other in a small booth, drank Guinness and dipped soda bread dripping with sweet kerry butter into the hearty stew. They chatted easily, enjoying each other's company.

Finally Zack asked the question that had been burning him all night. "Brenda, am I infringing on anyone else's time? Surely you weren't sitting home tonight with no plans. It is Saturday night."

She shrugged and smoothed her napkin with several long strokes. "Having plans isn't important to me anymore. I just do things as they come along. Or I do nothing and that's not too bad, either."

He grasped his pint of stout and took a big gulp. "What I'm asking is—"

"I know." She laughed at his fumbling around. "Am I attached?"

"Well . . ."

"I'm not involved with anyone at the present time, Zack."

"Good."

"Afraid that would interfere with business?"

"No. I wouldn't want it to interfere with us."

"Look, Zack, my job is first and foremost. Let's keep this to business, okay?" She gave him a firm expression and felt very proud of herself.

Zack, on the other hand, just eyed her for a moment with his daringly devastating brown gaze. Then his lips spread into a brief but devilish smile. "Okay,

Brenda. Anything you say. Just one thing, laughing lady. Are you made of steel?"

She chuckled delightedly. The man could actually joke! "No, of course not." And his eyes were amazing when they had that twinkle.

"Neither am I," he admitted in a low voice. "And I'm beginning to like the feeling I have when I'm with you."

"The laughter's getting to you?"

"You are getting to me, my fiery-haired beauty." His brown eyes softened and his gaze caressed her auburn hair. Something in those eyes told her he wanted to caress her all over and that his large hands could be gentle as well as commanding.

They walked home slowly, talking intermittently, yet at ease with the silences between them. Brenda shivered in the cool damp air, and Zack put his arm around her and drew her close. She felt his warm strength and knew that she hadn't wanted to be this close to any man in a long time. She wanted to be even closer to Zack, but didn't dare let on. She had the feeling he'd gladly oblige.

At her door, there were a few disquieting moments. Neither wanted the evening to end, yet there were no more reasons to prolong it. No business reasons, anyway. Brenda handed him her key with a silent, solemn look that said, "Please don't make this difficult."

Zack twisted the key easily and the door squeaked open an inch. He handed the key back to her, his fingertips lingering as they scraped across her palm.

She drew in her breath sharply, wanting—yet not daring—to invite him in. "Well, good night, Zack.

41

Thanks for supper. And welcome to the neighborhood."

"Thanks for a beautiful evening, Brenda." He sensed her trepidation and, shifting suddenly, stuffed both hands into his pockets. "And for the rosebud. It'll remind me of you."

She breathed a little sigh of relief. "I'm glad you like it." She took a step into her apartment.

Zack shifted again. "Uh, Brenda, what are you doing tomorrow?"

"Zack . . ."

"I don't know a soul in town. It could be a pretty lonely Sunday. How about a walk in the park?"

"I'm going . . ." she hesitated only briefly before blurting, "I'm going to the country to visit my great-aunt Brigid. She lives alone and loves to have company. Want to come along?"

"You sure she wouldn't mind if I did?"

"Heavens no. She'd love it. The more the merrier is her philosophy."

"How about you?"

"I'd like to have you along."

"Okay, you talked me into it. Or did I invite myself?"

"It doesn't matter. It'll be a great opportunity for you to get out of the city and see the countryside. It's really beautiful and the people are fun and wonderful."

"A chance for another lesson in laughter?"

"Yes." She smiled. "We'll leave around nine and have breakfast on the way. I have a favorite spot where I always stop to eat. I think you'll like it, too."

"I'm sure I will, Brenda."

42

"See you tomorrow, Zack."

"See you." He nodded and turned for the stairs.

Brenda slipped quickly inside her door and leaned on it. She grasped her heart, which was pounding a mile a minute and couldn't believe she'd actually asked Zack to go with her tomorrow. But she was wildly excited at the prospect. He made her feel so absolutely wonderful, she could hardly wait to see him again.

She'd wanted him to kiss her at the door and wondered if he could tell what she was thinking. The look on his face told her he'd wanted to kiss her, too. But he held back because of her reluctance. He could read her mind that much, anyway. Maybe he was just too much a gentleman to risk offending her.

Maybe he wanted to wait until there'd be no holding back from either of them. That thought was positively exciting!

CHAPTER THREE

"I borrowed a bike for you."

Zack stared sleepily at Brenda. "You did what?"

"Well, I knew you wouldn't have one yet, so I borrowed Mr. Flanagan's. He lives down the hall from me. It's an old one, but I think it'll be okay. You do like to ride, don't you?"

"Huh? Oh yeah. Love it." Zack ran a hand through his disheveled brown curls and gazed curiously at the shimmery red-haired vision before him. Her auburn hair tumbled darkly over both shoulders onto a pale fisherman's knit sweater, and she wore corduroy slacks of army green and shiny brown penny loafers. She looked like a young Irish girl, fresh-faced and just up from the farm. And yet, she also had the appeal of an American woman, attractive and self-assured. In the early-morning light, she was quite beautiful.

"Sorry to have to wake you, but we need to be heading out soon. Of course, you can still back out, Zack. If you'd rather catch a few more z's, I understand."

"Back out? Not a chance. Anyway, I'm awake. Can't go back to sleep once I'm awake."

She smiled and a happy twinkle lit her eyes. "It's going to be a beautiful day. No rain in sight."

"You say we're riding bikes on this trip?" He couldn't remember the last time he'd ridden a bike. But, what the hell, with the way Brenda looked this morning, he'd ride anything just to be with her.

"It's the best way to view the countryside. Actually, when you've been over here awhile, you may find it's the best mode of travel, unless you're going a great distance."

He shook his head. "I can't imagine."

"That's because you're fresh from the States. When you see how enjoyable this slower pace is, you'll change."

"Think so?" He propped his hands loosely on his blue-jeaned hips. "You know, Brenda, I think I'd like that. A change."

She gave him a slightly puzzled look, but decided not to pursue it. Not now. Still, she was curious about what part of his life he'd like to change. Suddenly she wanted to know all about him. What was his life in America like, his marriage, his business that failed? Maybe today she'd learn more about this interesting man and his elusive past. The fact that he was standing here today indicated he was already instituting changes in his life. Well, so was she. "You look as if you could use a cup of strong coffee before we get started."

"Yeah, I guess," he said. "What time is it?"

"We don't worry about time over here, Zack. When you're ready to go, come on down to my apartment. I have some freshly brewed coffee."

"Sounds like heaven."

She nodded and stepped backward. "See you in a

little bit. Just dress casually, in layers, so you can peel your jacket or sweater off later as you get warmer."

"How far are we going?"

"It'll take us about an hour." She looked at him curiously. "But we'll be stopping for breakfast. I'll introduce you to the famous Wicklow pancake—it's a fantastic omelet with scallions and herbs."

"Wicklow pancake is really an omelet, huh? Is that like the biscuits that are really cookies?"

"Mm-hm," she said, nodding. "And scones are like our biscuits. Well, come on down when you're ready."

"Will do." He stood in the doorway, watching her walk away. Her hips were small and slightly rounded in those dark green slacks and swayed just enough to entice him. She was tall and slender and those damned red curls tumbled down the middle of her back so alluringly he wanted to reach up and—Zack took a deep breath and halted his fantasies about Brenda O'Shea. He doused his thoughts in a lukewarm shower and wondered if the water ever got hot. But then, maybe what he needed was a cool shower to calm his raging blood whenever he was near this woman.

She sat with hands curled around her coffee mug, waiting for him. She felt the heat from the coffee move up her arms and radiate beneath the collar of her sweater. Thoughts of Zack Ehrens made her warm. His look was steamy. Oh, he didn't mean to be, she was sure. But he was, all the same. His dark brown eyes seemed to conceal hidden secrets. He even hinted of them occasionally.

She wondered about him, but if she knew all about him, maybe those wonderful eyes of his would lose their mystery. Maybe that's what she liked best about him. The mystery. The handsome, devilishly sexy, steamy mystery of him.

He had been so handsome this morning, with those heavy-lidded, bedroom eyes and pillow-tossed, brown curls, it almost took her breath away when he opened the door. It had been a long time since she'd seen a man in his early-morning disarray. And she found Zack quite appealing.

His jeans had been hastily pulled on, zipped but not snapped at the waist. And his shirt opened down the front to reveal a chest covered with a sensuous smattering of dark hair. The breadth of his chest narrowed to a flat, slender waist where a dark line of hair disappeared beneath his jeans. And his hair was a curly, riotous mess—a wonderfully sexy mess that made her want to run her fingers through it.

She found this man extremely attractive, and that scared her. After all, they were about to spend the day together. She reminded herself he was a client and tried to convince herself he was nothing more.

Brenda inhaled as she sipped her coffee, savoring the richness. Out the window she could see the two bikes, waiting on the sidewalk for her and Zack. She remembered his doubtful look when she mentioned riding the bicycles to the country. And she knew, instinctively, that he hadn't pedaled a bike in years.

She smiled at his reactions, typical for an urbanite used to the easy availability of cabs and cars in America. Well, he wasn't in America, and he had no car. Neither did she, and he'd just have to travel her way if he insisted on going with her. It would take him a while to become acclimated to the slow-paced Irish ways. But if he stayed long enough, it would happen. Just as it had for her.

In her heart, she hoped he would stay a good, long time. His business would be beneficial to the economy and good for the moral of the local Irish people. And perhaps he would be good for her. An American friend, after all this time in Ireland alone.

A light knock on the door interrupted her thoughts and she rose to open it. He wore a blue cable-knit sweater over a blue-striped, button-down shirt. His faded jeans hugged his lean body with a familiar intimacy that she envied. For the life of her, Brenda thought he was the handsomest man she'd ever seen.

"Am I all right? Spinach on my teeth or my zipper down?"

"Huh? No, of course you're fine. I didn't mean to stare, Zack. Come on in. Coffee's ready."

He followed her inside the attractive, modest apartment, thinking of those blue eyes of hers and how they mellowed when she stared. And, by God, she *did* stare at him with a certain look in her eyes.

He noticed she'd tied her hair back with a green ribbon. In a moment of wild abandon, he wanted to rip it off and watch her hair tumble down around her shoulders again. But he talked about her apartment instead. It was about the same size as his, but didn't look the same at all. "Is yours furnished, too? Looks nicer than mine."

"No," she said, motioning for him to sit at the small dining table beside the window. "I've picked up pieces here and there. Sometimes I go to an estate auction or to shops where wood craftsmen bring their products to sell. I love country furniture."

"This looks and feels very comfortable," he said, adjusting his length into the chair at the end of the table.

"It's worn too. But good wood improves with age and wear," she added with a smile as she served up two steaming cups of coffee. "Would you like something else with your coffee? A muffin or some juice?"

"No, coffee's enough. Brenda, uh . . ."

"Yes?" She paused and looked down at him,

"Did I tell you I appreciate you sharing this day with me? I realize I'm taking your day off."

"You aren't taking, I'm giving," she answered with a casual shrug and moved away to replace the coffeepot. Then she joined him at the table. "I want to show you the simple beauty outside of Dublin. Anyway, it's rural areas like this that will provide workers for your plant and you should learn more about them. And about the people who'll be working for you."

"I'm looking forward to today. Even the bike ride."

She laughed at his polite attempt because she knew he was lying about the bike ride.

Sturdy and jovial best described Brenda's great-aunt Brigid, introduced lovingly as "Auntie Brige." She was a big, comfortable-looking woman who stood beside her front gate until they parked the bicycles, then threw her arms around Brenda with happy enthusiasm. For a second, Brenda was lost in the ample folds of flesh, then she emerged with a flushed smile and presented her stiff-legged bike-riding companion.

Zack took Aunt Brigid's chubby hand and looked down into her smiling face. "It's a pleasure to meet you."

Her hair was downy white and her scalp shone pink beneath the curls. On her cheeks were rosy circles and her cheery blue eyes crinkled at the corners. Zack knew immediately that Brenda had inherited her own beautiful blue eyes from this side of the family.

The elderly aunt beamed as Zack kissed her knuckles, then gushed, "My, my, he does have the manners, doesn't he, Brenda?" She looked closely at him, then launched into a winding question in her lilting, Irish brogue. "Zack Ehrens, you say? I knew a family in Blessington named Ehrens. The father died, leaving that tiny, withered apple of a woman with six little ones, most girls I think. Before the poor man was laid out a day, God rest his soul, his wife'd sold the farm. In little more than a month she moved the girls to Kildare and opened a very fashionable dress shop. You wouldn't be related to them, would you?"

Zack dropped the aunt's hand. "No, sorry to say, I don't have relatives in Ireland." *At least, not yet,* he thought. *But you probably wouldn't want to meet the one I'm bringing over in a few months.*

" 'Tis a shame," she said, clucking her tongue. "Well, come on in. Tea's on and shortbread's fresh out of the oven."

Brenda looked at Zack, an unreadable expression on her face. He interpreted it as doubt and nodded reassuringly before placing a guiding hand on her shoulder. They followed Brenda's aunt toward the storybook cottage with its thatched roof and boxes of brightly blooming geraniums on either side of the door.

Inside the small house was warm and comfortable, just like Aunt Brigid. The furniture was simple and worn with age, and crocheted scarves covered the arm and head rests of the sofa and chairs. Sunlight poured in through a tall, narrow window, chasing shadows into the corners of the room. Strategically placed near the huge fieldstone fireplace was a large wooden rocking chair that looked ancient and worn and extremely comfortable.

At the old drop-leaf table, they drank tea and ate steamy sweet shortbread and listened to a seemingly endless stream of Irish stories related in Aunt Brigid's marvelous lilting voice.

"Have you heard about Sadie and her soldier and how he carried her away to America with a babe in her arms?" Aunt Brigid leaned forward and patted Brenda's knee. "You don't mind if I tell him about your grandmother, do you, darlin'?"

Brenda smiled reluctantly. "No, I don't mind. But Zack may not want to hear such a romantic little love story."

"Of course I do," Zack said, giving Brenda a reprimanding glance with his devilish dark eyes.

"Men fall flat in love, too," Aunt Brigid vowed, wagging her chubby finger at Brenda. "And your grandfather Walt was one who did. Though I was just a young thing myself, I knew the minute he laid eyes on your grandmother, he was a goner. And so was Sadie."

"He was a soldier stationed over here during World War Two?" Zack prompted.

"Walt was here with the Canadian air force before the Americans came. And a handsome one he was too in his uniform. Tall and dark and with the broadest shoulders you've ever seen." She paused and gestured toward Zack. "Almost as broad as yours. And as soon as Sadie got a close look at him, she was smitten."

Brenda chuckled at the old-fashioned word and glanced at Zack. But he dutifully gave Aunt Brigid his full attention as she rambled on with her love story.

"My sister was only sixteen when they first met at a dance in Dublin. She was worldly then, or so we thought. She had been going to school in Wicklow learning to be a teacher and some friends took her to Dublin for the weekend. I was just an innocent of fourteen, but I'll never forget how she talked about her Walter when she came home. He visited her often, driving all the way out from Dublin whenever he had the chance. Sure, we were as fascinated by that car he drove as by him. They married before the war was over."

"She was so young for marriage," Brenda commented wistfully. "Only seventeen."

"Ah, in those days she wasn't too young for marriage. Times were hard, and father saw to it they were married in the little church here in the village. Such love I've never seen in two people's faces. It was a beautiful wedding." Aunt Brigid paused to take a sip of tea. "By the next year, Sadie had a baby girl, your mother. And when the war was over and Walt took them away to America, we all cried like fools. Oh Lordy, wouldn't I just love to see my darlin' Sadie again." She wiped a tear from each eye with the corner of her apron.

"Maybe you can, Auntie Brige," Brenda said softly.

"Having you here so close has been a God's blessing, Brenda. You look so much like her, it's almost as good as having her here, and I'm grateful. Now—"

She slapped her large thighs with both hands, signaling an end to the sentimentality. "Are you two ready to go fishing?"

"I don't know if Zack—" Brenda answered hesitantly and looked imploringly at him.

"I'm game for anything." He shrugged.

"Well, good," Aunt Brigid said. "Because we've just got a few hours before Paddy O'Sullivan gets here with his flute. And when I told Willie Malone you were coming, Brenda, he said he'd bring along his fiddle and you two could play a little music. You did bring your fiddle, didn't you?"

"Yes, Auntie Brige," Brenda said obediently and gave Zack another doubtful look. "Do you like Irish music?"

"Course he does," Aunt Brigid answered for him, rising from the table in a flourish and gathering an armload of cups and plates. "Everybody likes good Irish music."

He leaned toward Brenda and winked. "I'd never admit it if I didn't. Do you play, Brenda?"

"I flail at the fiddle some."

"Bah!" Aunt Brigid scoffed. "She's a beautiful musician, considerin' she grew up over there. Wait'll you hear her! But first we're agoin' fishin'. I've found the best spot for catching. Down near the bend is a rapids and it pours into the nicest, laziest little pond you've ever seen. The fish just love it."

"How far is it?" Brenda rose to help with the dishes.

"Oh, we'll have to take the car, girl. It's too far for the likes of me to walk. But we'll need someone to look at that danged motor. Paddy says it's leaking oil and left me an extra can. It's parked out back and so's the can."

"I'll be glad to check it for you," Zack said, and headed outside to where a twenty-year-old Volkswagen bug was parked.

Brenda followed him outside. "Zack, I hope you don't mind. She likes to fish, and I usually take her."

"I don't mind at all. In fact, it's been ages since I've been fishing, and I think it sounds great."

"You're being very polite. I'm afraid Auntie Brige takes a lot for granted. And I indulge her because she's such a dear."

"Brenda, I find your aunt delightful and this is exactly how I want to spend my day. Otherwise I'd be alone in that apartment, sitting on someone else's furniture. And miserable. You wouldn't want your newest client to be miserable, would you?"

She grinned and shook her head.

"So quit fussing."

A genuine smile spread across her face, a grateful, beautiful expression that crinkled the corners of her eyes. "Okay. Thanks."

He took a step toward her, then halted, his dark gaze never leaving hers. "My pleasure."

Her eyes widened ever so slightly as she read more in his eyes than he ever stated. Her smile faded. "The fishing equipment is in the small shed around back. We'll be ready in a few minutes." Then, like a scared doe, she whirled around and went back inside the cottage.

They sat beneath a spreading oak, fishing lines dangling in the water. It was unbelievably quiet. A gentle

54

zephyr occasionally rustled the leaves and the low purr of Aunt Brigid's snoring was pleasantly lulling. Occasionally, in the distance, the sound of a sheep bleating reached them.

"I think Auntie Brige likes to come fishing because it's such a pleasant place to take a nap," Brenda said softly, nodding toward Aunt Brigid's form propped against a nearby canopied tree. Her chin rested on her ample chest and her head bobbed with each breath.

Zack relaxed with his long legs stretched out on the green, grassy carpet and his back on the broad base of a hundred-year-old tree. He'd peeled off his sweater and the angles of his shoulders were clearly apparent beneath the thin oxford shirt. "A nap isn't such a bad idea, you know." He was content to rest his tired, already-aching body and feast his eyes on Brenda's natural beauty.

"Zack, I hope you don't think the reason she told you that story about my grandmother is because she's trying to create something between us. It's because she lost a sister when Gran went to America, and that was very traumatic for her."

"I can imagine. Have they visited each other?"

"Gran made several trips back here over the years. But Auntie Brige couldn't afford it, so she's never been to America. Now they're both widows and not getting any younger. They'd like to see each other again."

A strange feeling came over Zack and he gazed transfixed into the lazy pond where their floats bobbed and fishing lines disappeared in the green depths. He thought of James and what he might be doing—might be enduring—at this very moment. Zack was certain his brother wasn't spending such a pleasant day as they were having now and an unavoidable pang of guilt tore at his heart. "I understand. That's only natural. Brothers . . . and sisters are sometimes very close and stay that way through life."

"I hope you don't mind Auntie Brige. Out of six brothers and sisters, she's my grandmother's only living relative and they were so close during their youth. I do love her, but she can be—"

Zack propped himself up on his elbow and checked his fishing line. "She's a wonderful lady. How can I convince you I'm having a very nice day?"

She gave him a wry grin. "We aren't finished here, Zack. You haven't faced the music yet. Literally!"

"I can hardly wait," he said with a grin. "Anything, as long as it delays that bike ride back to town."

She lifted her blue eyes to gaze at him for an absorbing minute. "Is that a smile, Zack Ehrens? On the face of the tense, uptight American who watches the clock and hurries through life?"

Unable to resist, he reached up and stroked the creamy softness of her cheek. "It is. You're a good teacher . . ."

She shivered at his touch and turned abruptly. "Oh! I think I've got a fish!"

When they returned to Aunt Brigid's cottage, a group of neighbors had begun to arrive. Some brought their instruments while others came to dance or just sit and enjoy "an afternoon session." The women brought covered dishes and Aunt Brigid bustled around like a clucking hen, speaking to everyone and introducing Zack as Brenda's friend from America who was "opening a plant for hiring soon. Tell everybody there will be jobs for the taking."

Later, they feasted on spatchcock, a specially flavored roasted chicken; creamed cabbage; Donegal pies, a sort of pot pie made of potatoes, eggs, and bacon. Then there was Irish whiskey cake and syllabub, a pudding made of sherry and brandy mixed with heavy whipped cream; and strong black coffee.

"Zack, I swear you haven't stopped eating yet!" Brenda teased as he sat beside her with another plate piled high with food.

"I don't want to offend anyone by leaving anything out," he said, diving into the syllabub and savoring it on his tongue with a blissful expression on his face.

"Well, you certainly haven't omitted a thing. I hope you'll be able to pedal yourself home in a couple of hours."

"This will give me fuel for the journey," he claimed and bit into a luscious Guinness cake made of spices and dried fruit and brown sugar.

"I hope it won't weight you down."

Just then, a lone fiddle started to play the beginning strings of "My Wild Irish Rose." Several couples started dancing on the lawn. Zack looked at Brenda, a question in his eyes. Then he didn't even ask. He simply took her hand and pulled her into his arms for the dance. He couldn't resist this opportunity to hold her, and she couldn't refuse his unspoken request. They moved together in one space, breathing and stepping in unison, their hearts pounding the same beat.

"My Wild Irish Rose . . ." he murmured into her ear.

She clutched his shoulder and tried to breathe

calmly. She inhaled his marvelously fresh fragrance and stayed close, feeling the movements of his muscular body against hers. And she was in heaven for the space of a song.

The next tune was the Irish classic "When Irish Eyes Are Smiling." But halfway through that one Aunt Brigid interrupted them. "Excuse me, please, Brenda. Wouldn't you like to fiddle a bit? Willie is asking for you."

"Oh, of course." She turned away from Zack quickly, so no one would see the regret in her eyes. And she could hear Zack's gentle offer to dance with Aunt Brigid. She turned in time to see the glow on her aunt's round face as Zack whirled her across the lawn. God, he was wonderful!

The music alternated between brisk dancing songs and haunting tales of rebellion and lost love. Zack felt he had received a great gift, an uplifting, happy gift from Aunt Brigid and her Irish friends. He even tried a jig or two, much to everyone's delight. When he and Brenda said their good-byes, the small crowd was still having a "roaring good time."

Pedaling home was painful for Zack, but he managed to keep up with the slender, energetic Brenda. Just barely. She stopped several times to rest and he was sure she did it especially for him. She wasn't even out of breath. It was dark when they reached the apartment building.

"You were a wonderful guest, you know." Brenda led the way upstairs. "Auntie Brige fell in love with you. And I can assure you all the ladies were impressed that you could eat so much. Even old Paddy thought you were a pretty good sport, trying the jig like that."

"I'll pay tomorrow, I'm sure." Zack groaned as he lifted each leg for the next agonizing step.

"I think you're already paying. Maybe it was too much for one day."

"No, it was good for me. I needed the exercise. It's been far too long since I've been so active." He reached for one of her hands, and warm, strong fingers entwined with slender, soft fingers. "I enjoyed every minute with you today." He gazed down at her, his brown eyes smoky and seductive. "Come upstairs, Brenda. Let's have a little brandy."

"Zack, I—"

He stepped closer and took her other hand. Their fingers clasped, though still hanging by their sides as if this link would sustain them, as if they didn't dare try for more. "Brenda, you're beautiful."

"Zack, don't . . ."

"Why not? You feel it too." He pulled her closer, lifting her hands to his waist. Their thighs touched. "Brenda, I want to kiss you."

She gazed up at him, speechless. She knew what he was thinking, knew what she was wishing. Their faces were close, their lips even closer. She tried to resist, to fight the feelings. But caught within Zack's power, she was weak. He was impossible to resist.

She turned her head up, a better angle for a kiss. *Just one,* she was thinking. Their heated breathing mingled, and she was lost . . . lost in the realm of Zack Ehrens.

His kiss was gentle at first, warm lips pairing, testing, liking what they felt. Then the pressure grew stronger. He wanted more than testing, he wanted to taste her sweetness, to savor her completely. And his arms encased her, his strong hands stretching along her back, forging them tightly together.

She went willingly into his arms, into the kiss that swirled her away into misty beauty, green valleys and along lazy rivers with rapids roaring around the bend. Her feelings rushed and tumbled over and over and she wanted to be lost forever in Zack Ehrens's arms.

A noise from down the hall tore them apart. A door opened and the grizzled old face of Mr. Flanagan peered out. "Thought I heard somebody out here. Expecting my daughter to bring my young grandson over for a visit any time."

"Oh, Mr. Flanagan, thanks for the use of your bike today. We parked it down in the store room." Flushed and slightly shaky from the kiss, Brenda managed to fumble in her backpack. "Here, a gift from my aunt."

His gnarled hand reached out to take the small package. "Her whiskey cake? Best in the county! Thanky. And tell her she made an old man's day." Smiling with pleasure, nodding to Zack and Brenda, he withdrew into his dark apartment.

Brenda walked back to her door.

Zack looked at her expectantly. "Sure you won't come upstairs for a brandy?"

"And make your day?" she teased and shook her head. "We'd better not, Zack. We . . . we have work to do tomorrow. I have several plant sites to show you."

"Brenda . . ."

Her blue eyes lifted and silently implored. "Zack, no. We have too much business . . . please, no."

His face tightened and he sighed and looked down the hall at Mr. Flanagan's closed door. *Damn the man for hearing a noise!*

She unlocked her door, then gave him a gentle smile. "Take a hot bath, as hot as you can. It'll help those sore muscles."

"Does the water ever get hot around here?"

She pushed back a stray curl and grinned. "Maybe you'd better heat some water on the stove and add it to your bath."

"Thanks for the advice."

"See you tomorrow, Zack. Around ten?"

"I thought you folks didn't watch the clock."

"When I'm doing business with Americans, I do."

"Sure . . . see you."

Brenda slipped inside her door and moved silently across the floor in the darkness. Switching on the kitchen light, her gaze fell on the coffee cups they'd left from morning.

Suddenly she wanted to have that brandy with him, wanted to share another hour. Wanted to feel his lips on hers again. Yet she knew that tonight it wouldn't stop at one brandy, one kiss, one hour. Sighing in resignation she put the cups in the sink and washed the coffeepot so it would be fresh for tomorrow.

Zack leaned his weary shoulders against the wall next to her door and listened to the soft sounds coming from within her apartment. *Damn Mr. Flanagan!* Then Zack realized that he was blaming an old man for nothing. This was between himself and Brenda. He felt a rush for her. She was attractive, alluring, sexy. Maybe she felt that rush too, and it was too fast. If she'd wanted to make more of the situation, she would have agreed to come upstairs. But she hadn't. Maybe she'd change her mind and come back out.

Maybe not.

He heard dishes clinking together and water running. She was *not* coming back out to him. With a heavy sigh, he took the stairs to his apartment. By the time he'd reached the top, he was thinking of heating hot water for a bath. His muscles were tight as hell. And he ached all over.

CHAPTER FOUR

The Monday-morning rainstorm invaded the tiny emerald island as the Vikings had a thousand years before, overtaking and embracing everything in sight. Grayness settled over the city, conquering the airspace and seeping down through the trees to the verdant valleys and rambling rivers and brick buildings, coloring them all gray. Gray everywhere. Rain slashed viciously at the windows, pelting the glass with high-pitched pings in a regular pace. It looked as if it would never stop.

From the safe haven of her warm, comfortable kitchen Brenda sipped coffee and watched the process that maintained the emerald lushness of Ireland. Rain was inevitable, but this time of year it was cold and bone-chilling. She dreaded the thoughts of tramping through this mess, but that's precisely what she and Zack would be doing soon. Today they were scheduled to inspect several prospective plant sites, and she knew he would be anxious to go. He'd been in such a hurry to get the project under way over the weekend, she was a little surprised she hadn't already heard from him this morning.

She finished off the last drop of coffee and moved

unenthusiastically through the motions of getting ready. Since it was raining, she'd forgo her bike and take the bus to the office, get the company car, and come back to pick up Zack.

Dressed to the teeth in rain gear, Brenda paused by the front door of the apartment and checked her watch. She didn't want to go outside and stand on the street waiting for the bus until the last possible moment.

"Brenda? Is that you? Wait up!"

Her heart skipped a beat as she recognized Zack's voice in the hall. She heard him shuffling on the stairs, then groaning low, then more shuffling. Puzzled over the curious sounds, she hurried back to the staircase. "What is it? I've got to catch a bus any minute, Zack."

"I would have called if I had a phone." His voice was more like a groan.

"I explained that may take several weeks. The Irish don't consider a home phone much of a necessity."

She looked up. There he stood midway down the first flight, a grimace on his angular face. He gripped the handrail with one hand and his thigh with the other. But his expression told her that nothing stopped the pain he felt. It hadn't occurred to her that today would be worse than yesterday. In fact, she hadn't thought of his physical condition at all.

"Zack, are you all right?"

"No. I'm going to have to cancel today, Brenda. Sorry, but—" He chuckled embarrassedly. "I'm in no shape to be hiking around a plant site."

"I was going to get the company car."

"Don't bother. Not for me, anyway. Crawling in

64

and out of a car sounds like a special type of torture to me."

"Oh my God, Zack!" She forgot about the bus and tore up the stairs. "Oh Zack, I'm so sorry."

"Why? It isn't your fault. I'm the one out of shape."

"But I should have known that was too much for a novice. I should have borrowed a car."

"And I should have been in better shape." He waved away her guilt. "I just need a little rest today. Sorry to cancel out at the last minute like this."

"I'm not," she admitted with a little smile. "I was dreading going out in this rain. It can be pretty cold and miserable. What you need is a good hot bath and I have just the thing for your sore muscles. Some liniment from Auntie Brige. Come on, let me help you." She took his arm and they walked back to his apartment.

Zack's gait was straight-legged and clumsy. "I can't believe I've done this to myself."

Brenda felt a wrenching inside, feeling a pang of guilt that she'd caused him such pain. It was the last thing on earth she'd wanted to do. "I'll make sure your water's steaming hot."

He let her take charge and watched helplessly as she filled a large pan with water, placed it on the stove, and lit the gas flame under it. "I feel like such a damn fool for letting myself get in such poor shape."

"Not everyone can ride a bicycle for hours without knowing it the next day. I'm a little sore myself. And I feel responsible for this, Zack. I had no idea the problems I would create when I made the suggestion."

"I suggested it. I wanted the trip in the country, and I enjoyed it. At least, this part of me enjoyed it." He motioned from his waist up. "But the other part wishes it were dead."

She muffled a laugh. "And the bike seat isn't very comfortable, either!"

"Oh, yeah. I thought it was just me." He rubbed his seat and gave her a rueful grin. "I've been so damned busy with my life, or rather, my life's mess, that I've neglected everything else, including exercising my own body."

"We all do that when we're under stress," she said gently, then looked up apologetically. "I mean, I assume you've been under stress with your bankruptcy and divorce and everything."

"Yeah, you could say I've been under stress the last few years. But the marriage was gone long before the business." One large hand unconsciously rubbed his thigh. "When one brick tumbled, everything went to hell."

"That's usually the way it happens." She began to unbutton her raincoat. "Now that this is started, I'm going downstairs to get out of this garb. I'll call my boss and then I'll be back up with that liniment." She paused at the door. "A hint about the hot water. Let it run a good five minutes before plugging up the tub. See you in a little bit."

He nodded and with an audible moan hobbled to the bathroom.

Brenda skipped downstairs, as much as someone could skip wearing rubber boots and a long trenchcoat with hood flapping on her back. Suddenly the day wasn't gray at all; it was excitingly sunny because she'd be spending part of it indoors with Zack.

66

He eased himself down into the tub. The hot water edged over his hair-roughened skin, reaching a stopping point as he settled into the steamy liquid. Soon he could feel the warmth seeping inside him, stimulating the blood flow to his sore, aching muscles. He ran his hands over his thighs, then all the way down to his heels and back.

Even touching them lightly hurt. But it also brought memories of yesterday, of biking through the rolling green countryside with Brenda, flocks of sheep ambling across the road, an old woman digging peat for her fire. And Brenda, beautiful Brenda with the laughing blue eyes and mass of red hair, pedaling ahead of him. Always ahead.

He thought of her long legs as they pushed the bicycle pedals around in a clean, circular motion. They were lean, shapely legs, kept that way by biking every day. Even now, in the midst of his pain, he would do it again. The idea of spending another day with Brenda sounded like heaven. But he knew he wanted more, wanted to kiss her, to hold her close again and feel her respond to him. Again.

Oh God, he *wanted* her, wanted to take her to bed and make love and yet he hardly knew a thing about her. She was like a dream who had come into his life when he needed her.

Yes, he did need her. He needed her laughter, her enthusiasm, her zest for life. Admittedly he'd lost his, as one problem tumbled into another. He'd forgotten how to have fun, how to laugh, how to love a woman. Losing Charmaine had diminished his desire for another relationship. He hadn't even wanted another woman, hadn't wanted the bother of getting to know anyone. Mostly though, he wouldn't risk the pain.

Until Brenda.

She threw all his old notions into a backspin. She was a welcome sunny face with laughing blue eyes and riotous red hair who immediately captured his imagination and made everything seem worthwhile again. Soon she would be back, rubbing his legs with her ointment, rubbing away the pain. God, he could hardly wait to feel her hands on him, long, slender fingers seeking the ache deep in his muscles.

But his physical aches were nothing compared to the pain deep in his heart. Everything had gone so wrong with his life and those close to him that he needed to know life could be right again. Right with the beautiful Brenda O'Shea; right with a new start in the beautiful Ireland. With her in his arms . . .

"Zack?"

His head shot up. *Brenda.* She was so close, she had to be right outside the bathroom door! "Yes?" Would she come in? His heart pounded at the thought.

"Excuse me for barging in like this, but you didn't hear my knock. I figured you were still in the tub."

"You figured right." He paused only briefly before teasing, "Come on in."

"I just brought the liniment so you could use it while your legs are still warm from the tub. That's when Auntie Brige says it works best. I'll leave it on the dresser."

"Hey, wait a minute! Don't leave, Brenda."

"Why? What is it?"

She was so close, just a door away. Why didn't she just open it and—

68

"Brenda, I thought you would do the honors. I'm not a very good nurse." He stood up and water dripped from his lean body onto the floor as he grabbed for a towel.

"Do the—" She laughed. "No, thank you. I'm not much of a nurse, either."

He stepped out of the tub. "But it would be so much better if you would—"

"Better? I doubt it. You do it. You know where your legs hurt the worse."

"I'll tell you." He opened the bathroom door. "I'll *show* you."

She looked up, trying to force her blue eyes to fix on his brown ones. Watch his face, not his *oh dear* bare body. "That's over and above the call of duty, don't you think, Zack? I'll be glad to fix you a little breakfast, though." Just before she wheeled around, her eyes dropped slightly to take in his towel-clad form. His chest was broad, but she knew that already. His muscular arms didn't particularly surprise her. But to see him in all his lithe, masculine glory, down to the towel knotted low on his lean hips, sent her into a tailspin.

"Yes, I guess that's asking too much. Even breakfast is."

"I don't mind." She gulped and tried to smile. Then, like a shy ingenue, she turned and retreated.

He sighed and picked up the liniment bottle.

In a few minutes he joined her, casually dressed in a V-necked sweater and jeans. She looked up and smiled, trying to blot out the image of him wrapped only in a towel. Beneath the soft sweater and worn jeans was the muscular body of a man she found very attractive. And she tried to dismiss her erotic thoughts about him. Even though she had rebuffed his offer to rub liniment on his aching legs, she had had to draw on all her strength to do so.

"Feel better?"

"Much. The liniment feels good. I expected some foul-smelling stuff, but this is nice and light."

"Herbs. Aunt Brige mixes it herself. It's good for lots of things. I don't know why I didn't think of it last night."

He folded his arms and leaned against the door facing, watching her move about his kitchen. "Could it have been the kiss that made you forget, Brenda?"

She bent down to pull a fragrant pan out of the oven. "Could have been. Or the fact that I was tired after the ride. Are you fishing for compliments on the way you kiss?"

"God, no! I just wondered if our feelings were the same last night. To see if you felt the way I did."

"Frustrated?"

"Very!"

"Look, you know already I responded. It . . . it was nice." She picked up a knife from the cabinet.

He took one step and gripped her arms, pulling her hard against his chest. "Only nice, Brenda? I think you're trying to hide the way you really feel, even from yourself."

"You're wrong, Zack," she said tightly. "I'm trying to resist. You're a client and this is dangerous."

"Dangerous? You mean because of these sparks flying between us might catch on fire? I think I already am!"

"Zack, we just can't ruin everything for both of us because of a quick fling."

"I don't want a quick fling."

"Yes, I'm afraid you do. Now let me go. I have to cut the shortbread while it's still hot."

He released her with a quick snap of his wrists. "You didn't have to stay, you know."

"I knew it would be a risk." She scored the warm, soft dough with practiced precision. "But I was willing to take it. After all, you are my client and my job is to help you get your business going here."

"And nothing more?"

She sighed and looked up at him. "Zack, I've already given you more time than usual. Surely you know that."

"Yes, and I appreciate it. But I want more."

"Soft-boiled or hard?"

"You or me?"

"Your eggs." She motioned to the pan of eggs on the stove and tried to hide a smile.

"Oh, uh, soft is okay." He grinned too and carried their cups to the table while she dealt with the eggs.

Brenda folded a napkin beside each plate. "Shortbread with black currant tea. Auntie Brige swears by it," she said crisply and averted her eyes from his.

He touched her hand, letting his fingertips trail gently over the top of hers. "Thanks, it smells great."

She quivered at his soft caress and drew in her breath. Slowly lifting her eyes to meet his gaze, she saw the blatant desire of an honest man. And Brenda wondered if he could read her eyes, too. She licked her dry lips and murmured, "I hope you like shortbread."

"Ever since my first taste yesterday at your Aunt

Brigid's, I'm hooked." He pinched off a corner and put it in his mouth. "You're a good cook, Brenda."

"This one is my grandmother Sadie's recipe. Easy as pie." She took a bite too, and quickly decided that constant conversation was the best way out of this. "She and I were always very close and I stayed with her a lot when I was growing up. If I wasn't feeling well, she would fix me a treat of shortbread. Some things stay with you forever, I guess. Every now and then I still make it for myself when I feel low. I guess that's why I thought about making it for you today. To me it's one of those comfort foods that always make you feel better."

"And it does. Between your liniment and fresh shortbread, I feel better already. But mostly, I suspect it's because you're here."

He gazed at her seriously until she laughed, then he joined her. He was teasing, and she had to admit, she loved it.

"Did you have one of those feel-better foods when you were growing up, Zack?"

"Yeah. Hot, sticky buns. My brother and I usually worked together on this project, so you can imagine what a mess we made in the kitchen. We'd pile them high with brown sugar and raisins and on rare occasions we'd add nuts. Then, we'd top each one with a blob of butter and bake. They come out oozing and delicious. Cures anything, especially loneliness."

"Were you lonely?"

Zack pinched his lower lip thoughtfully. "Sometimes. Mom worked a lot. Our father was long gone."

"But you had your brother."

"He wasn't always around."

72

"Oh." Brenda sensed she had stumbled onto a sensitive area with Zack and was reluctant to pursue it further. Obviously his childhood held lots of pain. "Well, the rolls sound positively wicked. Where did you live growing up, Zack?"

"Philadelphia. East side. We were street-tough, always proving our 'macho.'"

"Lots of fights?"

"Constantly." His brown eyes clouded briefly. "We were terribly poor. You know, some people claim that as kids they never knew they were poor. Well, we were poor and we damn well knew it. Everything was a struggle. And you, Brenda? Where did you live?"

"Baltimore, Maryland. I guess you could say we were middle class. If you were in Philadelphia, we weren't that far away, were we?"

"No, I guess not." He rubbed his nose and looked out the window at the rain. God, the way they grew up was probably eons apart. "Tell me about Brenda O'Shea. I know a little about your grandmother Sadie, but not much about you. Only what I see, which I like very much."

She shrugged. "What do you want to know? Sadie came to America with her soldier-husband and they settled in Baltimore. There were two children after my mother, one of whom died in childhood of polio. My mother also married young, at seventeen. Seems to be a family trend." She grinned ruefully. "My father was injured in Vietnam when I was young. It didn't mean much to me except that we got to go to the White House for an awards ceremony. Later, I discovered that my father had received the Medal of Honor for dragging a buddy through enemy fire."

"Medal of Honor winner, huh?" Zack was impressed.

"To me he was just a daddy who ran a hardware store. When he and Mom moved to the outskirts of Baltimore, I stayed with Gran Sadie and finished school. I always got along better with her than my mother anyway."

"Sounds like an impressive family. An audience with the President and everything."

Brenda chuckled. "Everything's relative, I guess. My Aunt Caroline works in Washington, D.C., and is always at the White House for special ceremonies or the Capitol for committee meetings. She's on the President's Special Council on Education."

"And you, Brenda? What special deed have you accomplished?"

She shrugged. "Muddled my way through college with barely passing grades. Married young. Too young, obviously. Divorced young. Decided to try again somewhere else. Ireland appealed to me because of my family ties here. Aunt Brigid offered to try to get me a job. And I love it. It's been my greatest success so far."

"A new life in the old country huh?"

"I needed a change, just like you, Zack. Now, I want to hear about . . ." She checked her watch. "Oops! I've got to get to work. I told Padraig I'd be there before noon. I have some paperwork to catch up on. Anyway, he's looking for more sites for your plant. So, I'll take a rain check on finding out about Zack Ehrens, okay?"

"It's a deal." He nodded, thinking he had no intention of telling her the whole truth about his miserable excuse of a family.

"Sorry to leave you with this mess, Zack, but you do understand, don't you?"

"After you fixed such a marvelous meal, the least I can do is clean up. And even though you wouldn't rub the liniment on my sore muscles, I appreciate you lending it to me. I feel much better."

"Good. Why don't we give you a day to heal before we start looking at land? I'll check back with you tomorrow and we'll plan to go see one or two sites then. Okay? I'm leaving several of these black currant tea bags with you. And the liniment. Please use them both."

"Fine." He watched her in masculine admiration as she whirled toward the door. "But I'd like to see you later."

She smiled apprehensively and reached for the doorknob. "Maybe, Zack." Without hesitation, she was gone.

He stared for long minutes at the brown door, feeling that just when things started to develop between them, she had to dash away for some reason or another.

Wednesday had rolled around before Brenda had time for Zack again. "You aren't my only client," she said, refusing dinner invitations for both Monday and Tuesday nights.

"Nor the only man pursuing you?"

"Is that what you're doing?"

"Almost as hard as you're running away," he vowed solemnly.

"Give us a little time, Zack." She shifted from one foot to the other in the doorway of her apartment. "I've got to go. Business meeting."

"Okay. Nobody's holding you." He stuffed his hands into his back pockets. Frustration was written clearly on his face.

"Zack, you're impatient. You need to learn to cool down."

Scowling, he looked down the hall toward Mr. Flanagan's apartment, half-expecting the old man to poke his head out the door to see what the ruckus was about. "Yeah, I guess I am. Sorry to be such a pest." He took one step before she caught him.

"Zack, you aren't a pest. You know that." Her hand slipped down to his wrist. "I'm just trying to be cautious. You understand, surely."

He looked back at her, his brown eyes deep and dark. "Sure, Brenda."

"Tomorrow," she promised.

They spent the next two days together. Brenda drove him through the city, showing him around. Then they scoured the countryside and tromped through endless acres of untilled farmland and empty pastures. She related the sad stories of farmers who had gone out of business and had been forced to leave the farms to ruin while they tried to find jobs in the cities. Many of them ended up on some freighter heading for America. Some were lucky enough to sell to an entrepreneur like Zack, a foreigner who might come in and build something profitable on the land.

On Friday, Zack went to Padraig's office and they discussed several possibilities. He had chosen a particular farm located just outside of town and was hoping they could make a deal on it soon. Brenda usually left land negotiations to Padraig, so she went on home.

That night Zack appeared at Brenda's door, champagne in hand. "I'm celebrating and wondered if you'd like to join me."

"Celebrating? Did you get it?"

Zack nodded. "Yep. We have a verbal agreement with the owner. Padraig is going to draw up the papers next week. Soon I'll be an Irish landholder, thanks to you, Brenda."

"Congratulations, Zack!" Her eyes lit up and spontaneously she opened her arms and hugged him quickly. Then, realizing what she'd done, she stepped back and murmured, "I'm so glad you're pleased."

"I'm more than pleased, Brenda, I'm ecstatic! Won't you join me?" On his face was a boyish delight that she'd never seen before. It was the pure joy of accomplishment. "This is my new beginning. Please share my celebration, Brenda."

"Well, why not?"

"I have some cheese and crackers to go with this upstairs."

She groped at her hair. "I should brush these tangles."

His eyes caressed her auburn tresses where her hand had touched. "It looks beautiful to me. Come on."

"You're the one who has to look at it," she said laughingly, joining him.

Happily they toasted Zack's decision to come to Ireland and Padraig's decision to assign Brenda to him. Another glass saluted their new friendship and yet another to the land that would provide new jobs for all the locals who were out of work. By the time they had toasted all that, they were giggling and feeding each other cheese and crackers.

"I'm going to need some coffee to sober me up, Zack," she said, laughing at her plight. "I might just tumble down the stairs to my apartment. Then, wouldn't old Mr. Flanagan have something to peek out his door about!"

"Anything you want, my sweet, wild Irish rose," he agreed and followed her to the kitchen. "Except no coffee. I have good, strong Irish tea, though. It's fabulous for sobering up."

She smiled up at him. "Okay, where is it?"

"Let me see," he said, opening door after door of empty cabinets. She could tell he was stalling. "Ah, here 'tis." He drew out one lone tea bag and let it dangle between thumb and forefinger. "Only one."

"Oh. I have more down at my place. I'll go down and get it."

She started away but he grabbed her arm and pulled her back against him. "No. Don't go."

She looked up at him, questioning.

"You can't make it down the stairs, remember? Anyway, I don't want any tea. I don't want anything to dim this feeling I have right now, this glow. This, whatever we're sharing tonight, Brenda. You and me. Together." His arm slid around her, pulling her even closer. "It's wonderful."

She caught her breath and leaned on the firm wall of his chest. Tonight his body was strong and eager against hers. And tonight, she was all too weak and willing for a taste of that strength. The way he held

78

her felt so natural, his arms surrounding her, his body pulsing with heat alongside hers.

She trembled and responded to that heat by molding herself even closer to his hardness. "Oh Zack, this is getting dangerous."

"I always did like playing with fire." His hand cupped her neck, then lifted her chin. His lips were amazingly close to hers. And still they didn't mesh.

"Are you going to kiss me or not?"

"Only if you beg," he whispered. His hand continued to cradle her chin and his arm remained nestled between her breasts. He moved the muscles ever so slightly, erotically rubbing his arm against both breasts at the same time.

At the moment, she thought she would die if he didn't kiss her. And do something about that arm! "Yes, oh yes—"

The kiss that had been on his lips all evening yet never fulfilled, brushed across her lips. Gentle and hot and promising more. "Brenda, Brenda, please . . ." he murmured, brushing his kisses across her chin and down the pale column of her neck.

She arched her head back. The pulsing in her neck sent heat waves throughout her body as he continued to kiss her.

"Zack, please—" she gasped and he covered her mouth with his, silencing her words. His hand dropped slowly from her neck, caressing one breast along the way. His thumb and forefinger found the tight nipple beneath her clothes and squeezed. She moaned softly.

His eyes were dark and brooding and filled with passion. That look excited her more than she ever dreamed, especially when she realized his passion was meant for her.

Their lips matched perfectly. His mouth met hers, seeking, sipping sweet nectar, then he backed off to look at her. "You're beautiful, Brenda. I can't believe you're in my arms at last." Then he was kissing her again, harder this time, stronger as his lips forced hers apart and his tongue drove between her teeth. He plunged into the honeyed depths of her mouth, his hands bracing her back, holding her firmly against him.

She opened willingly for his intrusion, welcoming the thrusting motion with a gentle undulation of her hips against his. The moment she noticed she was doing it, she stopped abruptly and drew in a surprised breath.

He lifted his head. "What's wrong?"

"Nothing . . . I'd better go."

"Why?"

"Things are getting too hot."

"I like it that way. Don't you?"

She shook her head. "Zack, I—"

"Brenda, don't go."

She looked at him, knowing full well what he was saying. Knowing in her heart what she wanted to respond. Knowing what she should do. Quickly that part of her brain shut down and she could only think of Zack. And how wonderful she felt with him holding her. And how she wanted more of this enigmatic man who held her so close. His hooded eyes promised more.

"Zack, maybe we should wait—"

"No excuses this time. I want you. You want me. Please stay."

Brenda looked into his dark eyes and saw herself, happy in the arms of a man for the first time in years. And she liked what she saw. She knew what she felt inside and didn't want to lose the excitement, the anticipation. "But I don't know anything about you, Zack. Except that I want to know everything."

"I'll tell you everything."

She smiled and her hands traveled lingeringly up his chest to rest on his shoulders. She couldn't help herself. "Show me."

"It'll be my pleasure."

CHAPTER FIVE

He kissed her slightly parted, waiting lips and felt her reluctance melt away. Instead, there was a willingness that he found wildly exciting. "My God, Brenda, you're beautiful. I've wanted to love you since the day we met."

"Oh come now, Zack. You were not pleased to see me there that day, and you know it."

"I took one look at you with your fabulous red hair and those long, sexy legs and it scared me. I could imagine us making love, but not working together. And you know how important this business is to me."

"I told you I'd work hard. Have I disappointed you?"

"Not one bit." His kisses played along her cheek and jaw line, then dipped to plot a sensitive path down the pale column of her neck. "You've been tireless. But making love to you is the most important thing to me right now."

He lowered his head to hers again and this time the kiss wasn't tentative or testing. There was a certain hungry power in his grasp, a shock wave of strength that reverberated from his body to hers. And Brenda felt it all the way through her limbs, spearing her very core with his burgeoning power.

It was thrilling, this rush of sensuality between them. Suddenly the rock walls were torn down, there was no holding back on her part, no resisting on his. They both wanted each other, both sought the same sensual pleasures. She surged against him, enjoying the feel of his taut masculine body pressed to the softer areas of hers.

Gloriously, neither seemed to want to hurry the moments, either. Their kisses were leisurely, their caresses soft, their exploration into intimacy slow. This teasing torment allowed the anticipation of what could happen between them to grow higher and higher with each touch, each kiss.

"When you kiss me like that, it leaves me weak," she admitted with a little laugh, leaning heavily on the fortress of his chest.

"I don't know any other way to kiss you. I'm weak, too. For wanting you."

"You feel strong to me," she said, sliding her hands beneath his sweater and running them over the corded muscles of his back.

"It's because you're here, so close. But you can't see my knees shaking." He chuckled low and playfully kissed her nose and chin and mouth again. "Let's get closer. There are better places for us . . . for this . . . than the kitchen." Reaching down, he easily scooped her up in his arms and walked through the living room and down the dark hall.

It was provocative to think he was carrying her off to his bedroom. Where he dressed and undressed and slept. Soon it would be the place where he loved her. Soon . . .

Brenda anticipated the moment with eyes closed and face buried against his chest. She reached up and nibbled at his neck, which tasted surprisingly like ginger. She inhaled his wonderful fragrance and, spontaneously, licked out her tongue for more of a taste of him. When he shifted her away from him, she opened her eyes to the undistinguished decor of his bedroom.

"This is where you belong," he murmured as he deposited her gently on the bed. "Where it's well padded, just for us." Bending over her reclining form, he kissed her while at the same time caressed the curves of her breasts and waist and hips. His hands set her on fire and for a moment Brenda wasn't sure she could wait for them to undress. She writhed in undeniable pleasure while his lips kissed sensitive places and murmured sweet, dark words of passion.

"Ohhh, Zack . . ."

"I want you, want to *see* you, Brenda. Want to *feel* you."

He helped her slip the sweater over her head and leaned down to kiss along the top edge of lace that scalloped her swelling breasts. Then he unlatched the front closing of her bra and freed her from the binding garment.

With breathless admiration, he caressed and kissed her enflamed skin. "Oh God, they're like pearls," he murmured as his hands lifted and stroked the soft mounds. His lips closed over each tip, suckling them to aching tightness.

She arched to meet his pleasure as he scooted his fingers tantalizingly inside the zipped front of her

84

slacks. "Wait, I'll take them off," she offered and shaky hands tore at her remaining clothes.

At last nude, she lay back on the bed and watched him undress in the shadows. Zack was a beautiful male; his very appearance left her breathing deeply, feeling very much a woman.

And Zack was very much a man. Well-muscled arms linked to broad shoulders. His back was a creation of masculine beauty, a latticework of muscles connecting and rippling as he moved to discard his clothes. He shifted and she saw the curly mat of dark hair that covered his expansive chest. The evocative hairline led downward to a flat waist before disappearing beneath bulging briefs.

Then the briefs were gone and masculine hips narrowed to strong, firm thighs. He turned toward her and her eyes widened at the glory of his vigorous arousal.

Her heart pounded wildly as he came to her, and she opened her arms and her heart to receive him.

His body radiated heat in the tiny space between them until there was no more space and he was erotically rubbing against her. Hot skin against hot skin. It was almost more than he could stand, yet he knew he had to pace himself, take his time, savor. "Your eyes are like sapphires. No, they're more like blue smoke. And sexy . . ."

She smiled with relaxed pleasure as his kisses circled her gently sloping globes. She felt a deep inner tugging as his lips suckled each taut nipple.

"And these are sweet, creamy pearls."

His tongue made a moist trail down her middle, stopping to lave her navel, then moved lower.

"Your skin's like ivory, so smooth and slick."

Strong fingers stroked the auburn tangle of hair at her delta and she gasped aloud as he found the diamond of her womanhood.

"Easy . . . easy, sweet Brenda," he said, kissing her parted lips. "Slow and easy. Touch me, Bren . . ."

Eagerly her nimble fingers stroked those masculine muscles of his arms and shoulders. "Hmm, Zack, you smell like ginger. I *like* ginger . . ."

With a satisfied groan he lay back on the bed and let her explore his body.

"You taste like ginger, too," she whispered as her hands roamed over the rough planes of masculinity. Then she planted moist kisses over him, letting her lips show instead of tell him of her admiration. Finally, when she had touched him everywhere and her feminine curiosity was sated she snuggled closer. "Hold me, Zack. You feel so good next to me."

His arms wrapped around her and the explosive energy of his heated body radiated passionate heat to hers. Passion which was barely under control. "You're like an exquisite jewel, Brenda. Sparkling with a rare beauty. I want to love you all night long . . ."

"I want to love you, too," she admitted shyly, spreading the fingers of one hand into the hair on his chest and scraping her nails along his skin. Then, she proceeded to drive him crazy as she stroked lower, more sensitive areas. "You know what I thought when I first saw you, Zack?"

"Hm?"

"I thought your eyes were very sad, and I wanted to make them happy again."

"They're happy tonight."

She lifted her head and kissed his lips. "I'm glad."

"With you, Brenda, I am always happy. You make me forget everything . . . everything that tears me apart."

"I'll make it all go away," she promised and undulated her hips invitingly against his. "At least for now, Zack."

"Now, Bren?"

She nodded. "Yes, now . . ."

He touched her most intimate and sensitive spot, caressing and stroking until she surged against his hand. She was moist and ready.

With an easy movement, his knee separated her thighs and he slipped between her legs. Framing her face with his hands, he kissed her, hard and long. As his lips opened hers, his tongue dipped between her teeth, and she moaned softly in response. She opened to him, and his hips thrust forward instinctively. The force drove his heated shaft inside her, merging them at last. Gently, slowly, steadily.

Together they twisted to reach the ultimate of feelings, legs tangled, arms grasping, bodies seeking, his masculine strength burying deeper in her lush femininity.

She rose to a higher plane than she'd ever been, her feelings crystallizing for him into a mingling of love and lust, of desire and incredible longing. Of a woman's desire to please her man, of Brenda's yearning to bring pleasure to Zack. To make him smile. To brighten his dark, sad eyes.

Then she was lost as all senses whirled together. For

endless time she was only aware of her own pleasures, her own desires being fulfilled.

Wildly they peaked, Brenda feeling a rush she had never experienced. Higher and higher, culminating in the utterance of a soft but uncontrolled cry. Slowly, like the easing of a magic spell, they drifted in each other's arms, settled into a quiet calm.

Eventually, he withdrew from her, and they lay wrapped in each other's arms. Content and sated. For now.

His sigh reassured her he was still awake and she ventured to speak. "Zack, what are you thinking right now?"

"That I'm the luckiest man alive. You're incredible."

She was quiet for a little while, then moved her head to pillow on his shoulder. "I've never felt so good, never known such . . . strong feelings for someone."

"I feel the same, Brenda."

"Zack, do you believe in . . . love at first sight?"

"I didn't. Before now."

She smiled and kissed his bare chest. And that night she slept in his bed, content in his arms with her lithe, bare body pressed to his. Once during the night, he woke her and they made love again in a burst of quick desire. Then they slept again.

Brenda had never been so positive in her life about anything as she was that this was exactly where she belonged. With Zack.

When morning came she was vaguely aware of doors opening and closing, of keys clicking in locks, of the fact that she was alone in bed. She slid her hand to the place where Zack had touched her and made most intimate love to her. And she was warm again, just thinking of him.

As her head cleared and she became more awake, Brenda realized fully what she'd done last night. To go to bed with a client was certainly not approved behavior. Normally she would be embarrassed and chagrined at such actions. Normally she wouldn't have done this.

Yet, with Zack, she had no regrets. She and Zack had been clearly attracted from the first. They were two Americans in Ireland, drawn together by fate and a kindred spirit. They belonged together. Last night had been absolutely beautiful.

Zack knew exactly how to elicit her deepest response, and he fit inside her perfectly. Thinking of the moment of their merging, she pulled up her knees and squeezed them together, recalling the way she felt when he was there. Making love with Zack was more wonderful than she had ever dreamed because she hadn't known how intensely her body would react. She had never known such feelings existed.

Brenda scooted under the covers and buried her face in the pillow with a silly smile that wouldn't go away as she thought about him and how he made love. And how he made her feel. *Fabulous!*

She dozed and woke again, wondering if he had abandoned her in his own apartment when she heard him unlocking the door. In a few minutes, Zack appeared in the doorway, wet hair plastered to his head and clothes obviously damp.

"Morning," he said lightly and crossed over to the

bed where she lay waiting for him. "Coffee's on. It'll be ready in a few minutes."

She smiled at the sight of him, looking so rakishly handsome with droplets of moisture still clinging to his hair and face. The ridge along the top of his broad shoulders was dark and wet. "You didn't go out in the rain to get the coffee, did you?"

"We needed some anyway. Actually, it isn't really raining. More like heavy mist. I picked up breakfast on the way home from jogging."

"Jogging?" she groaned. "How could you possibly find enough energy to exercise after last night?"

"Boundless energy," he said, sitting on the edge of the bed and bracing an arm on either side of her head. Slowly he lowered himself slowly toward her.

"Even the morning after?"

"I must stay in shape."

She grinned up at him, loving the anticipation of Zack's kiss. Her blue eyes twinkled merrily. "You were in pretty good shape last night, Zack."

"So were you." He stroked her disheveled auburn hair, tucking a strand back with the rest. It spread enticingly over the white pillowcase. "We were good together, weren't we, Brenda?"

"Fantastic," she said softly and pulled him down for the kiss he'd failed to deliver. His lips were cool on hers, and she framed his cheeks with her warm hands. "Ohh, you're cold."

"Just my face. Wouldn't you like to warm me up?"

"Of course."

"I think I'd better take a shower first. Join me?"

"Love to."

She waited until he'd adjusted the water and she

90

was sure it was warm before she dashed into the bathroom. "I was curious to see your shower. My bathroom is old-fashioned and just has a tub."

"Well, I'm a shower person myself, and I constructed this device. It's crude, but it works." He helped her step into the tub.

"Very clever. Americans are so inventive. If you need something badly enough, you'll find a way."

He pulled her under the makeshift shower head that connected to the tub's faucet. They stood beneath the pelting warm spray, his arms wrapped around her back, hers encircling his ribs. His hand slid around her lower back and pressed hard, pulling them together erotically. "What about if I need you?"

"You'll find a way," she murmured and ran her hands over his slick body, finally cupping his flat hips. "Hmm. Nice. You warmer now?"

"Not warm enough," he said bending his head for a drenching kiss. "I think we'd better finish here before the hot water runs out completely."

"I think you're right. Want me to wash your back?"

"No, that's not where . . ."

Soon they were laughing and romping in bed, warm and pressed together and making love again. And when they were finished, he rolled away reluctantly. "How about coffee in bed?"

"Sounds wonderful."

"I'll be right back." He donned a chocolate-brown robe that matched his dark eyes and strode barefoot out to the kitchen. When he returned, he had more than coffee on the tray.

"What's this?" she asked, delighted. "Hot sticky buns?"

"I passed a bakery a couple of blocks away that had them in the window, and I couldn't resist. I knew they'd be great with the coffee."

She inhaled the mingled fragrances of coffee and melted brown sugar. "You were right. Smells marvelous!"

They sat cross-legged on the bed, he in his brown robe and she in a dark blue flannel shirt from his closet, "This is probably the best breakfast I've ever had, Zack. Ever!"

"That's what I like about you, Brenda. Unabashed honesty! I'll confess, these sticky buns are far better than anything my brother and I ever made."

"But, at the time, I'll bet yours were best. Tell me about him."

"Him? Who?"

"Your brother. Where is he now? What does he do?"

Zack's dark eyes clouded immediately and the light mood between them changed. Brenda wasn't sure what happened or why, but it was a difference she could feel.

"He works in California."

"Oh. Did he work with you out there in Ehrens Enterprises?"

Zack's eyes darted to her, then down. He nodded abruptly. "Yeah, for a while."

Brenda took another bite of the sticky bun. "So now that the business has folded, and you're over here, what's he doing? Did he start another business?"

"Another business? No, not exactly. Uh, James . . ." Zack rose and walked to the window. It had

92

started to rain, harder than the mist of earlier in the day. "James works at various jobs now."

"Oh, so he has a variety of skills?"

"Yes, he's a hard worker, considering he never made it through college."

"But, you did, didn't you, Zack? It's in your dossier that you have a degree."

"I've always been driven, I guess." He chuckled self-consciously and glared at the rain driving against the window. *You're the great white hope, big brother,* James would say. *You with your fancy college degree. Go out and make it for the rest of us.* It was a taunt, but Zack took it as a challenge. After all, he was the big brother, the oldest male in the family. And he tried, oh God how he'd tried, to "make it" for them. He was learning, though, it was practically impossible. "It's impossible . . ." he muttered in a low breath.

"Zack? What did you say?"

He halted and clamped his jaws together.

Brenda stood beside him, looking up curiously. She touched his arm. "What's impossible, Zack?"

He glared at her. Had he really said that? How much had he revealed? "Huh? Oh nothing. Just nothing."

She squeezed his arm. "I didn't mean to pry."

"You aren't. No, it's okay. It's just . . ." He jerked free of her and stalked across the floor, then back again. His eyes were strangely fierce. "My brother and I are close. Real close. I don't want anything to come between us and now it's tough. Things are beyond our control."

She looked at him curiously. What launched this sudden defense of his brother? She didn't know what

93

he was talking about and decided to keep her responses to a minimum. "I'm sure it is, with you here and him still in California. I guess you miss him."

"Yeah, I miss him." Zack turned away and nervously massaged the back of his neck.

"Zack, you don't have to explain anything. When you're ready to talk, I'll be glad to listen." She touched his back, felt the muscles tightening across its breadth.

Slowly he turned to her. His eyes were still fierce and unreadable, except for the pain.

"Zack, whatever is bothering you can wait."

Suddenly he groaned and wrapped his long, strong arms around her, drawing her close to his pain-wracked body. "Oh Brenda, if you only knew . . ."

She didn't know how to respond to his strange behavior, other than to return the gesture, clasping her arms tightly around his ribs. His heart pounded against hers and she ached for him. For his unknown, inner pain. She fervently wished that she knew what was wrong with him so she could help.

They stood that way for a long time, wrapped together, seeking and giving strength to each other. The rain continued to ping against the window, and they drew into a tighter circle of themselves. Here was a place that was warm and dry and secure.

Finally he spoke, and it was a heavy rasping sound. "I didn't realize until today how hard it is for me to talk about my brother. About my family."

"You don't have to, Zack. I don't care about them or your past. I only care about you and me and what's happening right now."

"No, you deserve to know more about me, Brenda.

It's funny. I thought this would be easier to tell. I thought I could handle it." He paused and pulled back to look at her. With soft caresses, he touched her hair. "I've been reluctant because you come from such blue-blooded stock. Your family is so typically American—" He stopped and sighed heavily.

"What do you mean, typically American? Everyone is."

"Solid citizens who've made something of themselves," he interrupted. "An immigrant grandmother who married and made her life better. A father who was a Medal of Honor winner. A supportive mother, an aunt who works on the President's Council." He gestured as he talked. "They're all well educated, upright—"

"Please Zack, don't."

"Well hell, it's true." He sighed and moved away as if touching her prohibited this type of conversation. Touching her precipitated loving her and right now he needed to talk. So he sat in a chair and clasped his hands between widespread knees. "I couldn't tell Aunt Brigid if my ancestors came from Ireland because I haven't the slightest idea."

Brenda sat opposite him on the end of the bed. "That isn't important, Zack."

"Yes, it is," he insisted. "You asked, and you deserve to know before we go any further with our relationship. This may affect us, may even break us up. But you need to know." Zack looked closely at Brenda's oval-shaped face, trying to read what was going on behind her troubled eyes. But her expression was open and curious.

She shook her head negatively. "Nothing you could

say about your family could affect us. I only care about you."

Zack hesitated. Would she really want to hear all? Would he be able to tell her everything? The only one who knew *everything* was Charmaine. And she had eventually left him. God, he didn't want to lose Brenda.

"Don't tell me," she said urgently. "It doesn't matter, Zack."

"My father left us when I was four," he blurted. "James was only two. My mother raised us alone. She had no education and not much ambition. It was damn tough."

Brenda felt a pang of sadness tear through her as she pictured the two little boys, fatherless, living half the time on the streets of Philadelphia. "It must have been very hard for her, as well as for you boys."

"Damned hard. She never had a decent job that I could remember. And she . . . she drank a lot. We were in our teens when she died. I realize now that she must have been an alcoholic. See what a sloppy family I have?" He glared at her. Could he tell her more? This much was bad enough.

"Zack, I want you to know one important thing," Brenda declared with conviction. "This will not tear us apart. I think that I have even more admiration for you now. After all, you finished college. That, in itself, was a remarkable feat. I realize you couldn't have had any help from your family."

He shrugged. "I worked a lot. And was lucky enough to get a scholarship."

"Smart enough, you mean." Brenda's expression softened. Zack was truly a remarkable man and what

96

he'd revealed only made him bigger in her mind. "I'm glad you told me. I think more of you than ever."

You don't know all of it, my darling Brenda, he thought as his eyes sought hers. "But James . . ." He couldn't bring himself to tell her all. "James had a mind of his own. I was the responsible one, he was the rebel. Eventually, he passed a high school equivalency test and got his GED." *He was in prison, trying to seduce the attractive, young teacher. He didn't give a damn what she was teaching.*

"I think it runs in the family."

"What—"

"To have a mind of your own. You do, and it's a strength, Zack. To accomplish all you have, in spite of the lack of support or help, was quite an accomplishment. I admire you."

"I've certainly had my share of failures. You know some of them already, from my dossier. My business in California, my marriage to Charmaine . . ."

"I don't want to hear about her. Not now. I want to concentrate on you." Brenda moved toward him, kneeling close, stroking his forehead. "It must have been hard, to always be the responsible one," she said softly, then kissed his forehead and brows.

He closed his eyes with supreme pleasure as she kissed the lids gently, her lips feathering the tender skin. "Ahh, Brenda . . ."

"I don't care about your failures, Zack. We all have them. So do I. Some things in life just don't work out for us, and we have to try again. That's what we're both doing here, honey. Trying again. And this time, it'll work. We'll do it together."

97

His arms reached out to her, pulling her between his knees. "I've never known a woman like you, Brenda."

"And I've never felt this way about a man before, Zack. So close and caring."

"Brenda, my darling, my beautiful darling Bren . . ." His huge hands framed her face, then slowly burrowed into her thick mass of hair. "Oh God, Bren. You're good for me." His mouth sought hers in a fervent, feverish kiss.

She raised her face to him, absorbing all he had to give, giving all the love she could. *I hope so,* she thought fervently. *And you're good for me, Zack Ehrens.*

Brenda wrapped herself in the private cocoon of his arms, loving him with sweet, sensuous kisses and soothing, understanding words.

She thought about how this whole involvement with Zack had been fast and furious. One day they were business colleagues, the next they were lovers. Yet, strangely, she had no doubt about their love. *It was love.* Nothing could be so crazy, so wild, so real.

CHAPTER SIX

"Are you sure you want to go?"

"Yes, I'm positive."

Brenda propped up on one elbow and studied Zack's profile. "Why?"

"Because today's Sunday, and she expects you."

"I don't go to Auntie Brige's every Sunday."

"Anyway, maybe we can borrow her car and go look over the property again. Wouldn't you like to take another look? And Aunt Brigid might like to go along."

"Aha! I knew it! Your ulterior motive is to see the property! Okay, it's a deal." Brenda slid her hand over Zack's chest and snuggled closer, relishing the feel of him beside her in bed. Their one night of love had expanded to include the entire weekend. "I'd love to see it, and I'm sure Auntie Brige would, too. But shouldn't we borrow a car here? So you won't get crippled biking way out there again?"

"I'm not worried because I have the liniment."

She leaned close to his ear and whispered, "And this time I'll be happy to rub it on."

"I think I need some now." He took her hand and moved it along his lean, muscled frame. "My legs weren't the only problem, you know. That damned little seat was invented by an evil torturer!"

She laughed delightedly and caught him in a bear hug. "Oh no you don't! I have to see visible proof that you're in pain!"

"You're a hard woman, Nurse Cratchett. I'm in better shape for this trip. I'll be fine this time."

"Better shape? Let me see. Hmm, I don't know . . ." She ran an exploring hand over his chest and down to his waist.

"Lower!" he moaned, then turned toward her and wrapped her in his arms. "I love it when you touch me, Bren."

"And I love touching you," she murmured with a smile. "I think you're right, Zack. You *are* in better shape . . ."

"If you keep that up, I may never be able to get out of bed," he growled, tenderly nipping her lower lip with his teeth. "And I won't let you go without me. Aunt Brigid won't mind if we arrive after lunch, will she?" He drew her closer still, aligning their bodies as they lay facing each other.

"Not if she knew the alternative."

"We'll tell her you were busy with a client."

"Very busy . . ." Brenda murmured between kisses. Sliding one long leg over him, she playfully straddled his hips and pinned him to the bed. "Busy pleasing my favorite client." She smothered his face with kisses, then started in on his neck. When she moved lower, nipping each taut little male nipple, he grabbed her and merrily rolled them over and over. Sheets tangled in their long legs and the blanket fell to the floor unnoticed.

He pushed her luxuriant hair back from her face and held it there, gazing into her eyes with unabashed admiration. "You're very beautiful, Bren. Your complexion is like delicate pink roses."

"You make me feel like a new woman, Zack."

"Oh, Bren, you are a lovely woman to love." With deliberate leisure, he lowered to meet her lips, letting his body down to pair with hers. Firm to pliant, hard to soft, male to female.

"Then love me, Zack." She closed her eyes as he kissed the bare, quivering tips of her breasts and let her imagination take her away to a series of pleasures. Making love with Zack was like walking through a lovely Irish flower garden, full of delicate, fresh-scented buds and miraculous new blooms. Each time he touched her was another erotic pleasure, a sweet delight.

He leaned her back on the bed and kissed the most erotically sensitive places. His tongue scored the inner edge of her parted lips and slipped inside for a taste of honey. Then he was kissing her somewhere else, like a bee seeking honey, constantly moving, hovering, dipping into the honey spots. She writhed in pleasure.

His hard-muscled body framed hers, spreading out to touch her everywhere. He stretched her arms wide and kissed the white, inner flesh. His legs hooked around hers and forced them apart. She had never felt so desired and she responded completely. She wanted him as she had never wanted a man, as she had never known she could.

His lips were soft and pliant, kissing and caressing hers, his tongue playing with her senses, daring to go deeper each time. His body was hard and demanding, hers was pliant and willing. Her breath caught in her throat and hot desire surged through her as he touched her again and again. She arched upward to try to capture him, but he was maddeningly elusive. He moved between her thighs, kissing and caressing, rocking her with pleasure.

"Zack . . . oh, Zack, come to me," she begged, clutching at him.

He continued to tempt her, the firm strength of his aroused manhood seeking her warm nest, then pulling back to repeat the process.

Again she arched her back, rising up to meet him. Her hands clutched fiercely at his shoulders. He was vigorous and hard and ready. So was she. His teasing nearly drove her crazy.

"Zack, please—" She quivered all over.

As buds of desire blossomed within her, growing until she thought she would burst, she reached for him. Circling his maleness, she stroked vigorously.

"Oh God, Bren—" His hips undulated forward in response to her magic touch and moaned aloud.

She guided him to the gentle haven that awaited him and sucked in a tiny cry as he thrust into her. Harder and harder, faster and faster, he undulated out of control. And she moved with him, rapidly reaching the breath-stopping moment of climax. Then, she felt the spirals again and she thought it would never stop. Her small cries of ecstasy mingled with his low groans as they tumbled over the brink.

And when the wildness subsided, they lay there quietly, merged into one, enjoying the feelings they had shared.

After taking a quick shower, they dressed and borrowed Mr. Flanagan's bike again.

"Before the next trip, I'm buying my own bike," Zack vowed as he adjusted the seat height. "This one just isn't big enough for me."

Brenda stood on the sidewalk, holding her own bike and watching. "Well, Mr. Flanagan's legs aren't nearly as long as yours. But you don't have to buy a bicycle just for a few trips into the country. You Americans are so extravagant!"

"I expect to be making this trip frequently with you, my bike-riding beauty. Anyway, bike riders are like lovers. They should fit, part for part."

She grinned. "Words of wisdom from Zack Ehrens?"

He finished adjusting the seat and stuffed the wrench in his backpack. "Like us. We fit, don't we?"

"Perfectly," she agreed with a happy smile.

He looked up at her and his dark eyes grew serious for a moment. "It's nice being with you, Brenda. Comfortable and easy."

"Are you saying I'm easy?"

"I'm saying I fell for you easily." He tried out the seat and rode slowly past her. "And I don't usually do that."

"I'm glad." She slipped her bottom onto the bike seat and followed Zack down the street.

They took their time riding through the lush, multi-hued countryside, stopping at their favorite spot for a Wicklow pancake and again for water and to rest.

Brenda perched on a rock by the roadside and drank from her canteen. "They say a true Irishman can distinguish forty shades of green."

"Can you?"

"No." She laughed, swinging her arm out to encompass the stone-filled meadows surrounding them. "It all looks like green and more green to me."

"Then you aren't a true Irishwoman? You sure had me fooled. Red hair, blue eyes, a few freckles in strategic places . . ."

"You just forget about those freckles!"

"I'll never tell!"

She laughed, but couldn't help wondering if she was fooling Zack—and herself—when she looked at him with love. Was it too soon, or had it been, as he said, too easy for them? It *had* been fast and furious. Sometimes, though, that was the best. No time to develop problems. Just the two of them to enjoy each other. "Ready to go on? How are your legs holding up?"

He slapped his thigh. "Fine. I told you, I'm back in shape."

She laughed and pedaled away. This time, Zack followed, admiring Brenda's fine shape from behind as they traveled.

Aunt Brigid was delighted when they finally arrived and, after the requisite tea and shortbread, Zack offered to show them the property he was negotiating to buy. Both women readily agreed it was a great idea.

Zack cut the Volkswagen's motor beside an overgrown field full of weeds and bluish stones. A cross-timber fence was falling down in places and the house and barn were in sad disrepair. In the distance, on the crest of the hill, stood an old foundry building. The entire place was ramshackle and obviously had been abandoned for years. A breeze whipped eerily through

104

the weeds and whistled between loose boards in the barn.

"It's an excellent location for our plant," Zack said as they piled out of the tiny car.

"Why, it's the old Vaun place. Seamus Vaun, I believe his name was," Aunt Brigid said, shading her eyes.

"Seamus Vaum? Yes, that's the owner," Zack agreed.

"Do you know him, Auntie Brige?" Brenda asked.

"Indeed, I do."

"Small world," Brenda mumbled to Zack.

"Especially here in Ireland. Everybody seems to know everybody else."

"Poor Seamus," Aunt Brigid said, shaking her head sadly. "I knew him many years ago when he married that pretty woman from Kilkenny. She was always sickly and died when their firstborn son was but a wee fellow. After that, Seamus never could make the land give up its bounty. Too many rocks. He couldn't even raise sheep here. So he leased the land to a group of businessmen from Dublin, and they built the stove foundry. It provided work for many until it closed a few years back."

"Apparently the land went back to Seamus because he's now ready to sell outright," Zack said. "And we can use the old foundry. It'll have to be renovated, but our architect has already approved it for our first building."

"That's nice," she said with a satisfied smile. "The others just left Seamus's house and barn here. He lived here for years and worked at the foundry."

"I'm afraid we'll have to level them," he replied. "Even the rocks must be removed for the parking lot."

Aunt Brigid looked up at him with an understanding nod. "Every piece of land has a story, Zack. No matter which you chose, there'd be something to tell about it."

"Especially around here," Brenda added with a little laugh.

"That's just the way it is," Aunt Brigid affirmed.

"Oh, Auntie Brige, everybody here is a storyteller," Brenda teased. "If you don't know something, you'll make it up right quick."

But Zack pressed his lips together without humor. He looked around him. The land . . . so much a part of the people that even the land had human characteristics. This one wouldn't give up its bounty. Aunt Brigid said it as though the land had made a conscious decision to hold back.

Zack ran his hand through his hair. "You know, there were some very good reasons we chose this site for the plant. Besides having the old foundry building already on site, the location is primary. It's close enough to Dublin to draw employees. We may even be able to run a bus from town out here for them. Plus, there's good proximity to the Grand Canal for shipping." Zack ambled over the fence and propped a foot on a broken rail.

"I can see you've already thought it through, Zack," Aunt Brigid observed as the breeze whipped her dress around her substantial body. "I'll bet you know just where your future buildings will go."

"Yes." He nodded thoughtfully and looked off at the horizon. "How do you feel about people like me," he posed suddenly. "Coming into Ireland, turning perfectly good farm or grazing land into some kind of mechanical industry with modern buildings and parking lots?"

Aunt Brigid studied him for a few moments and her sharp blue eyes grew stern. "Ah, but you're wrong there, Zack. It isn't perfectly good farm land. It has no talent for growing things. Seamus had his chance to make something of it. Then the stove foundry. Now it's your turn."

Zack wasn't satisfied and looked away impatiently. "But I'm the intruder here. This land was meant for farming, not for industry."

"Ah, Zack, that's an old-fashioned idea," Aunt Brigid scolded. "New industry will help us catch up with the world and maybe keep some of our sons in Ireland. We've lost too many of them over the years because they couldn't make a living. Ireland's changing. It's time for a new day."

"But I'll change it drastically," he persisted, walking away from them and stuffing his large hands deep into his pockets. "Maybe not all for the best, you know? Certainly it won't have all this pleasantness. The quiet and calm, the peaceful landscapes, all this will change. Why, it's almost as if time has stood still here and that's the beauty of it. Once our processing plant starts cranking, all that will be gone."

Aunt Brigid looked firm. "This land is best used for a plant that will give men jobs."

"And women," Brenda added. "Ireland's daughters need jobs too."

"Yes, well . . ." Aunt Brigid cast her young niece a

107

fierce glance and added reluctantly, "As I said, Ireland's changing."

Zack lifted his head and inhaled. It smelled typical of the country, of farms and sweet-scented grass and colts frolicking across the fields. Best of all, there was no pollution. "I hope my efforts to build this plant don't become one of your sad tales, Aunt Brigid."

"If anything, it'll be a success story," she said brightly.

"God, I hope so."

"I don't think you will ever do anything to harm Ireland, Zack." She touched his arm with her pudgy hand. "They say if you stay here long enough, it will capture you."

"I think it already has, Aunt Brigid." He looked up and caught Brenda's gaze above her aunt's head. "It already has. But that's not bad, is it?"

Aunt Brigid smiled slyly at the exchange of glances between Zack and Brenda. "No, it isn't bad at all. It's good. We need your progressive ideas, Zack. And we need the work you're going to provide. That good for the people. The land can take care of itself." She turned and started toward the car. "Well now, if we're going to get any fishing done this afternoon, we'd better be going."

Brenda joined Zack and they walked slowly back to the car together. Neither touched, although they wanted to. Perhaps it was too soon for them to feel comfortable being affectionate in front of Aunt Brigid. Neither spoke, although they had a million things to say. For now, exchanged glances would have to say it all.

She looked at his dark eyes. They were haunting

and still sad at times. Like now. And she wondered why.

By the end of the week, Zack and Padraig had completed the land deal with Seamus Vaun. Brenda hadn't made it to the official signing, but that night she celebrated with him.

"Congratulations! It's official! You're now an Irish landowner. That makes you an honorary Irishman, at least." Brenda handed Zack a glass of wine, then snuggled beside him on the sofa. The television was on low, but they ignored it.

"Couldn't have done it without you, Brenda. And especially so soon. You're amazing. Thank you." He tipped his glass to hers.

"Why, you were in such a hurry, I had no choice. I've never seen anyone make a decision so fast. You looked at the sites and picked one. That was it."

"I'm a man of decision. But everything you showed me was prime property. You really do your job well."

She shrugged. "Padraig and I spent a good deal of time studying your reports before you arrived. We concentrated on your particular needs."

"Well, you've certainly taken care of my needs satisfactorily." He nibbled tiny kisses on her neck.

"I was referring to your company's needs," she corrected, grinning. "I must admit, though, my biggest pleasure is attending to your pleasures."

"Me too." His kisses strayed to her earlobe.

She shivered and moved her head. "Hold it. I want to hear all about the signing."

"I thought we were going to deal with my pleasures. And yours."

"Later," she promised. "Business first. Sorry I couldn't make it today, but I had to meet a new client. I know it was an important occasion for you."

"There weren't any hitches. Padraig and his staff are quite efficient and everything was in order." He paused and sighed. "I was surprised that the sellers were willing to settle so soon."

"What's wrong with that?"

"I don't know." Zack shrugged. "I just thought the Vauns would want to hold on to the family land as long as possible."

"Oh, you're a soft-hearted soul, Zack Ehrens. Just remember, they lost the ability to make a living on the land way before you came along. You're actually making it better for them."

"I may hire them. The irony is that they both need a job and intend to apply for a position as soon as we're open for business."

"See? You're making it better for them and lots of men like them, Zack." She smiled proudly at him.

"And women?" He raised his eyebrows teasingly at her. "Aunt Brigid wasn't too keen on the idea of women in the work force."

Brenda gave him a quizzical look. "Would you hire a woman? You know this is still a very conservative country."

"Of course I'd hire her in a minute if she was qualified. In fact, one of my best managers in California was a woman. I have no reservations about hiring the best person for the job."

"Good." She nodded with satisfaction. "I hope you get lots of applications from females." It was doubtful that any women would even apply, but at least Zack was open-minded about it. For a moment their attention turned to the flickering black and white television when the announcer mentioned something about the United States.

"Do you still look for news from home?" Zack asked. "Or have you reached a point where you don't really care because it doesn't affect you?"

"Oh no, I think you always care what happens back home. Sometimes I long for an announcer without an Irish brogue who will give me a complete rundown on the major news across the country, or to just watch something with good old American humor. I miss it terribly."

"How long has it been since you've been back?"

"I've only been back once in the two years I've been here. I guess I'm due a trip. But I hear from Gran Sadie often with family tidbits. She sends wonderful little packages with newspaper clippings and funny articles from magazines and chewing gum. It was her idea for me to come over here, you know."

"Was that after your divorce?"

"Yes. My whole life had crashed in around me, and I went to stay with her for a little while. She has been pretty lonely since Gramp died, yet refused to move from that rambling old house they'd had all through the years. She spoke glowingly about Ireland and how she'd love for me to see it some day. But I had no money nor time for a vacation. Worse yet, I had no job. It was an impossible dream."

"So how did you get the job over here?"

"With a little help from Auntie Brige. She had written that American entrepreneurs were starting businesses here and how a friend of hers, Barrister Padraig

111

McGuinness, was looking for an American to serve as a liaison between the two cultures. Both Ireland and the businesses benefited, but the Americans needed someone to pave the way and keep both parties happy. It sounded perfect for me, being American with a little bit of an Irish background. So, I applied and here I am."

"You said earlier that you were in business in the U.S. Was it anything like this job?"

"No, not at all. Ken, my husband, and I were in real estate, specializing in investment properties. When the business fell apart, so did the marriage. Or was it the other way around?"

"That sounds familiar."

"Is that what precipitated your divorce, Zack?"

"It seemed that way. I was plagued on all sides with bankruptcy and numerous lawsuits. There was no money, and I went a little crazy. Started selling everything in sight to pay expenses. Whoever said bankruptcy was the cheap way out?" He sighed and shook his head. "It cost me everything."

"I know. It's awful." Brenda's laughter was hollow.

"Charmaine didn't say much until the Porsche went. That's when she bailed out, too. She was furious having to lose that car. Can't say that I blame her, but the car was just one of many disasters."

"Was it the money?"

"No, not really. It was the deciding factor, the final blow. But our marriage wasn't strong to begin with, and certainly couldn't withstand such a storm. Ah, I was disappointed that we couldn't make it, but in all fairness to Charmaine, I was a lousy husband."

"I doubt that."

"I was," he said absolutely. "I could see the end coming and turned into a workaholic. I spent almost every waking hour at the plant. I didn't do much toward salvaging our relationship."

"Every story has two sides. I'm sure she wasn't great, either."

He nodded and took another sip of wine. "Charmaine was not the type of woman to stand behind her man. If she couldn't ride alongside him in their Porsche, she wouldn't go at all. Well, so much for my ill-fated marriage. What about yours, Brenda? As long as we're spilling guts, we may as well get it said and done."

"I suppose I was the workaholic in our marriage," Brenda admitted. "Our situation was different, but we also could see the end coming. My reaction was to work harder, and run faster on the treadmill. Ken's response was to seek solace elsewhere while I was out trying to drum up new clients."

"Another woman?" Zack sat up stiffly. "How could anyone do that to you?"

Brenda plastered a wry smile on her lovely face. "Ken did. Funny thing. Even after admitting to me that he was having an affair, he claimed he loved me. That he was in love with both of us, for different reasons. Can you believe he thought I'd be foolish enough to believe that?" She laughed bitterly.

Zack was quiet for a few moments, watching her reactions in the growing shadows. "That must have hurt you terribly, Bren."

She drew back to look at him. "You don't think it's possible to love two women, do you, Zack?"

"Not when you're one of the women, Bren." He

held her close and kissed her cheek. "No. It would be impossible for me." His kisses were sweet and convincing. They told her he could love only her.

And she melted in his arms, knowing she could love only Zack. He gave her the solid, unconditional love she needed and his sweet, hot kisses were her proof. At least right now.

"Hold me, Zack. Don't leave tonight," she asked.

"I don't think I could ever leave you, Bren."

"Oh, Zack, don't say that. It's too soon."

"Not for me. I know how I feel."

"Don't," she begged. "Just hold me. And love me. We've both been hurt too badly for the wrong commitment too soon. Let's just enjoy what we have."

He kissed her again. "I love what we have, love being with you. Whatever you call this, it's wonderful, Brenda." And his arm slipped around her and pulled her over him. Her hair tumbled shapelessly, curls tousled, making a sensuous veil around their kisses.

CHAPTER SEVEN

After the acquisition of the land, activities started to accelerate, and time together became scarce. Zack was either busy or exhausted. He consulted for days with an architect to make sure the rendering would be correct. Then they worked endlessly with the building contractor haranguing long hours before the ground was even broken.

Presently, Zack was using every spare minute to interview for management positions for the plant. Brenda was occupied with a new client. They had hardly seen each other all week. So when he appeared at her apartment door late one afternoon, she was delighted to see him.

"Close your eyes. I have a surprise for you!"

"What is it?"

He took her hand and pulled her close for a quick kiss. "You're beautiful, you know that? And I've missed you like hell this week. Come on with me. I'll show you."

"Show me here."

"Can't. It's too big."

"What in the world? Where are you going?"

"Out front. Come on, Bren!"

She grabbed a sweater and scrambled after him, down the stairs and out the front door of the apartment building.

He leaned proudly on the front fender of a green Volkswagen sedan, arms folded, legs crossed at the knees in a cocky stance, a big smile on his face. A man's pride.

"A car!" She gaped at the man and his vehicle. Suddenly she remembered Ken and his Cadillac and how obsessed he was with the car. He'd spend every Sunday afternoon waxing and shining it, while she longed for his attention and love. But he showered it on that damned car instead. And when it all fell apart, that damned Cadillac was the last to go. She hated the vehicle because of what it represented.

"How do you like her? She's a few years old but has low mileage. And she's in real good shape. And the color is appropriate for the country." He paused and placed a hand tenderly on the fender behind him, stroking the metal a couple of times.

"She?"

"Yeah, well." He chuckled. "Habit, I guess, to think of a car as female. Want to take a ride?"

Brenda stopped beside the car and surveyed it. "This is quite a surprise, Zack." *Shock* was more like it.

"Why? Don't you think it's about time I got something decent for us to ride around in? To keep the rain off us?"

"There are other ways to travel, you know. I've managed for two years with public transportation."

"Brenda, you sound as though you don't want us to have a car."

116

"It's so sudden. You're just getting started here, got the property signed, the building started, and now you want a car, just like an American."

"I *am* an American."

"I thought you wanted a bicycle."

He shrugged. "It's getting cooler. This seemed more practical."

"More practical to spend more money on something you don't really need anyway?"

"How can you say that? I need a car. I have no means of getting anywhere, unless I borrow Mr. Flanagan's bike."

"Why, everybody here rides one. Or takes the bus."

"The bus just isn't my style, Brenda."

"Style? I've never heard you talk like this, Zack."

"And I've never heard you kick up such a fuss before. How can you deny me this car? My life has gone to hell, I lost everything important to me, including my business and my marriage, and now I've bought this cheap little used car and you're objecting? I can't understand your logic."

"Well, it's not like the expensive cars you drove in California. Your wife drove a Porsche. What did you drive? A Cadillac?"

"A Mercedes."

"Oh, well. The VW isn't quite that elite. I guess it doesn't matter, Zack. It's none of my business, anyway."

"Yes, it is! Of course I want you to like the car. Hey, don't you want to ride in her?"

Brenda turned away, her head down. In a low voice, she murmured a low, "No thanks. Maybe another time. I'm busy now." And she ran back upstairs to the modest escape of her apartment.

Zack watched her go, staring after her in amazement. When she disappeared inside the wooden doors, he slapped the green fender with his palm in frustration. "Women!" he muttered. "What the hell am I supposed to do? Charmaine left when we lost her fancy car. And Brenda turned her back on this one! What the hell!"

The next night Brenda knocked on Zack's door. She drew in a quick breath at the sight of him dressed casually in jeans and sweater. He looked wonderful, even with tired lines beneath his dark eyes and his square jaws tight. And she had only made things worse with her inane objections to the car. How could she have been so stupid? She'd missed him like crazy this week. Right now, all she wanted was to feel his arms around her. What difference did everything else make in the scheme of things? Just the two of them mattered.

"Want to talk?" She lifted apprehensive blue eyes.

"Sure." He stepped back.

She entered quietly and turned around to face him. He'd shut the door and was leaning on it, his hands behind his back. There was nothing arrogant in his stance tonight. God, she felt terrible for arguing with him.

"I was afraid of this sort of thing happening, Zack, when we started being together so much and uh . . ."She paused and pressed her lips together, searching for the right words. "I'm sorry" just doesn't come easily, even when you know you're wrong.

"And sleeping together?"

"Yes. I don't want any petty personal differences to interfere with the business you have here."

"No, we don't want that."

"You're still my client, and I want what's best for you and Ehrens Enterprises."

"That's a relief."

"Don't be snide." She squeezed her hands together. "Look, I don't know what got into me today but, when I saw that car, I went berserk. I'm sorry, Zack. I had no right."

"It's okay. No big deal."

"I made it one."

He shifted and folded his long arms across his chest. A defensive stance. "I'm just trying to understand why, Brenda."

She longed to take his hand, to put her arms around him, to kiss him. But he wasn't inviting any of it. "I don't know, exactly. I guess I saw it as changing the simple, halcyon relationship we had. But in the last few weeks, things between us have been changing. Now with the new car, things will be quite different. No longer is it most important that we're together, even if we have to take a simple bike ride. Now, you have to have a car."

"So it's a symbol?"

She shrugged. "I guess. I wanted our relationship to be based on simple pleasures, instead of material ones. We've both had that in the past and it didn't work. Or, at least, when the material stuff fell apart, there was nothing left. I don't want that to happen to us."

"I don't think buying a Volkswagen puts me in the high-spenders category. I look at it as a necessity." He frowned. "You want us to remain with no material possessions? That's crazy, Brenda. I came over here without even a stick of furniture! Nothing but my clothes!"

"No, not at all. It's just—" She gestured futilely. "I only know that I care for this new Zack, the one who's starting over again in Ireland. The one who's escaping the old life. And I don't want to see you change back."

He dropped his hands to his sides and they flexed nervously. "What about the Zack who wants you very much. Wants to please you and only you. I don't need any of the extra trappings, I only need you."

"Oh, Zack—" She flung herself against him, burying her face against his chest until he lifted her chin up so she could receive his kiss. And she opened her lips eagerly with a small whimper.

"Bren . . . Bren . . ." he murmured and dropped his kisses to her neck. "I need you . . ."

"I need you, too." She clung to him, returning his kisses, murmuring words of affection and love. "Hold me, Zack. Hold me close."

He obliged willingly and the closeness grew to something more. "Brenda, I want you . . ."

"Yes." She was breathless as desire for him grew like a spiral within her, urging her to press him into her very soul. Oh God, how she loved him, how she hated what she had done today. She only wanted to show him how much she loved him.

"Stay, Bren—"

"Yes."

In the next instant, he whisked her away to the bedroom. Their lovemaking that night was fierce and contained a desperate quality. She clung to him, pledging that nothing would come between them again, hoping she was telling the truth. He wrapped his great arms securely around her and promised they wouldn't change, hoping he could make it happen.

The next morning, she rose early and sat on the edge of the bed and pulled on her stockings and jeans in the twilight. A masculine hand caressed her back before she had a chance to don her sweater. "It's nice to wake up with you in my bed, Bren." His voice was thick with sleep and she found it extremely sexy.

She smiled. "But everything has to end, even good things. I have to go to work."

"I'm glad you stayed."

"Me too. And this afternoon, I'd like to go for a ride in the green monster."

"Monster, huh?"

She turned around with a grin. "It brought out the monster in me, didn't it? Or should I say 'she brought out my monster'?"

"But you turned into a kitten before it was over." He laced his hands under his head and watched her with a pleased smile on his face.

"So did you, Mr. Ehrens." She bent to put her shoes on, then straightened and walked over to the dresser to comb her hair. "I'm screening three women today that have good qualifications for Ehrens Enterprises."

"Women?" He pursed his lips.

"What's wrong? You said you were an equal opportunity employer."

"Nothing's wrong. It's fine. I'm looking for people with certain specifications, though. She must be qualified, Brenda, or I could be in a bigger mess after she's hired."

"I know that. I won't send you anyone who doesn't meet your specifications. These three women have excellent qualifications. Well, gotta go. See you later."

"Brenda!" His voice was demanding and he sat up in bed, baring his chest as the covers fell down around his hips.

With a smile of secret understanding, she walked back to the bed and gave him a lingering kiss.

"That's better."

"Much," she agreed. "Have a good day. See you later."

"Dinner tonight?"

"Love it."

Brenda spent the morning screening the three applicants. They were all well qualified and she found herself vacillating between them. Finally, it came down to family situations and instinct based on the face-to-face interview, and she chose two of the women to interview with Zack.

In the afternoon, she felt at odds with herself and strangely restless. When she finished her paperwork, she left work early and pedaled out to visit Aunt Brigid.

"What's troubling you, darlin'?"

"I've put myself in a strange position with Zack."

Aunt Brigid was kneading dough and looked up for a moment. "Yes?"

"I'm spending a lot of time with him. We enjoy many of the same things. We—now I know you probably won't approve, Auntie Brigid, but we've been lovers for some time now."

"I know you have." The elderly lady gave her a sly

glance. "If you think I don't understand these things, then you don't know me very well. But I'll have no judgment on it."

"Thank you, Auntie Brige. I just had to talk to someone about Zack."

"Do you love him? That makes a big difference, you know."

"I think I do. He makes me feel better than any man ever has, including Ken. I feel that he cares for me, too. And being with him gets more wonderful every day."

"Ooo!" Aunt Brigid's blue eyes danced and she smiled happily. "Sounds serious!"

"It's so serious that I don't want anything to change between us. I'm afraid if we do anything, we'll ruin it. And I don't want to ruin anything. Yesterday he bought a car."

Aunt Brigid pounded the dough. "He did? Great! What kind?"

"It's a fine car, a Volkswagen similar to yours. But I took one look at it and went a little crazy. And yet I know it wasn't the car. It was the inevitable change I feared."

"True love will adapt to change, Brenda."

"I know. But we both come from pasts that were based on financial success. When all of that fell apart, so did the marriages. We're both over here in Ireland to escape, to start new. I don't want anything interfering with what we have. It's too precious."

Aunt Brigid pounded the dough one last time, folded it into a bowl, and covered it with a towel for rising. Then she settled her large body at the table opposite Brenda. "I think you're dreaming if you believe things or people never change. Even the way a man and woman treat each other changes, as life changes. It has to change so it can grow. Don't worry about this one. If it's love, real love, it'll hang on." She reached over and patted Brenda's hand.

"Oh, Aunt Brige, you're such a romantic!" Brenda laughed and grabbed her aunt for a quick hug. Just talking about her relationship with Zack was such a relief that she now felt slightly giddy with happiness. "And you have all the answers."

"I didn't get these gray hairs for nothing!" Aunt Brigid chuckled and her massive bosom jostled beneath her print dress. "I've lived a long time and endured my share of joys and sorrows. Of it all, love is the best."

"That's nice to know. Guess what! I screened a couple of very smart ladies, *Irish ladies,* this morning for possible jobs with Zack's new company."

"Oh?" Aunt Brigid's eyebrows shot up. "What do you mean, screened?"

"It's like a pre-interview. I talked to them about the kinds of jobs Zack needed and if their experience and qualifications would suit his standards. He'll be interviewing two of them next week. It's very exciting."

"Yes, I imagine. Do you think women would be good at this? Are they strong?"

"Oh, this isn't in the processing area. These would be the bosses."

"Women bossing men in their jobs?" Aunt Brigid fanned herself with her apron. "What is this world coming to?"

"It's all part of the changes, Auntie Brige," Brenda

said, giving her aunt another squeeze. "I've got to head back home now."

"Not before supper. I have lamb stew."

"I'm afraid so. I'm meeting Zack tonight."

Aunt Brigid took her hands and squeezed affectionately. "Glory be, your eyes are every bit as blue as your grandmother Sadie's. At least the best I remember. You don't have to visit me this weekend, Brenda. I'm sure you'd rather spend it with your man."

"Visiting you is a delight for us. Zack enjoys it too."

"Ah, now, girl, I was young once. I know about these things. You'd rather be together, and I understand."

"Wouldn't you like to take a ride in Zack's new car?"

"Next week. You two spend this one with each other. You need it."

Brenda kissed Aunt Brigid's warm, cheery cheek. "Besides being an absolute dear, you're also very wise."

"It takes years," she said, chuckling.

"I love you, Auntie Brige."

That night Brenda met Zack for dinner in high spirits. They went to O'Shaunessey's Oyster House for fresh seafood served up with Irish songs and gaiety provided by the green-vested waiters. It was a rowdy evening, one that Brenda loved and knew she would always cherish.

The waiters took turns singing Irish tunes, mostly outrageous ditties with bawdy lyrics. Occasionally they asked patrons to join in a song or to try an Irish jig. Everyone participated, including Brenda who even played a short tune on the fiddle. The crowd responded enthusiastically to her talent, and when she finished, the waiter played "My Wild Irish Rose" just for her. Spontaneously, Zack took her hand and whirled her around the dance floor.

The crowd began to clap with the music as the couple danced with sure, athletic grace. They were the only ones on the dance floor and from the looks in their eyes, were alone in the world.

Zack held her close and whispered, "You're my wild Irish rose, Brenda. Even when we're apart, I think of you."

She smiled up at him. "And I always thought you were preoccupied."

"You are never far from my thoughts."

When the song was over, the other guests applauded wildly. Zack and Brenda bowed and took their seats, flushed with the glow of happiness and sudden shyness. Before long, he squeezed her hand. "Let's go home."

She smiled and nodded her agreement. She knew what he meant, for he had that enticingly warm look in his eyes, and she could hardly wait for him to hold her.

When they were alone, he fulfilled that promise in his eyes, loving her and holding her close all night long.

Brenda relished every precious minute with Zack. A thrill of excitement coursed through her when she realized that he thought of her even when they were apart. They stole every possible moment to be together. Time stretched out to a period of months, but it seemed to fly past in a blur because they were so busy.

Zack hired one of the women Brenda had screened, a recent graduate with a degree in business from Cork College. Like most of the prospective employees, Betty McKee's family was poor and she was eager to work.

"I'm glad you hired a woman," Brenda commented as they relaxed together one Sunday afternoon. "Maybe she'll be the first of many."

"Many employees or many women?"

"Women, of course!"

Zack chuckled good-naturedly and she knew he was teasing her. "Betty'll make a good salary, by local standards. But she has a big responsibility as our accountant and financial adviser."

"That's an important position. I hope she does well." Brenda snuggled onto his shoulder. "How's the construction coming along?"

"Moving slowly," he answered. "What a mess we've made of that beautiful little farm. The house and barn are completely gone now and the whole place is taking on the look of an industrial site."

"Which it is, and those changes can't be helped," Brenda said sympathetically. "Ehrens Enterprises is the wave of the future, and I'm proud to have been a part of the beginning. Why you'll provide much-needed jobs for the people of Terenure, Clondalkin, and Rathcoole, from the heart of Dublin, and as far away as Cork. Maybe some of the locals can even keep their farms because they worked for your industry, Zack."

He nuzzled her neck and kissed along her chin. "You make it all sound so noble."

"It is." She responded to his gentle nudging with a small quiver. "Noble and worthwhile and . . ."

He stopped her rambling with a long, sweet kiss. "Hush. You're the only noble person I know. And this is the only thing worthwhile to me . . ." His hand slipped beneath her sweater and massaged her breasts, first one, then the other. "I like you like this, Brenda. Free and eager."

She turned on her side to face him. "This is the way I like you. With me . . ."

He took off his sweater, then helped remove hers.

"Hold me like this," she urged. "Close."

He ran his hands sensuously over her bare back, clasping them together, pressing her pliant breasts to the masculine structure of his unyielding chest. He kissed her again, this time his tongue played with her lips until she eagerly tried to capture it. She moaned softly as his tongue sought the inner recesses of her mouth, deeply and with a special urging.

She responded with a gentle rocking of her hips and his hand slipped beneath her panties to cup her buttocks and stroke the sensitive skin between her legs.

"Brenda, you're so soft here. Like velvet."

"I want you in me, Zack. Want you . . ." she said huskily.

In a moment they were stripping off their clothes with feverish hands. Zack whispered, "Kiss me, Brenda."

She knelt before him, her lips making moist forays over his taut, rippling body. His arousal was a feminine delight, and she grew excited by the mere sight of his maleness as she touched him.

With a groan he pulled her over him as he lay back

on the sofa. She sprawled along his length, writhing with pleasure as he controlled her and guided her movements carefully. He steered her hips with firm hands and planted himself inside her with gentle force.

She wriggled impatiently as her own passion rose to meet his. When he moved in a fierce, pulsing rhythm, she quickly joined.

His thrusts grew harder and faster, plunging with a desire beyond his control. Her passion rose, and she accepted him fully, in blessed unity with the man she loved.

They reached the summit and, with a groaning shudder, he grasped her fiercely as he throbbed within her. She clutched him to her and felt her own passion soar out of control. She held him for as long as possible, unwilling to let go, unable to slow the rush of her emotion.

Finally, they drifted apart, lying side by side in a close embrace.

"Brenda, I need you so . . ."

"I'm here, Zack. Whenever . . ."

He sighed heavily and after a long pause, said, "This is probably not the most appropriate time, but I need to talk to you about something, Brenda."

"Sounds serious," she murmured lazily, drawing a line of moist kisses across his chest.

"Listen to me, Brenda. This is important." He shuddered unavoidably at her touch. She could make him respond, even when they had just made love. Sometimes he even wanted her again. But not just now. She could feel his tense resistance. She obediently relaxed in his arms. "All right. What do you want to talk about that's so serious?"

"This is something I've been putting off telling you for some time. I wasn't sure how to say it."

"Nothing's wrong, is it?"

"No, not really." His dark eyes clouded and he leaned back, loosening his hold on her. *Not yet.* "It's just a matter we have to deal with."

"Well, what?"

"My brother's coming to Ireland."

She smiled in relief, wondering why that would make him so tense. "Zack, I think that's wonderful!"

"You do?"

"Of course. You're going to give him a job, aren't you?"

"Yes. He, uh, I may as well be honest with you, Brenda. He's had trouble holding jobs in the past. He needs my help and I'm going to give it. I hope you understand."

She slid her arms up his chest, letting them rest on his shoulders. "Of course I understand. He's part of your family! Look how many times we've visited Aunt Brige, just to check on her, when I know you would have preferred doing something else. I don't know why you've been so reticent about this."

"Because I know how you feel about things between us changing. And having James share my apartment is bound to change things."

She smiled sweetly and nuzzled his cheek. "Well, we'll just have to stay down here more often. When is he coming?"

Zack paused. He hated to tell her, but he knew he must. He'd already waited too long. "Tomorrow. I pick him up at three."

"Don't worry, honey, having James here won't change things at all. I won't allow it."

Zack leaned his head back and absorbed her warm touch and sweet kisses. *Ah, my sweet, ignorant Brenda. Thinking that James won't change things is like believing a rattler might not bite. The fact that he's coming will make a difference in all our lives, my beautiful Brenda. I can only hope it won't change things too much.*

CHAPTER EIGHT

Brenda and Zack walked through Dublin Airport together. His hand rested with casual familiarity on her shoulder. Although during the past three months they had developed a warm and comfortable relationship, neither had verbalized a need for commitment.

It seemed that they had both been hurt too much in their marriages and were protecting themselves by avoiding a commitment now. No commitment, no hurt. For now, Brenda was satisfied with their relationship. She cared deeply for Zack, probably loved him, and knew that his feelings for her were the same. That was enough for her. For now.

She made a concerted effort to keep up with his long strides as they navigated through the crowds in the terminal. Finally she halted, gasping tiny breaths. "Zack, wait a minute, please. I can hardly keep up with you. I know you're anxious to see your brother, but we have plenty of time. We don't have to run."

He looked at her with a bewildered expression. Had he been running? He had no idea. His mind was a million miles away. No, in truth, only a few air miles. He wondered how James had fared through the last few months in prison; how he looked; if his thinking was any clearer; if they could make it this time. *If James was still susceptible to those elements that tipped him over the edge of the law last time.*

Brenda watched him with gentle eyes. "Zack?"

"Yes? Sorry, Brenda. I didn't mean to rush."

"Thinking about James?"

"Huh? James? Oh, yes."

"It'll be all right, Zack. I'm sure of it. When you two get together, it'll be like old times. And I'm sure James will like Ireland. We'll see to it that he does." She shifted the bouquet she had bought for James: roses mixed with sprigs of fragrant heather and rosemary. Taking Zack's hand she gave a warm squeeze. "It's my job to see he likes it here, remember? My techniques worked with you, didn't they?"

Zack's eyes flickered with a tiny bit of teasing. "You'd better use different tactics for my brother, though."

"Don't worry, honey. There are certain methods reserved just for you, Zack. Besides, James has both of us to keep him company while he adjusts to a new country. You only had me."

"Which was plenty," he said with a smile. "Ready to continue? The plane is due any minute."

"At a more leisurely pace, please."

"Is this the same lady who always leads the way bike riding, while I struggle behind?"

"When I have wheels under me, I'm a fast cat!"

"Well, come on, fast cat. We have a brother to greet."

They needn't have hurried. James's plane was late, and by the time he made it through customs, they had waited nearly an hour.

When James Ehrens stepped through the double green doors that separated international travelers from local ones, Brenda gasped softly to herself. She knew him immediately, even though Zack didn't identify him. She blinked, hardly able to believe her own eyes. The man before them could be Zack's twin.

As he approached she began to notice differences between the two men. Although he was younger, James's dark hair sported more gray at the temples than Zack's and he had a harder look in his dark-brown eyes. His sunken cheeks framed a jutting jaw, and his shadowy beard made him look weary and somewhat harsh. James was also slightly shorter than Zack, an inch or two height difference that wasn't even noticeable until they stood side by side.

The most striking difference between the brothers' appearances however, was that James was pale and less robust than Zack. His jacket hung shapelessly on his broad, lanky shoulders. Then Brenda noticed the front zipper was broken. The jacket flapped open to reveal an extremely slender body. His worn slacks failed to fit his narrow hips and he carried an old green duffel bag that was worn on the edges.

Zack muttered James's name and stepped forward in a rush to embrace his brother with a bear hug.

Brenda stood back and watched the reunion. She had no intention of interfering with the moment. The worn, tired-looking man was probably Zack's only living relative and even though Zack had insisted he wanted her along, she still didn't feel she was a part of his family.

The reunion wasn't particularly emotional, but Brenda sensed a definite tension between them. The two men broke away from their embrace and stood there laughing nervously, exchanging a few comments she couldn't hear. Then they hugged again and slapped each other heartily on the back. Zack kept an arm around James's shoulder and led him to where Brenda stood holding the bouquet of flowers.

"This is Brenda O'Shea. Brenda, my brother, James."

James took her outstretched hand in a formal handshake, but his eyes never left hers. Brown and beautiful and a flicker of hard arrogance. "Brenda. My pleasure. You're almost as pretty as your name."

She cleared her throat and smiled, trying to brush away the penetrating, more-than-casual greeting she was receiving from this man. His eyes, his handshake, his body language all said more. But maybe she was reading too much into it. She pulled her hand away from James's and thrust the bouquet of flowers into it. "Welcome to Ireland, James."

"Why, thank you." He inhaled the heady fragrance from the bouquet, then looked back at her, a sly smile on his thin-edged lips. "Smells like a little bit of heaven. And you look like an angel."

His blatant admiration caught her by surprise and she wasn't sure just how to respond.

Zack broke in with a mundane question. "How was your flight, James?"

"Just fine. I slept a lot." James's deep brown eyes traveled up and down Brenda until she burned. Damn him, anyway! Then he nudged Zack. "She's quite a beauty, big bro. Why didn't you tell me you had such a doll?"

Zack gave Brenda an apologetic glance, then patted

135

his brother's shoulder. "Hey, old buddy, you'd better watch what you say to Brenda. She's too liberated for such sexist remarks."

"Liberated, huh? That's a shame."

James laughed with a guttural, earthy chuckle, and Brenda noticed a jagged scar marring one cheek. It wasn't a straight line like a cut from an accident, but more like a tear zigzagging across his face. One made by a fist brutally tearing into a smooth skin. What made her think that? The scar was probably old, for it blended with his pale complexion. It was probably something acquired in childhood, one of those street fights Zack had told her about.

"I've heard so much about you, James. It's nice to finally meet you," Brenda said in an attempt to change the subject.

"You have, huh? Not everything, I hope," he said, emphasizing the word "everything" and looking back to nudge Zack. "Every man needs a little mystery, doesn't he, bro?" Without waiting for an answer, James addressed her again. "Well, I don't know anything about you, Brenda. Zack kept you a big secret. Tell me all about yourself. Liberated, huh? And you aren't Irish, I take it."

"No, I'm from Maryland . . ." she explained as they began walking back through the terminal.

When they reached the escalator, Brenda pointed. "I think we have to go that way for luggage pickup."

"Don't bother," James said, lifting the duffel bag he carried. "This is all I have."

As they headed out into a light Dublin drizzle, Brenda wondered why a man would move to another country to work, presumably to stay indefinitely, and not have more possessions than what one small duffel bag would hold. Perhaps he's shipping the rest over later, she reasoned. She dismissed the thought as they dashed through the rain for the car.

Brenda clipped the single remaining rose from her tiny patio garden and brought it inside with a whoosh of cold air. "This is probably the last of the roses," she commented, half to herself as she snipped a few leaves off the stem and stuffed it into a bud vase. "It's getting too cold for them to keep blooming. But they've been beautiful this summer. Maybe I should plant mums. They'd bloom longer into cold weather."

"Hmm," Zack mumbled. He hunched at Brenda's table and continued to study a typed report.

"What are you reading, honey?"

"A financial planning report from Betty." He paused and looked up. "You know, she's a very smart lady and has some good, solid ideas. I want to thank you for recommending her, Brenda."

"I'm glad she's working out so well, Zack."

"In fact, I've had a chance to work with my managers in a few planning meetings and idea sessions. So far, I'm very impressed and pleased with the local people. I think it's going to work out fine."

"That's good to hear. I'd hate to know you had doubts at this point."

"Not about coming here to start the business. James is the only one I have doubts about. He's my only problem employee so far," he muttered, half-audibly. *He's always been my problem.*

Brenda didn't usually interrupt Zack's work at home, but she could sense that he needed to talk. She slipped into a chair opposite him. "What's wrong, Zack? It's not that silly business about the sticky buns, is it?"

She was still furious at both of them over the incident. She had planned a "welcome to Ireland" dinner and she'd gone out of her way to prepare some specialty Irish dishes. Dessert was a pan of gooey sticky buns that she had hoped would cap the evening with brotherly warmth, reminding them of the good old days.

Damn it, they'd ended up arguing over who made the best buns when they were kids and whether they were with or without raisins. Two grown men yelling about raisins! Brenda had joined in the melee by telling them they had reverted to their childhood and she had no intention of baby-sitting. James pushed away from the table and left her apartment in a huff. Zack pouted half the evening. And she was left with a pan of sticky buns that nobody wanted.

"That was silly, wasn't it?" Zack shook his head in embarrassed regret.

"Yes. I think it was just an excuse to argue."

Zack sighed. "You're probably right. James has been here only a couple of weeks, and it hasn't been my greatest time."

"Maybe you should insist that he get his own apartment."

"He doesn't have the money. And he won't have much until we start full production, which is weeks away. God, I hope we can last that long. My biggest complaints have to do with work, though. He's supposed to be my executive assistant and half the time he's late to planning meetings. Sometimes he doesn't even make it to the meetings. Later he says something about it not being important that he be there every time. Anyway, he finds the meetings dull and boring. He isn't dependable. And now that we're so close to starting production, I need for him to be completely reliable."

"Have you told him all this?"

"I've hinted strongly. He claims he needs time to adjust. Maybe he's right and I should give him more time." Zack paused and ran his hand roughly over his face in an attempt to ease away the tension. *Adjust?* he thought bitterly. *Adjust to what—freedom? Hell, that wasn't fair. Of course James needed to adjust to freedom. To the new situation of living with his brother, to being in another country, to having Zack as his boss again.*

And Zack had to adjust to having James around again.

Brenda propped her forearms on the table and leaned forward. She knew Zack wanted this deal with his brother to work out and she was eager to help make sure it did. "Maybe he isn't in the right job. Could you reassign him to something he might enjoy more? Sometimes we had employees who did poorly in one area but when we reassigned them, they did great. Or at least they did better than before."

Zack considered her proposal, then nodded slowly. "Maybe . . ." It wasn't a bad suggestion from a managerial viewpoint. In California James had a good deal more latitude. But this time, Zack had made sure that James worked close to him. "In the California operation, he was in charge of foreign shipments coming in from Colombia." *Before he got mixed up in drug dealing from Colombia.*

"Did he do a good job for you in that position?"

"Yeah, he did all right with the raw platinum imports for the company," Zack had to admit. *It was the illegal imports he had trouble with.*

She spread her hands. "Well, then . . ."

"Maybe you're right, Brenda. I should give him more responsibility. And get him out from under my nose."

She placed her hand over his and slipped two fingers between his thumb and forefinger to caress his palm. "Some people function better with more trust."

His dark eyes softened toward her. "You're right, Brenda. Again. We already have imports covered, but I could use a good salesman in exports. That's what I'll do. Assign him to exports. In fact, we have an important meeting next week in London. A company there is considering buying our finished product. It could be a profitable account since shipping would be so convenient."

She ran her hand over Zack's forehead. "You have so many things running through your head, Zack, you need to relax more. And to delegate responsibility. You're doing everything, and it's too much for one person."

"Is this a lecture?"

She laughed and leaned across the table to kiss him, letting her lips tease his into pliancy. "No, it's a therapy session on relieving tension. There, that's better."

"I like your techniques, Doctor."

"What happened to Nurse Cratchett?"

"I lost her. I like the new one better. Better boobs."

She pinched his nose and sat back down. "You wolf!"

He looked at her, a half-grin on his face. "You know, you're beautiful when you're riled. And I'm glad you're here. Just talking to you and knowing you'll be here when I get back after a day of headaches is a blessing. I'm a lucky man." He stood up and their lips met across the table again. For a glorious moment the financial report, the hassles of opening the plant, the problem of dealing with James, were all forgotten. Only the immediate moment was real, the sweet, sensuous moment of gentle touching, reminding them of all they had to offer each other. Of tender love . . .

A knock on the door jolted them back.

"I'll finish that later . . ." Zack promised as she drew back from his embrace.

Brenda opened the door to James. "I have an important message for Zack. Mind if I interrupt?" She pointed to the dining-room table, where Zack had picked up the financial scheme again.

"There's a commotion at the plant," James said. "Just got a call from O'Kane. He's the new plant manager, isn't he? Anyway, he says one of the converters has arrived and the crew insists on unloading it tonight while they're out there. Something about saving time and money. He wants you there to make sure they have the right equipment and that it's set up correctly."

Zack frowned. "It's there now? Shipment wasn't due until Friday."

"I know, but it's here. And they want to set it up now. Makes sense, Zack. We'd have to hire the crew to unload it. No sense paying them to wait until tomorrow, if they're ready to go tonight."

"Yeah, you're right. I'll go right out. Do you want to come along, James?"

"Me? To stand around and watch a crane lift a hunk of metal? Not really."

Zack shook his head. "Don't need you, anyway. But I do want to talk to you sometime tomorrow."

"Sure, bro." James gave Zack a mock salute.

Zack strode rapidly for the door, pausing to give Brenda a quick kiss. "See you later."

"What about supper?" Suddenly she felt like nurturing Zack, making sure he had enough to eat and soothing away his worries.

"No time for that now. Anyway, O'Kane's wife always sends enough for three men and a pup. I'll grab a sandwich from him." And he was gone.

Brenda stared at the door, then sighed and turned back to James. He had taken Zack's seat at the table and was scanning the financial scheme. She wanted to jerk it away from him, then realized that was silly. James was a part of Ehrens Enterprises. Zack had never mentioned keeping anything from him. Why should he?

She walked over. "Would you like a drink, James?"

"Love it. Got any Scotch?"

"Sure." She poured them both one and, despite a strange uneasiness at the thought of James taking Zack's place at her table, joined him.

He lifted his shaggy head and gazed steadily at her for a moment, a half-grin on his face.

She was again struck by the similarities between the two brothers, yet fully aware of their differences. Although James hadn't moved, she was also cognizant of their closeness and the electricity in the air. In an effort to dilute the charged currents, she picked up her glass and tilted it to his. "Here's to a new life in Ireland, James."

His glass clinked against hers. "And to the beautiful lady who met me in Ireland with flowers."

She smiled and drank without answer.

He took a sip, then placed the glass on the table, caressing the sides slowly, sensuously. "You know, Brenda, when I saw you at the airport, I was sort of shocked." He chuckled self-consciously. "It had been so long since I'd seen someone as pretty as you and the sight almost took my breath away. I want to apologize for my boorish behavior."

"It's all right, James."

"Zack took offense."

"I know. But he's uptight about a lot of things these days. Has a lot on his mind."

"Did you take offense?" His brown eyes were like a tiger's with flecks of gold that sparkled when they caught the light.

"No, of course not. I'd already forgotten it," she fibbed.

He took another sip of the drink and lifted his head to gaze wonderingly into space. "You reminded me of one of those brochures that say 'Come to Ireland for her natural beauty.'"

"Why, thank you, James," Brenda murmured, lowering her eyes momentarily. It was just a compliment, nothing more. He meant nothing by it. So why did she feel her face flush as his eyes flickered over her?

"Oh hell, I've embarrassed you. And I didn't mean

to. Not at all. I just meant to say something nice to someone who's been nice to me. Flowers at the airport. Dinner the other night. You don't know how much I appreciated that, Brenda. It's been so long since I've had a good, home-cooked meal. You're a darn good cook, lady." He paused and gestured. "Here I go again. Was that a—what did Zack call it— a sexist remark? Sexy I understand. But sexist?" He shrugged and grinned devilishly at her. "I didn't mean it to be."

She shook her head. "If you didn't intend it—"

"I only meant to say you're good—" He halted abruptly and looked into his drink, swirled it, then turned it up and finished it in one large gulp. "Real good. And I apologize for ruining the evening at dinner by arguing with Zack. We were like two little boys. Forgive me?"

She nodded. "Of course. Another drink?"

He shoved his glass toward her and Brenda gratefully whisked it off the table. As she poured, she attempted casual conversation. "James, how do you like it here? I realize you probably haven't been in Ireland long enough to make a fair judgment, but what do you think so far?"

"I like it a lot," he answered readily. "It's beautiful. Rains a little too much, but otherwise, it's a neat place. Nice sounds."

"Sounds?"

"The people. Their funny language. Sounds you hear in the city. Even the rain is different. And things are slower here than in LA. I like it better. How about you?" He accepted the drink with a nod of thanks.

"Me, too. I enjoy working here and hope you do,

too. I'll admit I miss the United States occasionally, though."

"How long have you been over here?"

"A little over two years. I came after a divorce."

"So you're like the rest of us."

"You mean, starting over? Yes."

"Only you have a head start on Zack and me." He nursed the second drink until it was almost gone. "It seems like a good place to get your head straight about a lot of things."

"Yes, it is."

His dark, exploring eyes caught sight of the single rose in the vase on the table and he reached for it. "This is like the ones you gave me at the airport."

"Yes, I grow them. I have a little patio with two rose bushes. This one is the last rose of the season. It's getting too cold for them."

"I saved the dried petals of the ones you gave me."

"You did? Why?"

"They keep their sweetness for a long time and smell nice. Plus they remind me of the day I arrived and . . ." He hesitated before continuing in a low voice. "They remind me of you."

She didn't know what to say and tipped her glass for another sip of the stinging Scotch.

James pulled the rose out of the vase and ran his rough finger gently over a single burgundy petal, then took it between his thumb and forefinger and rubbed. "Looks like velvet, feels like silk . . ."

"What?" She watched his action, mesmerized by the large, rough hands that stroked the tender flower, almost as if trying to absorb its beauty into the callused fingers. He continued stroking and murmured something she couldn't hear. She leaned closer.

James stared into the darkness beyond the kitchen window, still rubbing the flower. "Soft and smooth, gems made of silk, too precious to discard. Beauty in an ugly world, truth among dark secrets . . ."

"James?"

He looked up at her, his dark eyes suddenly sad, much like Zack's had been the first time she saw him. Gone was James's arrogance, his rugged façade, his cheeky dominance. And her heart went out to him in a way she would never have expected.

"Like you, Brenda." Unexpectedly his hand reached out and touched her face. Ever so gently, his rough thumb caressed her cheek.

She drew in a sharp breath at his touch, but didn't move. Maybe it was shock, or just that she didn't want to break the contact yet. Whatever the reason, she just sat there.

He blinked, as if suddenly snapping out of a trance, and pulled his hand back. "I shouldn't have done that. Didn't mean to scare you."

"You didn't."

"You look scared, Brenda."

"Well, I'm not. What you said about the roses sounded almost like poetry, James. It was beautiful."

"I . . . I do that sometimes."

"Do what? Write poetry?"

"Yeah." He gave an offhand chuckle. "Sometimes, not often. Hell, here I go again. Spouting off when I shouldn't."

"Why not? I'd love to read your poetry sometime, James."

He looked at her, his lips slightly working. "You would? Well, I'll let you. Sometime . . . when the time's right."

"Okay, I'd like that." She smiled nervously and turned away from his tiger's eyes. "Are you hungry? I, uh, haven't had supper yet."

"Me, either."

"Would you like to go somewhere to grab a bite?"

"Yeah, that's a good idea, Brenda." He finished his Scotch. "Real good."

He helped her on with her coat, careful not to touch except through sweater-padded shoulders. They walked out into the black night and entered the cheery yellow warmth of the pub on the corner. They were careful to keep the conversation benign.

Afterward, they walked home quietly and he stopped beside her door as she fumbled for her keys. "I really enjoyed tonight, Brenda."

"I'm glad. So did I, James." She shoved the key into the slot and turned. The damn thing stuck, and she wiggled it frantically.

"Let me." His large hand took over the key, and with the other pressed flat around the lock, turned it smoothly. The lock clicked and her door swung open.

"Thanks."

"Brenda."

She sucked in air through her teeth, almost afraid to look up at him. "Yes."

"You don't have to worry about me. I look at you and I know you're Zack's and that's that."

"I'm not Zack's." Her blue eyes shot up to meet his with alarm. "I mean, we've never made, that is, we aren't married and—"

His eyes became hooded as he looked down at her. "Then, what you're trying to say is that I can look, can't I? Look, but don't touch?"

She shrugged. "I guess . . ."

"Good. 'Cause I *like* to look at you, Brenda. Like it a lot." He wheeled around and took off upstairs at a trot.

Brenda whisked inside her door and locked it quickly. Oh dear God, what was she getting herself into? Why did she let this happen tonight? But what happened? Nothing. *Nothing!*

She ran to her bedroom and began getting ready for bed. As she searched for her flimsy nightgown in the drawer, she thought of James's tiger eyes on her.

He probably looked right inside her heavy sweater and saw what was underneath. She looked up at her reflection in the mirror. Did he see this puzzled woman's face? These eyes that looked scared? This woman's body that strangely responded to him, even without a touch! No! Not really! Zack would be home later and—

Zack!

She jerked her gown over her head and grabbed her robe. She would wait up for him, meet him and show him how much she cared. Then an awful thought struck her and she halted mid-step. Was this a guilty reaction?

Guilty? Guilty of what? Eating supper with Zack's brother, that's all. *And enjoying . . .* But it was only because he reminded her so much of Zack, she told herself.

Zack was late, and she fell asleep on the sofa waiting

148

for him. She didn't even feel him lift her in his arms and carry her to bed.

He laid her gently on the bed they shared. Then he began to undress, watching her sleep. She was quite sensuous in this relaxed, vulnerable state and he felt a tautening in his groin just looking at her. He showered, thinking the warm water would douse his energy. But it didn't.

Vaguely she felt him, muscular arm curling around her waist, cool hand cupping one breast. And she responded with a deep inner glow and a sigh. She loved the feel of his body against hers. He was lean and hard, like an unyielding fortress giving her a place of refuge. And his masculine fragrance surrounded her, all warm and inviting.

His breath brushed her neck and his lips pressed her skin, then nibbled tender kisses in the darkness. "Did I wake you?"

She stirred. "Zack, thank goodness you're back. Did they finish the job all right?"

"Yep. The converter's set in the way it should be. No problems. Just tired as hell." He sighed and wrapped both his arms around her.

"What time is it?"

"Around three."

"I'm glad you came here." She arched slightly to better align their bodies, make hers fit closer to his. Her back rested on the wall of his chest, her buttocks nestled snugly against his groin, her legs framed his firm thighs. Thank God he was here where he belonged. Here in her bed to push away all disturbing thoughts of James.

"You're the one I need, Brenda . . . here waiting

för me." He surged against her, seeking her warmth for his tired, aching body. His grasp tightened, pulling them closer, mingling their heat.

Tonight she was the fortress.

Soon she felt the steady rhythm of his relaxed breathing and knew he was asleep. She drew solace from the way he had instinctively sought her and then drifted off to sleep. Brenda knew this was the way it should be. She belonged here, curled up with Zack. The two of them paired. There was no room in her heart for another. Only Zack.

CHAPTER NINE

"Come with us, Brenda."

"Why should I?" She sprinkled burgundy rose petals in a small dish and set it on the back burner of the stove.

Zack squinted his eyes at the dish, then gazed back at her curiously. "What are you doing? Cooking roses?"

"No." She laughed and stirred them with her finger, then added a couple of sprigs of fragrant rosemary and a cinnamon stick. "They aren't cooking. They're drying. The natural heat from the stove's pilot light will help them along. When dried, they retain some of their fragrance and make a nice potpourri. You can even steam them and they give off a nice, light fragrance."

"Then you do cook them." Zack gave her a preoccupied look. "Sounds like something Aunt Brigid would do."

"It is, if she had the roses. In fact, I'm making this for her. It's something I learned from Gran Sadie."

He shook his head as if to clear his mind of distraction. "We were discussing the business trip. I want to show you London, Brenda. Have you ever been? Wouldn't you like to cross London Bridge with me?"

"Sure, but . . . oh, Zack, why do you have to go to London with James? If you have some free time, I'd rather rent a little house by the sea for just the two of us, honey. Then we can be all alone."

"I don't have any free time. Anyway, I can't trust this meeting to James alone. It's too important to the company's future. This could be our first big account. Surely you understand."

She nodded silently and he took her hands.

"Come on, say yes. Piccadilly, The Strand, Hampton Court Palace with its beautiful flower gardens. King Henry VIII lived there. We'll have a ball, Bren."

"But James is going, isn't he?"

"It'll be a good experience for him, a little family affair. And there'll be time for us to be alone, too, I promise."

"A family affair?" She shuddered. But then, how could she object, after all the time Zack had spent with Auntie Brige and never uttered a complaint?

"Look, Bren, I'm breaking him in to his new position. It was your idea, and a good one at that. He seems more enthusiastic about it than anything we've tried. I think it's going to work out fine. In time."

"Then why not give him the responsibility now?"

Zack dropped her hands and shook his head. "Not yet. He needs to work into it. I'm going to London on this trip. You can either go along with us, or stay here alone. I have no choice. Remember, the buck stops here." He aimed his thumb at his own chest. "It's my business and I won't risk losing this one by not knowing everything that's going on."

"Is that what happened last time?"

His lips tightened. "I trusted too many people."

"Well, if you're going to be so stubborn about it, I'll talk to Padraig and see if I can get a few days off."

"Whoopee!" Like a madman, Zack grabbed her and swung her up in his arms, kissing her face and cheeks and the sensitive skin of her neck. "This is just great! We're going to have a wonderful time together, Brenda! We always do."

Brenda went to London with Zack and James. However, she did not have a wonderful time. It rained on the one afternoon Zack had free to sightsee with her. Zack rented a car, and they drove twelve miles out of the city to see the stately geometric beauty of the gardens surrounding Hampton Court Palace. They slogged through the rain and dripped through the halls once inhabited by Henry VIII.

By the end of the tour, Brenda was chilled to the bone. Miserable, she bought a postcard with an aerial view of the Pond Garden so she could appreciate the colorful flowers later, when she felt better.

Although she started sneezing the next day she walked and shopped The Strand, anyway. Zack and James had meetings all day. That night, the three of them went to see Shakespeare's *Much Ado About Nothing*. Brenda sneezed through the first two acts. By the third act, Zack insisted they leave. When they got back to the hotel, he ordered hot tea to be brought to the room.

The next day held more meetings for Zack and James. Nursing her cold, Brenda took a few snapshots from her hotel window. She was extremely grateful when Zack returned early and announced that James was arranging an immediate flight for them back to Dublin.

"Incidentally, our trip was a success. We got the account!"

"Great," she moaned as she struggled into wool slacks and shivered into a sweater. "I'm glad something was a success."

Zack enfolded her in his arms. "Oh, honey, I'm sorry you feel so awful. This damn cold ruined your trip to London. We'll do it again when you aren't sick."

She pinched her nose with a tissue and snuggled against his shoulder, nodding. But she knew the trip would have been miserable, even without the cold. Zack had been too busy for her. She was suddenly struck with a horrible thought. Was she losing him? Is this the way it was for Charmaine?

Brenda spent the rest of the week sipping spiced tea and eating potato soup and cabbage soup and pea soup and chicken-in-the-pot soup, all provided by Padraig's wife. Brenda had never known a boss's wife who took such good care of sick employees and she kept saying, "This is wonderful, Mrs. McGuinness. Please don't get too close and catch my cold." And by the end of the week, she was sick of soup.

To ensure that he didn't catch her flu, Zack spent the week in his apartment. Although he stopped in to see how she was getting along, he slept upstairs and was away most of the time. Brenda understood. She kept telling herself it was the sensible thing to do.

James was off somewhere in Sweden. And Brenda

was lonely as hell. On Friday, she hauled herself in to work, mainly because she was so bored at home. The soup must have done the trick, for her cold was better. Now she had to chase the blues. Returning that evening to her cold, empty apartment didn't help, so she treated herself to a Scotch and water, switched on the television and curled up with a crocheted afghan over her lap.

When she heard someone at the door, she bounded up, thinking Zack had decided to call it quits, even though he'd told her he would be working late.

It wasn't Zack. It was James.

"Hi. Zack here?"

"Hi, James. No, he's working late. The other converter arrived and he's supervising its installation."

"I might have known." He stuffed his hands into his pants pockets.

"Did you just get back from Sweden?"

"Yeah. I thought he'd like to hear a quick report."

"Sorry he isn't here, but I'd be glad to listen."

"You would? Hey, how are you feeling, Brenda? You were a pretty sick cookie when I left on Monday."

"I'm better, thanks."

"You sure you don't mind if I come in?"

She looked at him for a minute. It had been a miserable week for her and now that she felt a little better, she was left to entertain herself with the TV. That was not what she wanted to do tonight. After a moment's hesitation she said, "Sure, come on in, James. I was just having a Scotch and water. Would you like one too?"

He followed her through the door. "A drink sounds great right now." He continued after her into the kitchen. "This place is so warm and inviting, you know, Brenda? Kind of like you."

She poured his drink and handed it to him. "Doesn't feel too inviting to me. It has been pretty bad all week."

"Bad?"

"Lonely." She shrugged and moved into the living room to flip off the TV and get her abandoned drink.

James stayed in the kitchen. She folded up her afghan and laid it on the back of the sofa, then settled into a cushiony chair. When she looked up, he was watching her, a strangely tranquil expression on his hard features.

"Well, come on and have a seat, James. Tell me all about Sweden. Is it cold up there? And how did your meetings go?"

He snapped into vibrancy and strolled into the living room. "Is it cold there? Like an icebox. Snow everywhere. Makes a stark environment. Even indoors, the decor is sparse." He shook his head. "I didn't like it at all."

"This is probably a bad time of year to go. I'm sure it's beautiful in the spring."

"Ah, but the women! They're real beauties! Blond hair and blue, blue eyes, and tall and slim—oh God, I could die for the women."

The tension that had been building since the moment Brenda opened the door was released and she started to laugh. "Oh, James, I knew you'd notice the women. At least there was something to like about Sweden!"

He laughed, too. "And the meetings went well."

"Oh yes. Business. Your real reason for going."

"They strike a hard bargain, but they're ready to negotiate. I set up some meetings for Zack and me next week."

"You're going back?"

"Zack wanted it that way. This was just preliminary. He wants to be in on the final deal."

"Oh, I didn't know he'd be going."

"I'm sure he wouldn't mind if you went along, especially since you've never been to Sweden. There are some beautiful things to see."

"After London, I'd be a fool to try it again!" she scoffed and took a gulp of her Scotch. "No, thanks."

"Then what—" He halted and raised a hand, palm out. "Never mind. I sense this is personal, between you and Zack. I don't even want to know."

She gazed away, not wanting to meet his eyes, his all-knowing, deeply penetrating eyes.

Suddenly his tone changed. "Are you hungry?"

"What?"

"I said, 'are you hungry'? I brought some stuff back and it's no good unless you share it. How does smoked salmon and Swedish dill bread sound?"

A slow smile spread over her face. "It sounds fabulous, James. Do you know that all I've had to eat all week was potato soup and hot tea? And I'm sick of them both. Salmon sounds delicious. I even have an unopened bottle of wine my new client gave me. Let's have a party!"

He started to rise and paused long enough to pat her hand affectionately. "Great! I'll be right back."

Brenda sat there for a brief moment, listening to James's heavy footsteps as he bounded up the stairs, thinking of his eagerness to make her feel better. She realized that she felt better already. The next instant she was scampering after the wine bottle she'd stored in the bottom of the cabinet to await the right time. This *was* the right time!

When he returned, she had poured the wine and set the goblets beside napkins on the coffee table. He placed his treasures of food there and they sat on the floor Japanese-style beside the low table.

"Here, want a pillow?" She grabbed one for each of them from the sofa.

James slipped off his shoes and settled on the pillow. "Ah, better." He picked up the glistening goblet and held it out for a toast. "A feast for a beautiful lady!"

She laughed and held her goblet to his. "And to the generous man who provided it."

She began to pick at the food he'd brought. "This is great. I'm glad you brought it."

"You don't think Zack would mind?"

"Why should he?" she asked, popping a piece of luscious salmon in her mouth. "A person's got to eat, hasn't she?"

James lifted his goblet with a teasing grin. "And drink!"

"Of course!" she agreed, laughing, and poured them each more of the light, fruity wine.

By the time they had finished off the salmon and bread, most of the wine was gone too, and they were in high spirits, laughing at almost everything. Brenda wondered briefly if they were acting too silly and what Zack would think if he came in right now. Her worry was forgotten as James started spouting another funny poem about the delights of Irish stout.

If Zack came back, he could join their party. He

would probably think James was as funny as she did. She knew he'd enjoy the food and wine. And they would be just one big happy, funny family!

James leaned against the sofa and let his head fall back on the cushion. "Brenda, she's like a rosebud, closed tight and hiding her beauty. Give her a little party and she becomes a rose, opening up with laughter and exposing her beauty." He took her hand and began to stroke it as he talked, his voice low and smooth. "Each petal is like a scrap of velvet, too precious to let go. Like Brenda, too precious to let go."

Brenda watched his Adam's apple bob as he talked with his head flung back. Suddenly it occurred to her that it was the funniest thing she'd ever seen. She collapsed in fits of laughter and leaned her head helplessly on his arm. His other arm wrapped around her and they huddled together and laughed until they even forgot the reason for their hysteria.

"Oh my God, Brenda, I think I'd better go." He looked at her warily. "This is . . . too much fun."

"How can anyone have too much fun?"

"When the person you have the most fun with is your brother's lover."

"Oh, James, we haven't done anything but eat. And laugh." She giggled. "And have a party."

"But I want to do more. And I'm afraid you do, too."

"No, I don't."

"You don't want to kiss me?"

"Well . . ." She started laughing.

He leaned forward and let his lips meet hers gently. Ever so gently. Then he moved back. His eyes were dark with desire and longing.

"I want more than a kiss, Brenda." His hands tightened on her arms and he pulled her into the shelter of his embrace. And he kissed her with such fierceness that there was no mistaking his intent. There was nothing gentle and tender about this kiss. It was the kiss of a man who wanted a woman, a man who was strong and overpowering and capable of having his way.

Brenda struggled. She put her hands up between them, pressing on his chest. Finally he relinquished his hold and drew back slowly.

"I want you, Brenda . . ."

"No!"

"I can make it good for both of us."

"Please, James . . ."

He put his lips on hers, but she twisted and refused another kiss. "I won't breathe a word of this to him."

She strained to keep them apart. "I think you'd better go now, James."

He swore in a low rasp and moved away from her. "Yeah. I know."

Slowly he eased away from her and gathered his shoes. She followed him to the door. "Thanks for everything, James."

He looked down at her. "I hope I didn't spoil the party."

She tried to smile. "Of course not. You made the party. I . . . I appreciate it, more than you can know."

"And I appreciate you more than you could ever know. It isn't often that I feel this way with a woman and walk away to sleep alone."

She blinked helplessly at him as he left her apartment and shut the door quietly behind him. She shivered and knew he was probably being truthful with her. She knew he'd been aroused by that kiss. And that she'd felt the tug of unwanted desire, too. Only her emotional ties to Zack had held her back. She was sure those ties had restrained James too. Then a horrible thought struck her. Perhaps she'd led him on, even though the evening had started out innocently enough.

Dammit, she'd had a terribly miserable week. In fact, the last few weeks hadn't been great. Zack was working all hours of the day and night. He didn't have enough time for her. The disappointing trip to London didn't help, and her bout with the flu made it worse. Everything had come together wrong and caused tonight's confusion.

Was it so wrong that James and she came together tonight? Right now, as she thought of Zack working late and trusting her, Brenda was filled with guilt.

She cleaned up the remains of their little supper and left a small lamp on in the living room before going into the bedroom to get ready for bed. Then she heard a familiar footstep on the stairs below. It was dragging tired and slow. But it was Zack! Zack!

A rush of joy surged through her and she raced to the door. When she reached for the knob, however, she heard his footsteps continue on, mounting the stairs to his apartment. He wasn't even going to stop and see how she was feeling! And damned if she was going to open the door and call him back.

Brenda slumped against the door facing and heard him open the door to his own apartment and greet James. Two brothers, laughing and talking business.

Planning another trip together. Zack obviously didn't need her tonight.

And she didn't need him!

Brenda stormed back into the bedroom and tore her clothes off. She struggled into her nightgown and looked in the mirror while she brushed her teeth. She watched big, sad tears form in her blue eyes and trickle down her cheeks. Yes, damn it, she did need him! She needed him tonight!

But he wasn't hers to have. Not tonight. He was too busy for her.

In despair Brenda hurled herself into bed, eventually falling asleep to dream of Zack scooping up handfuls of dried rose petals and letting them fall through his fingers. And she wondered if their relationship was like those velvety petals, slipping through their fingers. And in her dream, she hugged her pillow and cried for Zack. But he was gone.

CHAPTER TEN

"A drunken brawl will immediately follow the funeral! What kind of crazy invitation is that?" Zack waved his arm, bemused at the absurdity of two such contrasting activities.

Brenda smiled tolerantly at him. She had to admit, it did sound strange. "It's the Irish way. They'll have the wake all night, the funeral, then there'll be a get-together afterward. An Irish gathering."

"What do you mean by that? Is it a wake or a party?" Zack looked at her askance. "A drunken brawl after the funeral?"

"Well, it might develop into a party, sort of. Depends on the mood of those attending. But it's what ol' Willie Malone would have wanted. He loved a party, always came to Auntie Brige's and fiddled for the dances. Surely you remember him, the tall, skinny fellow who fiddled a duet with me that day you ate so much. For the wake and funeral, people will come from miles around and bring food."

"And drink?"

She grinned. "Have you ever seen Irishmen get together and not lift a few pints of stout?"

"This sounds like as much fun as a hog killing," Zack groaned.

"Oh no, not at all," she said seriously. "That's an honest-to-God, fun celebration. The typical wake and funeral is something the Irish people do to chase away the sadness of losing a friend or relative. I think you should go, Zack. The wake's tonight. The funeral and —whatever follows—is tomorrow. It'll be something to see since it's an important part of the culture here."

Zack ran his hand through his dark wavy hair and stalked around the living room of her apartment. The stress of getting the business started was beginning to show on his face. And he looked as though he'd lost a little weight. Dark shadows beneath his eyes and deeper lines beside his mouth made him look more haggard. *And more like James.* As Brenda watched him, she was struck by the increased resemblance between the two brothers.

"Honey, I'd love to go with you. But I just can't take the time off. Not now. It's a crucial time at the plant and you know it."

"But Zack, just a couple of days."

"I can't," he said resolutely. "Betty and I have to work out the financial plan for the new Swedish account tomorrow. And I have meetings that I just can't postpone. But, if it's as important as you say, James can go along as my envoy. He doesn't know much about the culture over here and needs to learn more. It would be a chance to make community contacts for Ehrens Enterprises and show we care about them and their families. After all, we'll probably be hiring some of these people within a few months. Yeah, good idea, take him along." The more Zack thought about it, the better the idea sounded.

Brenda, feeling a sudden panic swelling inside, shook her head vehemently. "No, I don't think so."

Zack countered with a strong nod. "Yes, he should go with you. I'll talk to him about it today. Anyway, it'll give you some sober company if everybody's going to be sitting around mourning or, worse yet, nipping the booze until they're half drunk."

Sober company? She almost laughed out loud. "I'm sure James wouldn't be interested in this sort of event, Zack. You, as head of the new plant, should be the one to go. Padraig will be there with his wife."

"Padraig will be there?"

Brenda nodded enthusiastically. "He sent me the message from Auntie Brige that Willie had died. They're all old friends. Padraig's originally from the same town and knew Willie Malone for years. You know how it is in such a small place, everybody seems to know everybody else."

"Seems that way." Zack pressed his lips together firmly. "Then James should go for sure. Introduce him around as the representative of Ehrens Enterprises. Please apologize to the proper people for me. I'll feel better having him with you."

"Why does James have to go? I could go alone."

"No, I think it best if he goes. Could Aunt Brigid put him up for the night?"

"I suppose so." Wildly, Brenda tried to imagine where James would sleep. And how she would explain all this to Auntie Brige. Why was Zack being so stubborn about this?

Brenda was suddenly an observer, listening to her-

165

self argue with Zack over whether James should go with her or not. It was ridiculous! If she didn't cool it, he would wonder why all the fuss over a funeral. And, if confronted, what would she say? *I don't want to be alone with James.*

Zack was still talking. ". . . and please, take the car. The green monster will come in handy."

"What'll you use?"

"I'll use the company car. Didn't I tell you? I got a Volkswagen van, big enough for hauling equipment or workers out to the construction site. It's great. I'll show you next time we get a chance."

"No. You didn't tell me . . ." She wandered to the window and gazed out at the small park across the street. When Zack first arrived, they used to walk along the wooded paths in the park together. Now he jogged over there in the early morning before she even got up.

At first, the trees were thick and green and when they walked the paths, it seemed as if they were hidden in a world of their own. Now the trees were bare against the gray sky and she could see the buildings beyond the park. Things had changed, in spite of her efforts to keep them the same.

She turned around, her voice as firm as Zack's had been. "Okay, Zack, I'm leaving this afternoon. If James wants to go along, tell him to be ready."

"He'll be here," Zack assured her. Then he crossed the room and silently took her in his arms and held her close. He stood there for a long time. "I'll miss you."

"I'll only be gone two days."

"One night."

166

"You're spoiled."

"Granted. I always want you close, Bren."

She could feel his warmth, his heart pounding against hers. She needed his warmth and reassurance and opened her arms to receive it and all it signified. "Me too, Zack."

"Don't be angry with me, Bren. I'll make it up to you. I know I've been working long hours lately, but when the plant opens, that'll change. Oh God, I hope it does. Maybe we can go somewhere in the next few weeks. Bear with me, baby. And understand."

"I do, honey. I just wanted . . ." She melted against him and slumped against his shoulder.

He kissed her neck, then sought her pouting lips. "I know, honey. I know . . ." The kiss was lingering and filled with passion and unspoken emotion. It said more than mere words, more than apologies and promises. It expressed a deep, desperate longing of a man for a woman, of his need for her understanding and support. Of his yearning for her love.

She listened to the unspoken words of his kiss and had to be satisfied with the touch.

She hadn't seen James in the week since that night in her apartment. *Since the kiss.* As they settled into the green monster with James behind the steering wheel, Brenda turned to him. Her blue eyes were serious, her face tight.

She closed her eyes for a flickering second and willed herself strength. "James, this is a business trip. I appreciate you going along, but I do not want anything to happen between us."

He looked at her quizzically for a moment. His

brown eyes seemed to glimmer with dark sensuality and curiosity. Then, he smiled, ever so slightly. "If you don't want anything to happen, Brenda baby, it won't."

Her heart pounded, for he was clearly indicating that whatever happened last week had been her fault, with her full consent. And all this time, she had been blaming him for taking advantage of her at a vulnerable time! But she wouldn't argue the point with him. She just wouldn't let herself get in that position again.

"Well, I don't. And don't call me baby."

"I can see Zack's really put his stamp on you." He reached down and started the car.

"He's put no stamp on me. This is the way I want it."

"Whatever you say." James's dark eyes raked over her with a taunting glance. "Now, which way?"

Brenda gave him directions, then slumped into her seat and fumed silently as they drove away.

Aunt Brigid greeted Brenda with a tighter hug than usual and Brenda could feel the sadness in her aunt's large body. Death, when it struck, did that to people. It drew them together. And instantly she was glad she had come for Aunt Brigid's sake.

The white-haired lady turned to James and started to hug him, then pulled back in surprise. "Saints preserve us—you aren't Zack!"

"No," he said, laughing and turning on the charm. "But we have lots of the same genes."

Brenda smiled and introduced them. "This is Zack's brother, James. We told you about him. Zack sends his regrets, but business is keeping him very busy these days. James is his envoy, representing the company."

James took Aunt Brigid's chubby hand and kissed the back. With a devastating smile, he greeted her warmly, instantly winning her with his charming style and masculine good looks.

"My, my, you certainly have many of the same good qualities as your brother," she gushed, her blue eyes crinkling with pleasure. "You two aren't twins, are you?"

"Hardly!" he said, grimacing mockingly. "I'm sure our poor mother couldn't have stood two of us at once!"

"Ah, but you're close."

"Two years. I'm the baby brat."

She stood back and admired him. "My, but you surely have the family traits, especially in the eyes. Doesn't he, Brenda?"

"Yes, the eyes . . ." She let the subject drop and followed her aunt and James into the thatch-roofed cottage.

"Come on in, now. We'll have a little tea. Zack loves my shortbread. I hope you will, too, James."

"I'm sure I will, if it's homemade." He smiled over his shoulder at Brenda.

That one little glance from him sent Brenda's heart plunging. It wasn't an arrogant motion at all. If it was, she could continue to be angry with him.

On James's face was the look of a little boy who was about to embark on something pleasurable, a chance to choose anything he wanted from the candy counter, or a double-dip ice cream cone. Brenda knew he really meant it. He was a lonely man and genuinely appreciated Aunt Brigid's attentions and the chance to enjoy her good cooking. It was an honest expression and it captured Brenda's heart, just as it had in the past when she gave in to that appeal. Gave in to his advances. Oh dear God, would she manage to make it through these next two days without anything happening between them?

He'd said it was up to her. So, what did she want? Could she resist him? Or follow her heart? Which direction did her heart lead? Loyalty to Zack? Or giving in to James?

Right now, her heart was wrenched into a huge knot in her breast.

"Brenda? You coming?" Aunt Brigid called.

"Yes, Auntie Brige. I brought you something." She opened her purse and pulled out a plastic bag. "Potpourri made from the last of my roses."

"Why, how nice! Smells like a little piece of heaven!"

Brenda's eyes drifted to James's. His eyes were dark and sensuous and directed toward her. The message was unmistakable. Heart pounding, she turned away quickly.

The first thing Brenda noticed when they parked near the Malone home was the large crowd milling in and out of the house. The second thing she couldn't avoid was the dog that didn't stop barking.

"Drew quite a crowd, didn't he?" James observed dryly.

"Everybody liked Willie," Aunt Brigid answered. "And if they didn't, you won't hear about it tonight. Only praise for the one who's gone."

170

The sound of the dog seemed to come from behind the house. And it was constant.

"Willie's hound," Aunt Brigid observed. "Poor lonely soul doesn't know what's going on. I'll bet he misses Willie more than anybody."

"Probably," Brenda agreed. The dog didn't cease its yelping. It was a sound she quickly grew to despise.

As they accompanied Aunt Brigid to the house, Brenda told herself her aunt needed her, otherwise she wouldn't be here. But, oh how she wished she were anywhere else! Unconsciously she held back as they reached the threshold. Her body was reacting, overruling her reasonable mind. Suddenly she was overwhelmed with the wild desire to turn around and run.

Then she felt a strong hand on her shoulder. It was a man's large hand, secure and supportive. She looked up to catch James's nod and brief wink. He squeezed her shoulder and she felt his chest supporting her back. He was close and he knew that she was in trouble. He said nothing, but his expression told her more than she dared to know. And his body language assured her he was there for her.

Bravely they walked inside together.

The living room was full of people chatting and Brenda caught snatches of conversations as they tried to edge through the crowd. ". . . good man, old Willie . . . I remember one time when . . . I can see his eyes now, staring in every black window . . . looks nice laid out, doesn't he?"

Brenda shuddered and gazed in the other direction. Her eyes fell immediately on the coffin in the adjoining room, of polished wood so shiny it reflected the faces that passed by. She cringed against the wall and grasped James's hand with a steel grip.

He was there for her and she clung to him, her only source of security in this strange death house. Then she felt his arm around her and she leaned gratefully against his strength. He was her "sober company" and thank God he was there.

Aunt Brigid went ahead into the room where Willie "lay waking" but Brenda held firm. She couldn't move forward another step, and felt a strange panic rise within her breast. She looked around frantically. They were completely hemmed in by people. Some were serious and sad, other laughing and telling little jokes about poor Willie. Expressive faces loomed everywhere, and woolen-garbed bodies jostled her.

She looked beseechingly up at James, her frantic eyes pleading *Do something!* "I . . . I need to get out of here—"

Immediately he took charge. "Let's step outside and get some air, Brenda." Using his broad shoulders, he cleared a path through the crowd and ushered her to the nearest doorway.

She let him propel her away, silently grateful for James and his ability to read her mind. They emerged on a small porch and she grasped the rail and took deep gulps of fresh, damp air.

Quietly he waited a few minutes while she calmed down. His voice was low and gentle. "You okay, Brenda?"

"Yes. Thank you." She shivered in the night air and stared out at the darkness. The dog continued to yelp, only now it seemed to be a part of the natural sounds, blending in with the crickets and the occasional distant bleating of sheep. "I don't know what happened to me in there. I just felt I had to get out."

"Oh, you had a little panic attack. It's perfectly normal in a situation like this. Real unpleasant, though."

"Thanks for being here with me, James. I mean it."

"That's what I'm here for. Support."

His arm stayed around her for a long time, binding them together until she felt better. Finally she spoke in a low, shaky voice. "You know, I thought I'd be fine with this. I came along for Auntie Brige, and I don't even know how she's doing."

"I can see her from here and she seems to be okay. She's used to this, Brenda. You aren't." He squeezed her shoulders reassuringly. "You know something, Brenda? I think they might have the right idea, after all. What we need is a good stiff drink of whiskey. I'll be right back."

In a minute he returned with two small glasses of Irish whiskey. She reached out with a shaky hand and he smiled and murmured, "Let me help." He kept his hand on hers and guided the glass to her lips. "Just take a little one at first. This stuff's pretty potent."

She followed his instructions. The first sip took her breath and she gasped and looked up somewhat shocked.

"See? I told you," he said. "Take another little one now. You'll get used to it." He helped her drink again.

She looked up into his eyes, brown with tiger-flecks, gentle and caring, smiling at the corners. He knew exactly how to handle her. She dropped her eyes and murmured, "I can hold it now." She took the glass and half-turned away from those mesmerizing eyes.

But he put his finger under her chin and caressed and lifted at the same time. "Feel better?"

She nodded, captured by those marvelous eyes. "Thanks."

"Then let me see a smile."

She lifted her eyes to meet his smoldering gaze again. And she smiled.

They stayed on the porch talking and joking until Aunt Brigid found them. "I'm ready to go. Are you, Brenda?"

"Yes, Auntie Brige. We're ready." She extricated her hand from James's and placed her arm around her aunt's shoulders. "Let's go home."

James went after the car and Aunt Brigid lifted her lips to whisper in Brenda's ear. "Where do you plan to sleep tonight?"

"I'll sleep in your room with you. We'll make James a bed on the sofa."

"Good. That's good." Aunt Brigid nodded with satisfaction.

Later, after beds were made and lights were out, Brenda lay awake for a long time. Finally she heard her aunt sigh heavily and shift in her bed. "Auntie, you asleep?" she asked softly.

"No, Brenda. Thinking about old Willie, I guess. It was a good wake, though."

"Yes, it was. I think more than just his hound dog will miss him. He had lots of friends and family."

"Yes, he did."

They were quiet for a moment. "Auntie? I never thought it possible, but now I don't know. How can a woman be attracted to two different men?"

"I don't know, Brenda. Is that what you've done?"

"Oh Auntie Brige, I'm afraid I've gotten myself into a terrible mess. I care very much for Zack. You know that. But, I have a strange feeling for James, too."

"These two men of yours are quite something, I'll say. They're both handsome and alike in many ways. Yet different in nice ways."

"I know. I'm so confused. I care for them both, like them, even feel attracted to them both. How can a woman be true to one man and have secret feelings for another?"

"You have to know your own heart, girl."

"That's just the problem, Auntie Brige. I guess I don't know it right now."

"Look inside your heart and you'll know which one is the true love. And you can throw away those secret feelings. It isn't worth the hurt it could cause."

"I'm trying to understand it all."

"I can't tell you, girl. Only your heart can."

Brenda nodded silently. Huge tears formed in her eyes and rolled down her cheeks in the darkness. Finally she murmured, "I'm afraid I'm losing Zack."

But Aunt Brigid didn't hear her. She was already asleep.

"Good night, Auntie Brige," Brenda whispered.

She thought of James in the next room, sprawled on the sofa. And probably looking sexy, as usual. He'd been there for her tonight, standing strong beside her. He'd read her eyes and understood even before she did, what was wrong and what to do about it. He'd been wonderful, taking charge as he did. He'd given her support and even made her laugh a little. Tonight

175

James had done everything for her that Zack should have.

Except make love to her. But even that was in his eyes.

Zack was back in Dublin, too busy for her. Always working late, putting in long hours. But when he kissed her, her heart sang. And when they made love, she was in heaven. That much she knew.

Tonight she missed him, needed him terribly. But he'd let her go willingly. How did she know he felt the same as she did? How did she even know how he really felt? He'd never made a commitment. Never said "I love you." Suddenly that was very important to her.

She turned over and buried a sob, wishing Zack were here, sleeping next to her. Wishing his arms were securely around her. Wishing she knew her own heart.

CHAPTER ELEVEN

They decided not to stay for the drunken brawl after the funeral the next day. The wake and funeral were quite enough.

Brenda was quiet on the ride back. She couldn't get Aunt Brigid's advice out of her thoughts. *You have to know your heart . . . listen to your heart.* She glanced sideways at James and felt the old wrenching in her gut that had plagued her since meeting him. What was it with this man, anyway? Did she really care for him, or was it purely physical attraction? Or did he remind her so much of Zack that her feelings transferred to James? Perhaps he filled a void in her life that was missing because of Zack's preoccupation with the new plant.

Oh, what was her heart telling her?

Admittedly, she was glad that James had come along on this trip with her. He'd been gentle and understanding last evening at the wake. Thank God he'd been there to stand beside her and give her strength. She'd been able to rely on him, and when she needed him he'd come through with no demands, no pushing.

Today at the funeral, he'd been the perfect gentleman, meeting and talking to community members, making a quiet, positive representation for Ehrens Enterprises, giving condolences to the family. Yes, Zack couldn't have done any better today, and she had been proud to have James by her side. So what did her heart say to that?

James slowed the car and let it roll to a halt beside a huge and ancient willow tree. If it had been spring or summer, the limbs would have been green and lush, spreading a dripping canopy over the narrow two-lane road. But now, most of the leaves were gone and the gray sky was visible through the dark-etched, drooping branches.

"What's wrong?" She lifted her eyebrows and glanced at the gas gauge.

"Nothing. I just think we should talk privately before we get back. We never seem to have any time alone, especially now that I'm traveling so much for the company."

"Actually, I think it's better that way, James."

"Well, I don't. I'd like a chance to clear up a few things."

"There isn't anything to clear up. We have no problems. I think you did a fine job representing the company, James. I appreciate you being so supportive last night, and I'm glad you were there. I will certainly tell Zack what an excellent job you did."

He sighed and rested one long arm over the back of the seat, behind her head. He was close, but he didn't touch. She could feel his tense energy immediately. James's appeal was strong, all right, and he exuded a well-controlled vibrancy that was impossible to ignore.

"Well, thank you, Brenda. But that isn't what I want to talk about. It's us."

"There isn't anything to discuss."

His eyes closed then opened slowly, as if he were in some sort of pain. "Oh yes. There's something here, between us, and you know it. You can feel it as well as I can."

"No, James—"

"And you're fighting it, Brenda. Even right now, you're fighting it."

She knotted her fist against her thigh. "Damn right I'm fighting it. Zack and I have been lovers for months. And I care very much for him. Now, you come into the picture and suddenly, you expect—"

"Now wait a minute! I only expect what your eyes are promising."

"I'm not promising anything!"

"Oh, now, Brenda," he said soothingly, rubbing his thumb on her shoulder.

"Don't—" She jerked upright, away from his hand, from his magnetic touch.

"See? You're so sensitive to me, you can't stand to be near me. You don't want to be tempted by me. And Brenda . . ." his voice lowered sexily, "I can assure you, I'm beyond temptation with you. I'm fascinated by those blue eyes of yours, enticed by that gorgeous red hair, and I'm ready to be seduced by your—"

"James, please!" She looked wildly at him, wondering if he would dare try to seduce her right here in Zack's car, on the road, in the middle of the day! But he wasn't moving toward her. He just looked at her, the old hardness in his dark eyes returning to pin her to the car seat. And strip her of an adequate defense. He wanted her, all right, but he would wait for her acquiescence. At least, today he would wait.

"I'm just being honest, Brenda."

"Please, don't be. I don't want to hear it."

"Why? Don't you trust yourself?"

"Zack's your own brother, for God's sake!"

"You said he didn't own you. And he doesn't, either. Not by a long shot." He reached over and fingered the tips of her hair. It was such a gentle touch that she only felt a slight tugging on her hair. It was a wildly sensuous feeling and she wanted to jerk away from this new touch, but where was she to go? Jump out of the car and run down the country road?

"Neither do you, James. I . . . I don't want you to think there's nothing between Zack and me. There is!"

"Oh really? What is it? Undying love? I doubt it, and so do you." He chuckled sardonically and, with a final, firmer tug, released her hair. His hand moved to rub his thigh erotically and he dropped his head back against the head rest. "Let me tell you a little about brother Zack. It might change your mind. Or help you decide, if that's what you're trying to do."

Brenda stiffened. Was she trying to make up her mind? And how did James know what she was thinking? Could he really read her mind with those dark, penetrating eyes? Or was he feeling lust and hoping that's what he was seeing in her eyes, too?

Regardless, she wasn't about to sit here and let James tear Zack apart. "I know about Zack. He's always been reliable and hard-working. He's had a tremendous amount of responsibility during his lifetime and has always followed through, carrying his load and more," she spouted defiantly.

"Yep, he's done all that." James's lips were tight as he spoke. "He's a workaholic."

"That's no sin."

"Depends," he drawled. "Zack becomes obsessed with his job at the exclusion of everything else. *Everyone* else. Including those closest to him, like his wife. Or, in your case, his lover."

"He has a lot at stake here, and I understand that."

"I've been through this with him before, Brenda. And I know more about his habits than you do."

"I don't want to go through his past."

"Don't you want to hear why he and Charmaine really broke up? It's a pattern I can see developing here with you. And I hate to see you hurt the same way. Only he was married then and divorce is so messy and time-consuming. Now, though, it would be so easy to drop you. Or for you to bail out."

"I have no intention of bailing out, James. He needs me—"

"Maybe. Maybe not. He needs this plant. Needs for it to be successful. But I'm not so sure he needs you, Brenda. Oh, it's nice to have you waiting around. But *need*?"

"Damn it, James! Say it! Whatever you're getting at. Then let's get on with it. I want to get back home."

"Okay," he drawled. "From my observation as a not-so-objective outsider, Zack has been through so much pain from his past losses, from what Charmaine did to him, that he'll never risk the hurt again. With you. Or anyone."

"What are you talking about?"

"She left him. Charmaine walked out, took the keys to her Porsche and said *adiós*. That hurts a man beyond reason." He shrugged. "Now, maybe she had good cause to leave, because of his obsession with

181

work, but the end result hurt him more than I can say."

"It had to do with money."

"It had to do with a lot of things, not the least of which was affection, if you catch my drift. If I were in Zack's shoes, I don't think I would risk it again. No, I'm sure I wouldn't, if a woman did that to me. I'd say to hell with them all." He grinned. "But nobody's ever left *me* for lack of affection. I know how to treat a woman."

She turned away from those devilish brown eyes of his. "I don't want to hear any more about Charmaine. Zack and I are different."

"You're a woman, aren't you? You're no different."

"I resent the implication that I'm like all women. Any more than you're like all men."

"Oh, forgive me. I forgot you're a liberated woman. God help us, that's different! I certainly would be the last one to put you down, Brenda. I appreciate all your assets and distinguishing qualities more than you know. But, I'm not so sure Zack can set you apart. You see, from the beginning, women have a bad history with him. Our mother was . . ." he paused, "less than what mothers should be."

"I know about her drinking. But she loved him. Loved you both."

"Sometimes love isn't enough."

A breath caught in Brenda's throat, and she listened as James continued. "Then, there was beautiful Charmaine. *Very* beautiful Charmaine. Zack was crazy about her from the time they met in college until . . . well, when did he fly over here?"

"He said their marriage was over long ago."

182

"So he said. I saw him just before he came here and, believe me, the pain was still there. I don't think he's ready to risk it again. With you or anyone. It may take him a long time to trust again. Maybe never."

"He trusts me."

"Did he say that?"

"He doesn't have to. I know it. I know how he feels about me. That's why I can't—won't—betray that trust. Now, please start the car. I'm ready to go home. I have work to do today."

"Suit yourself. But when you're ready to be appreciated, really appreciated, just call. I'm not afraid of risk. The benefits, especially with a beautiful woman like you, Brenda, outweigh any emotional risk." He moved slowly, deliberately, his large hand reaching up to grasp the key. He kept his eyes steadily on her while he turned the key and shifted into first gear.

His eyes clung to hers and for the first time Brenda saw in them a dark, desperate evil that sent a chill through her. She was someone he wanted, and she was telling him "no." What would he do? He held his foot on the clutch then slowly released it, and the car started to roll.

With his eyes still on her he pumped his legs as he continued to shift. When they surged forward, he tore his eyes from her and watched the road. By the time he had shifted to fourth gear, they were flying down the road at a high rate of speed.

James's profile was sharp-featured and a lot like Zack's. The muscle jerked in his jaw. What would he do next? Brenda wondered.

When they arrived at the apartment, Zack was just driving up in the new van. He bounded out and threw open the door on Brenda's side. "Had enough of Irish wakes?"

"That one should do me for a lifetime," she said, smiling up at him. She was so glad to see him, she wanted to fling her arms around him.

He took her hand and helped her out, then pulled her close for a quick kiss. "I missed you."

"But you were working."

"In between working. With every breath."

She felt slightly giddy with happiness. Just to hear him admit it was enough to block out that entire miserable conversation with James. "Oh, Zack." She slid her arm around his middle and hugged tight. "I missed you, too. Like crazy."

Keeping his arm securely around Brenda, Zack took a few steps toward James and shook his hand. "How did it go, James?"

"As funerals rate, it was up there around seven or so. If we'd stayed a little longer for the real party, it might have been higher. We certainly would have been."

"That's the Irish for you," Zack teased. "I understand they do know how to celebrate or mourn, as the occasion requires. Come on in. I've got another trip lined up for you." Zack hugged Brenda close. "And one for you, too."

"What? A trip for me?" For an instant, she feared he had plans for her to accompany James somewhere else.

"Yeah. How does a weekend overlooking the Irish Sea sound?"

"With you? Oh, Zack—"

"Who else?"

"Oh, it sounds great! When?" She laughed at her foolishness. Who else, indeed!

"This weekend . . ." Zack led Brenda up the steps to the front door into the apartment building.

James leaned against the fender of the green monster and folded his arms across his chest. His brown eyes narrowed with envy as he watched Zack and Brenda walk inside, arm in arm.

"Oh, Zack, it's beautiful here."

The wind carried her words away and no one heard them. It vigorously whipped whitecaps over the slate-gray water and blew the salty spray toward the shore. The spray was like a heavy cloud that coated and chilled everything in its path. Brenda stood alone on the rocky edge, spellbound by the beauty.

She could feel the damp cloud on her cheeks, the unceasing tug of the wind on the ribbon tying her hair back. It insisted on having its way, of taking charge of her hair and blowing it skyward. Yet the ribbon held stubbornly. And the wind continued to tug.

Zack went ahead and opened the cottage and hauled their overnight bags inside. When he joined her on the windy slope, he too felt the salt spray. His eyes swept over Brenda. Unable to resist touching her any longer, he reached up and caressed the beads of moisture gathering on her auburn hair like a misty crown. "You're getting wet," he murmured, kissing her damp cheek.

"You are, too." She smiled, glad to see a small bit of relaxation settling over Zack's face, as if the stress were being carried away by the wind. She stood on tiptoe and kissed his lips. They tasted salty and she laughed and licked her lips. "This place is beautiful, Zack. How did you find it?"

"A friend recommended it."

"Your friend has good taste."

"Wait'll you see the cottage. Beat you there!"

Yelling with delight, they raced to the small arched door of the quaint house by the sea. Zack allowed her to stay a step ahead of him until he was ready, then he caught her and swung her up in his arms and around in a circle.

She shrieked and clung to him as he carried her across the threshold and into what appeared to be a gingerbread house. He stood in the middle of the tiny living room for a moment and let her absorb the antique beauty. It was like a little dollhouse.

Blue and white chintz curtains gathered at the windows, two stuffed tweed chairs framed a large bluestone fireplace, a hand-hooked rug embraced them all. A worn oaken table offered a bottle of wine between the burgundy tweed chairs and a neat stack of wood promised warmth from a crackling fire.

"A lighthouse watchman lived here years ago with his wife. The lighthouse was destroyed in a storm one night, but the little house remained intact. The heirs have turned it into a rental."

"It's like a little fairy-tale house," Brenda murmured breathlessly.

Zack deposited her gently in one of the chairs. "I believe this place was made for lovers. For us, Bren . . ." He bent to kiss her. When he lifted his head, the glow of desire lit his dark eyes. "I'm going to make love to you right here."

186

"That should be interesting since I can barely fit in this chair myself."

"I'll find a way. Don't leave. I'll be right back."

"I wouldn't miss this for anything."

He bounded upstairs and returned with a blanket which he spread on top of the braided rug and said teasingly, "There. Is that enough room for you? All we need is a fire."

"And the wine. I'll do the honors while you rub two sticks together."

By the time he had the fire blazing, she had poured the wine.

"To us."

"To us, all alone, with no interruptions."

They settled on the hard, warm blanket, watching the flames flicker and lick over the logs. Just as it takes a fire time to get started and burn easily, it took time for them to wind down and feel comfortable with one another again. They sipped wine, talked very little, and kissed occasionally. Even the kisses, though, were brief. It would take them time to relax enough to make love.

But they both knew they would . . . eventually. It provided a sense of growing anticipation as time went on. The wind whipped angrily around the corners of the little house, but they were safe and warm inside. And looking forward to love.

"This has been too long in coming, Brenda. I've been too preoccupied."

"I understand, Zack. Let's not get so far apart again." She was afraid of what might happen.

He began to undress her slowly, first with his eyes while he kissed her tenderly and deeply. When they

187

were both burning with desire, he took her half-finished wineglass and set it aside.

He started with her hair, untying the ribbon and tugging it loose. He removed the combs that held the tousled strands back from her face and caressed the moisture from the outer layer of curls. Then his hands dug into the thick mass, and he pulled her close for a kiss. "Oh, God, you're so warm underneath," he murmured as his kisses trailed from her lips to the arched column of her neck and around to the back of her neck. "Your hair is beautiful, Bren. I could happily bury myself in it and never come up for air . . ."

She laughed and laced her fingers in his dark, wavy hair, slowly easing her fingers down to his nape. "I like it when you're too busy to get a haircut. Gives me something to mess up."

"Just looking at me that way will do the same thing," he murmured. "Your eyes mess me up something crazy." He lifted her sweater over her head and unsnapped her bra.

Inadvertently she shivered as he massaged her breasts, then bent to pay homage to each swelling mound. She felt a rush of intensity surge through her veins as he suckled each pouting, pink tip. He tugged with gentle teeth, then laved each with his soothing tongue.

"You cold?"

"Getting warmer by the minute."

She felt the cool air on her nipples as he left them damp and wanting more. His hands were already stripping off her slacks. She lowered to the floor and helped him remove all her clothes. By then, she wasn't aware of hot or cold, only her soaring senses as he touched her intimately with soft, exploring touches, followed by moist, searing kisses.

She was burning with desire for him and knelt before him demanding, "Now you!"

He crossed his arms to pull off his own sweater and she stopped him. "I get the pleasure of this."

He stopped and looked at her. And a slow, wicked smile spread across his angular face. "It has been a long time."

She grabbed his sweater and pulled roughly, kissing him, arousing him with her eagerness. She planted kisses in the hair on his bare chest and nipped his skin lightly. She ran her fingers under the band of his slacks, all the way around to his back, then to the front. She chuckled deep in her throat as her fingers quickly unbuckled and unzipped. "Ah yes," she murmured as her hand plunged lower to grasp him.

He was already aroused and hard; she was panting with need and suddenly they were together, clinging as they knelt on the dark blanket, two pale bodies meeting and merging, seeking each other. Evening shadows grew long and dark around them; the fire crackled and the sound of the tide washing ashore drifted vaguely through the thick walls of the cottage.

Their world was small, just the two of them, alone in a love nest by the sea. Brenda wished it could last forever.

His kisses were sweet and searing, inflaming every part of her. His arms swept around her, bracing her, lowering her to the floor. And she smiled up at him, ready, eager, and knowing at that moment that she was wildly in love with him.

No one had ever made her feel this way, made her

know of love without saying it. She had no doubts that Zack was the man who spoke to her heart. And she lifted her arms to embrace him and pull him closer to her breast.

Warmth from the fire lit their bare bodies to a rosy glow. He caressed the feminine curves, touching her gently, almost reverently. And she responded with increasing fervor to every stroke. Finally, when she could stand it no longer, she pushed him back. "Let me," she whispered and proceeded to love him.

Her lips taunted and caressed, teased and kissed. The taut lips of her breasts brushed his body as she bent to kiss him everywhere. He groaned softly and murmured sexy love words. Her lips were like silk, his body like hard velvet. She smiled as his body responded to her magic with a joyful shiver and ran her tongue languidly over his most sensitive skin.

"Ohh, Bren . . ." He buried his fingers in her hair and gripped her scalp.

"Shh. Can you wait?"

"Oh God, barely—"

She settled over him, cherishing the hot hardness of his manhood thrusting against her. She slid her knee to either side of his hips and lowered herself until she captured him with her warm folds. A soft noise escaped from her throat as they merged.

But he wasn't so reserved. "Oh God, Bren! Come on!"

She moved up and down, undulating slowly until she was filled with the shaft of his love and tongues of fire leaped through her body. She started the rhythm and he joined her wild dance, matching thrust for thrust, lunge for lunge. Soon the momentum was furious and uncontrollable.

Her sensual delight and eager abandon enhanced his erotic pleasure and he felt his well-modulated fervor growing until he exploded.

She savored his release and tightened around him. Her life swirled with his, and she pressed forward to receive the full force of his long, upward thrusts. Again and again she felt the shattering riptide of ecstasy radiate through her body as she joined in his climax.

Waves crashed all around them, the sound reverberating in her ears, until she wasn't aware of anything but the storm they were creating together. Perspiration glazed bodies; two arching high with the tide; crashing and overflowing; cries of utter joy; bare forms glowing red-gold in front of the fireplace. Then, glorious silence and drifting love.

"Zack, I . . . love . . . you."

"Bren . . . my love—"

She slumped against his chest, panting for breath and murmuring her love. Oh God, how she loved him! Did he hear her? Did he believe her, trust her? The need to reassure him of her love grew to a gigantic swell within her and she had to convince him.

He held her that way for a long time. Eventually, the embers cooled and so did the room.

"I'd better stoke the fire," he muttered. As he rose, he reached for a crocheted afghan and tossed it over her.

"Ah, it's toasty warm in here now," she murmured.

He left the fire blazing and refilled their wineglasses. "Room for two under there?"

"By all means." She opened one side of the cover and he slid down beside her again.

They propped on pillows from the armchairs and watched the fire and sipped their wine quietly.

"Hmm, peaceful. And nice."

"Zack, do you know how much I like this, just the two of us together?"

"Me, too."

"How much I care for you?"

"Sure."

"How much I . . . love you?"

She watched for his reaction. His dark eyes flickered in a wince, but he didn't look at her. He kept his gaze on the fire. And he didn't answer. Not right away.

"Please, say something, Zack."

He drew in a shallow breath through his teeth. "I don't know what to say. You know I care for you, too. But love—God, Bren, I don't know."

"I only want you to trust me. The rest will come later, Zack." Her hand reached for his and clasped them together tightly, palm to palm. "Just trust me."

He lifted her hand to his lips. "It's hard for me to love now, Bren. I can't explain it."

"I know you've been hurt." She raised up on one elbow. "I've loved and lost everything, too, Zack. But I'm willing to try again."

He looked away, his eyes feasting on the fire. "It hurts like hell. I don't know if I'm ready, Bren. Don't push me."

"I won't push. I will only love. And believe me, I won't hurt you." She lowered her head and kissed his chest, then rested her head over his heart.

He held her close, stroking her arm.

The weekend was filled with happy, loving moments. They seemed intent on making memories and spent every waking moment pleasing each other. And when they were ready to leave, there was a definite feeling of sadness in the air.

Hand in hand, they walked through the little house and said a silent good-bye, then out by the rocky shore that looked over the Irish Sea. They laughed as the ocean squirted them with a misty spray and ran through the damp salt air to the dry car. And they drove away with vows to return. Soon.

She nestled against his shoulder, reassured and happy with the old Zack she was first attracted to, renewed in their love.

But the closer they got to Dublin, the tighter his expression got until they were there and he walked inside her apartment and immediately picked up the phone.

That night he stayed with her, but it was business as usual. She'd fallen asleep while he was studying a new report Betty had delivered that evening. And Brenda woke up to the blare of the telephone in the wee hours of the morning. She could hear his alarmed responses.

"Huh? When? Where? Anybody hurt? Oh hell, I'll be right there!" He threw down the phone and tore into his clothes.

"What is it, Zack?"

"An explosion. At the plant! I'm going—" And in less than ten minutes, he was gone.

And Brenda was left alone in bed, wondering what in the world was happening.

CHAPTER TWELVE

Brenda couldn't go back to sleep. Finally at daybreak she got up and fixed a pot of coffee. Zack might return and want some breakfast and a little rest. But he didn't return and she was getting ready for work when he called.

"The good news is that no one was injured in the explosion. The bad news is that it blew a hole in the side of one of the converters and looks like the damn thing will have to be replaced. It'll delay production time by several weeks, maybe a month."

"Zack honey, I'm so sorry. What happened?"

"Don't know for sure yet. But they think it's sabotage."

"Sabotage? You mean, like set purposely?"

"Yep, exactly. Investigators are here now. And as soon as they're finished, we have to get the insurance company in here to assess damages. Then, I have to put together a replacement crew—oh hell, somebody's looking for me. Don't expect me until late."

Brenda hung the phone up feeling as helpless as she ever had. Zack was back in his old stressful routine. She could only be thankful they'd had a chance to relax in the little house by the sea over the weekend. It had been a chance to be alone and rejuvenate their relationship. Right now, they both needed that.

She finished work early, with intentions to go out to the plant and see the damage for herself. But before she had time to change clothes, there was a loud pounding on her door. Only one person hit her door like that. James.

She opened to greet him.

"What the hell is going on, Brenda? I just got back into town and heard on the news something about an explosion at the plant!"

"Yes, Zack has been out there since four this morning."

James followed her inside. "Tell me what happened. Anybody hurt?"

"No, fortunately it happened at a time of the morning when there were no crews working. Only a night watchman, who called it in."

"So what caused it? Something malfunctioned?"

"The investigators think it was set. They found evidence to that effect."

"Set?" James's dark face clouded and he was visibly shaken. "Dynamite? For God's sake, why?"

"Apparently to delay production. At least, that's what will happen now. Zack says one of the converters will have to be replaced."

"Oh hell! How could they—"

"What?"

He looked at her distractedly, his dark eyes intense. "Who? Do they know who did it?"

"Not that I know of. At least, not yet. According to Zack, it may take days to finish the investigation and before they know anything for certain."

"What—what did they find? What kind of evidence?" James ran his hand through his hair, in much the same gesture that Zack did when he was upset.

Brenda watched James's reactions. It seemed that he was as upset as Zack had been, maybe more so. But then, maybe that was just normal. She, too, was upset. However, the vibrations coming from James seemed extremely intense. It was something she just couldn't put her finger on so she tried to shrug it off.

"Tell you what," she suggested. "I had planned to drive out to the plant site and see what's going on now. Why don't you go with me, and you can present all your questions to someone better able to answer than me."

James practically jumped at the chance. "Yes, yes! That's a great idea. We'll go in my car."

"Your car? Why, James, I didn't know you had a car."

"Yep. Bought it over the weekend while you two were gone on your little lovers' retreat. Come on, I'll let you drive it if you want to."

Brenda grabbed her coat and followed James outside. She halted with a start when he opened the door of a brand new red Jaguar. "Is this yours? Oh James! It's . . . amazing!" She wanted to ask how a man who came to Ireland a month ago with frayed cuffs on his jacket could suddenly buy such an expensive vehicle. But she didn't dare. It was none of her business.

He shrugged with a proud grin. "I thought so, too. Been wanting one for a long time. Come on." He dangled the keys toward her. "Let's see what it'll do on the open road."

Reluctantly Brenda got behind the wheel. The engine purred to life and, as they whizzed down the road, she couldn't help wondering what Zack would think of James driving this expensive car when the opening of the plant—and possibly all their jobs—were in jeopardy.

The next day, Brenda made her initial report on the explosion at Ehrens Enterprises to Padraig.

"This is just preliminary, Padraig. The investigation is continuing and further development has been halted. There will be a delay beginning production, originally scheduled for two weeks. It'll be at least a month, maybe longer." She handed a typed memo across the desk. "I'll add updates to the report as I receive them."

Padraig took the report and scanned it quickly. "It's too bad. Ehrens Enterprises seemed to be running along quite smoothly, going forward according to plan. Then—boom! And they think it was sabotaged? No chance it was just an accident?" His bushy white eyebrows furrowed in a frown.

"I don't think so. They found traces of explosives, which indicates it was set purposely. But what difference does that make? Regardless, damage has been done and production will be delayed."

"That's the bottom line, of course. Delays mean loss of revenue to businessmen. But it isn't Zack's only problem. You understand, Brenda, we have to report this to the Bureau of International Commerce. They govern all foreign business affairs. Now, whether Ehrens Enterprises was sabotaged or had an on-site accident makes a big difference in the way the BIC looks at it."

"You mean it might affect the future of Ehrens Enterprises in this country? They might not renew his license?"

He nodded his bushy white head. "Precisely, lass. They might not be inclined to renew production after the first year."

"Oh no! This could be disaster!"

"Well, let's hope the constable gets to the bottom of the problem and solves the crime, if one was committed. Otherwise, things could look quite bad for the continuation of this particular business in Ireland. An unsolved mystery will not be tolerated."

"Why, that's unfair. It wasn't Zack's fault."

"Nay, fairness to individuals has nothing to do with it. They're looking out for the good of the country. That's the way it is, I'm afraid. You can't expect the BIC to approve some foreign business that invites trouble."

"But, he doesn't! Zack is the most conscientious, hard-working man I've ever known."

"Yes, I know that and you know it. But facts are facts. Now, this makes two strikes against him."

"Two? If this accident's one, what's the other?"

"The BIC frowns on admitting ex-convicts into the country and you can't blame them. This isn't a rehabilitation program."

Brenda froze. "What are you talking about? Who's an ex-convict?"

"Why, didn't you know? Zack's brother, James, spent some time in prison in America before coming over here."

She felt dizzy, her head and her heart swirling, her stomach flip-flopping. "No, I didn't know that." Suddenly it all came back to her. The way James looked when he got off the plane, his worn jacket, his paleness, his slender physique, his hardness, his eyes . . . "Oh dear God, no. I didn't know!" She gripped the sturdy wooden arms of her chair. "Why wasn't I informed of this? He's my client."

Padraig leaned forward with a comforting look. "Zack talked to me privately about it and asked that I keep it confidential. I agreed to respect his wishes because I could see no purpose to telling you before now."

Brenda tried to separate her inner agony from her professional indignation. "What . . . what was he in prison for?" She didn't want to hear, yet couldn't leave without knowing more.

"I think it was bribery. Nothing very damaging."

"Noth-nothing?" Brenda held her forehead with a shaky hand. "Is that all you know? How much time did he spend in prison?" Then she realized it was a stupid question, although one that popped up. What difference did it make?

"I just have this one-page report, filed by Zack when James was applying for a visa. Through Zack's American attorneys we got special approval for his entry because Zack took full responsibility for his brother. Zack's reputation and future rest on this ne'er-do-well brother. I hope Zack realizes the full ramifications of all this. You can see my position, lass. It's right in the middle. I have to answer to the BIC. And they are looking out for Ireland's interests."

"Yes, I understand. I'm glad you told me, Padraig. And I'll keep you posted on the explosion investigation."

"You do that, now. And don't feel personally responsible for all this mess. I'll see that it won't reflect on your record. I'll vouch for your work record and assure them that you had no connection with or knowledge of any of these foul elements connected with Ehrens Enterprises."

"Thank you, Padraig." No connections except love, she thought miserably.

Brenda stumbled out of his office, her mind a whirlwind of emotions. Tears of anger and frustration stung her eyes as she grabbed the first bus heading toward home. She stared blindly at the buildings spinning by and tried to sort it all out. But she was numb.

The first, most pressing and painful question was *Why didn't Zack tell me? Why?*

She ran inside her apartment and quickly changed her clothes, putting on her heaviest sweater and wool slacks. She grabbed gloves and a lined coat. She had to get outside and walk—and think. If she had time, she would have biked out to Auntie Brige's for a sympathetic ear. But it would soon be dark and she had to iron this out in her own mind.

What did she think? What did she feel?

The numbness was beginning to wear off and conflicting feelings were emerging.

Disappointment, anger, frustration, sadness, anger. Anger! Anger! Lots of anger, strangely directed at Zack, not James.

As Brenda tugged her gloves on, she paused by the window that overlooked the park across the street. She didn't know why she stopped. Why she looked. But she did. Maybe it was habit. The place reminded her of happy times with Zack. Or maybe some tiny voice inside her head told her to look. But what she saw was puzzling.

James was standing at the edge of the park, beside his brand-new Jag, talking to two men. Talking and waving his arms, as if he were angry. One of the men stepped close to him and jabbed a finger into James's chest. Obviously they were both angry. Even in the distance, she could see his knotted fists by his side and wondered if there would be a fight. Yet James just stood there, flexing his fists, taking it.

Brenda was locked into position by the window. If she hadn't just learned the disillusioning facts about James's past, she probably wouldn't think a thing about this little scene.

But things were different now, and she was damned curious about who James talked to, what he did, where he went, and why he was angry with these two characters.

Suddenly, she wanted to know more and get closer to them. Maybe she could hear what they were saying if she slipped outside and sat on that park bench nearby, with her back turned, of course. Brenda hurried out of her apartment and down the steps and across the street.

But by the time she got there, James was gone and so was his car. The two men who argued with him were nowhere in sight.

There was nothing left to do except what she'd planned to do in the first place. Walk. And think. And decide what to do about the newest developments.

James, an ex-con? She could hardly believe it. Unfortunately, now he was suspected of everything. Did he have anything to do with the explosion at the plant?

But why would he do such a bizarre thing? What could he possibly have to gain from that? Zack was employing him there. It didn't make sense to think he would try to destroy the very vehicle that might salvage him from a life of crime: a new job.

But some things still plagued her. Where did Crane get the money for the new Jaguar? Was that purchased with "dirty money"? And who were these men he was confronting in the park?

She walked for hours and it was completely dark when she returned. She was cold and hungry and still trying to sort it all out in her head when she unlocked her apartment door.

Zack practically lunged at her. "Where have you been, Brenda? I've been worried sick! I called Padraig's office and even considered driving out to Aunt Brigid's. She isn't sick, is she?"

Brenda shook her head and started peeling off her scarf and gloves and heavy coat. "I've been walking."

"Walking? In this weather?"

"I had some thinking to do." She hung her coat in the hall closet. "Some heavy thinking."

"About what? What's wrong, Brenda?"

She lifted large, sorrowful eyes. "Thinking about why you didn't tell me James had spent time in prison."

The room went dead silent.

Zack sighed heavily, more like a groan, and stuffed his hands in his pockets. "Oh, God . . ." Then he turned away and walked over to the window, looking out over the park. "So you found out."

"I did. And I'm disappointed that you weren't the one to tell me. I had to hear it from Padraig."

He turned around. "I wanted to. Believe me, I wanted to tell you, Brenda. But the time was never right."

"I suppose not. It just doesn't pop up in normal conversation, does it?" She turned the flame up under the tea kettle and began fixing herself a cup of hot tea.

"After James arrived here, he requested that I not tell you. I felt that he wanted to be the one to do it. And I knew it would affect your relationship with him."

She drew in a sharp breath and looked up quickly. *Relationship?*

Zack paid no attention to her reaction and continued. "Anyway, we both felt this was a new start for him and his past didn't matter."

"But it matters now, Zack. You realize he becomes an immediate suspect in this explosion business."

Zack knotted a fist and pounded the back of a nearby chair. "Why? Damn it! Why does he become an immediate suspect for this? It has no connection to him. He's paid his dues to society! He's through! He deserves a chance to go straight! And he will, with my help."

"Where did he get the money for the Jag?"

"That isn't something for you to worry about."

"You're right. It isn't. And if it were anyone else, I wouldn't question it. I'm sorry, Zack." The tea kettle whistled shrilly and she poured her tea. "Want some with me?"

"Yes, maybe that would help. Apparently we need to get some things straight here."

They sat at the table, stiffly facing each other. "I'm

203

trying not to judge him, but suddenly it makes a difference, Zack."

"Why? The man is innocent! Innocent until proven guilty, remember? And when he's served his debt to society, what do you expect him to do? Go into hiding?"

"No."

"Brenda, he's my brother and I intend to help him. I have never turned my back on him and I won't do it now."

"I . . . I don't expect you to. It's just that I'm disappointed that you didn't trust me enough to tell me about him. You let me . . . let me go along, thinking he was like everyone else."

"He is."

She looked down at her steaming cup. "But he's served time. That makes him different."

"Let me tell you about that."

"Now's a fine time, when your back's against the wall." She was still angry and couldn't hide it.

"I want you to know that James is innocent of the charges that put him in prison."

"Innocent? Then, why—"

"It was a deal with the DA. Plea bargained. You see, he was also involved in some drug dealing from South America. And he pleaded guilty to the lesser charges and fingered a few drug kingpins. But I don't believe he was involved deeply in any of it. I refuse to believe it."

"Did it involve your business in California?"

"They tried to say that he was funneling money out for his own profits, but they didn't have enough hard evidence. I never believed it for a minute."

"Why?"

Zack's dark eyes grew intense. "Because James denied it. And I believe him."

She nodded. Brother to brother. Of course, Zack believed his brother. That's the kind of man he was. Honest, faithful, trusting.

But what kind of man was James? Would he lie to his own brother? She didn't know. Right now, Brenda was confused, and she felt that Zack had defied their trust by not being completely honest with her.

He finished his tea and shoved back his chair. "I think I'll spend the night in my own apartment, Brenda. James needs to know the new developments and he needs my support, especially since he has no one else's around here."

It was a stab in her heart and she felt it deeply. "I don't mean to be so cruel, Zack. It's just . . . I don't know. A natural reaction, I guess."

"You want to know why I didn't tell you sooner? Just because of this kind of reaction! James wanted a new beginning here and trusted me to keep his secret. He's trying to start a new life, not drag around the old one. Give him a chance to do it."

"I wish you trusted me enough to tell me that."

"This has nothing to do with trust between us."

"It has everything, Zack. Don't you see?"

"No, I don't. What I see is you looking at my brother with suspicion just as everyone else does. He's just trying to make it in this world and people like you won't let him."

Tears welled up in her eyes. His words hit like stones. "I'm sorry you feel that way, Zack."

He made an indistinguishable rumbling sound deep

in his throat and stalked out, slamming the door behind him.

And she stood there, staring at the door, letting the tears flow freely down her cheeks.

The next day, she sat before Padraig again. This time she was composed and calm. "I'm requesting approval to go to America and do a complete investigation on Ehrens Enterprises. And especially on James Ehrens."

"You think there's more to it than what's here on this paper?"

"After talking to Zack, I'm sure there's more to it. But, for some reason, I feel that we don't have the full story. And we won't until someone does an investigation."

"And you want to be the one? You sure, lass? You might find out some things you don't want to know."

She nodded, tightlipped. "Then I need to be the one to know. Before . . . before anything else happens."

"Maybe you're right. You Americans certainly have strange, curious minds."

"I think it's important to get the full truth, so the wrong ones aren't blamed. And the innocent don't lose. Zack's business, and hopes of him making it successful here, are very important to me. Also important is the possibility that I've helped established an illegal business here in Ireland. That goes against everything I've ever done for you and the BIC."

"I told you, lass. You'll not be blamed."

"I appreciate that, Padraig. But I need to know for myself just where we stand."

"Okay, I'll take it up with the board. But, in a case such as this, I'm sure they'll approve."

"Thank you, Padraig." She stood up and walked steadily from the room. But inside she was a quivering mass of jelly.

What if she found out some things she didn't want to know? What if she learned that Zack was involved? No one had mentioned it, but privately she had considered it. What if Ehrens Enterprises was a front for some illegal business. What if . . . a thousand what ifs.

They could only be answered by a full investigation. And she was the only one to do it.

CHAPTER THIRTEEN

"I know what you're thinking, Auntie Brige. That's why I wanted to come out here and explain."

"You do?" Aunt Brigid's blue eyes grew sharp beneath raised eyebrows as she watched her rather agitated grand-niece pace the old braided rug. "Now how do you know what's in this old lady's head, huh?"

"You're wondering if I'll come back, aren't you?"

"Oh." She paused and nodded with a teasing smile. "Yes, I did think about that, darlin'."

"Let me assure you, I'll be back within the week. This is strictly a business trip."

"Business? You're making a trip for Padraig? What in the world would he need from America?"

Brenda reached down to the rocking chair where her aunt sat rocking and hugged her quickly. "I'm going for information. Something's come up and we, that is, Padraig and I, need to know the full story."

"Well, I surely don't understand that."

"I figured. That's why I want to tell you before I leave. And to reassure you I'll be back soon. I'm not even going to take time to visit my family."

Aunt Brigid raised her eyebrows again. "You aren't? Why not, pray tell?"

"Oh, don't worry. I'll call them and give them all our love. Especially from you. Baltimore isn't close to where I'll be in California, and I don't have the money or time to fly over there. You see, Padraig has arranged for the trip to be paid for by his company, since I'm going strictly on company business."

"I didn't know there was such a thing," Aunt Brigid said, shaking her gray head slowly.

"Anyway, I wanted to wait until I have more time for a visit back home and maybe . . . just maybe we can work it out so you can go with me. Wouldn't you like a visit in America?"

Aunt Brigid drew up sharply. "Me? Why, what an idea you have there, darlin'! What a strange idea."

"Wouldn't you like to visit Gran Sadie?"

"I don't know. Never thought about it."

"Aunt Brige! Of course you have!"

"Well, if I ever thought about it, I dismissed it quickly enough. A woman of my means can't go traipsing around the world any time she pleases."

"What about if I gave it to you as a gift?"

Aunt Brigid's eyes grew round. "Ah, I couldn't let you do that, Brenda. That's too much."

"Well, we'll see. Meantime, I'm going to California, which is on the other side of the country from Baltimore. And there's something I have to tell you about what has happened."

"You're going to tell me about your business? I'm not so sure I'd understand it."

"Part of it concerns you."

"Me?" She smiled curiously and pushed her toes to make the chair rocker higher. "Which part concerns me?"

209

Brenda perched on the edge of a kitchen chair and leaned forward on her thighs. "A few days ago, there was an explosion at Zack's plant. It tore up several pieces of equipment."

"Saints preserve us! Was anybody hurt? Was Zack?"

"No, luckily there were no crews working at the time. Or maybe it was planned that way."

"Planned to tear up equipment? How awful! Who would do a thing like that?"

"The police are investigating it, Auntie Brige. They think someone slipped in and set it purposely. They found evidence. They know it wasn't a pure accident. It looks as if someone set it, knowing there wouldn't be anyone at the plant at that hour in the morning."

"So whoever did this vicious deed didn't really want to hurt anyone. Then why on earth would they do such a thing?"

Brenda shrugged. "I don't know. Maybe as a warning. At any rate, the incident has delayed the opening of the plant. Several large pieces of equipment must be replaced and they have to be shipped in. It'll take several weeks."

"Is that why you're going to America?"

"No," Brenda said, chuckling. "What I've been telling you is background information. The reason I'm going to America is to check on James."

"What's wrong with him?"

"I have to see the District Attorney of Los Angeles County." Brenda saw the confusion in her aunt's expression. "The District Attorney is an important lawyer who knows about all crimes committed in the whole county. We've just learned some new information about James. He spent some time in prison in America, and I need to find out more about it."

"Saints above! Why, I can't believe it! That nice young man who was out here only last week? He's a criminal?"

"No, not exactly, Auntie Brige. You see, he's served his time and in America, that's all that society expects of him. But Padraig wants to know more about his record, his history. And I do too."

"I see. So you're going over there to find out?" She sighed. "He seemed like such a nice young man, too."

"Well, he is, Auntie Brige. James is . . . just a little troubled, that's all. Now that Zack is having problems at the plant, it seems even more important to know as much as we can about James. And neither he nor Zack is willing to tell everything. I want to make sure they aren't hiding anything."

"You don't think James had anything to do with the explosion at Zack's plant, do you?"

"We aren't sure. Probably not. It's much too vicious an act to think James did it. Anyway, he was out of town when it happened. Mainly, I think Padraig and I want to know the full story, what we're dealing with here."

Aunt Brigid shook her head. "I'll bet Padraig is pulling his hair out!"

"Well, he isn't happy." Brenda was glad to see her aunt understood their position. It might make it easier to convince Zack later. She continued. "We've brought a foreign industry into Ireland that is already having terrorist-type troubles. And a close associate of that business, James, has spent time in prison before coming here. It's important to know as much as possible about that. It may affect the future of Ehrens Enterprises in Ireland."

"The future? How?"

"The Bureau of International Commerce may decide to revoke Zack's license over this."

"Oh my. Then this is serious, isn't it?"

"Yes, especially to Zack. I'm not sure he realizes just how serious, though."

"Does he know about your business trip to America?"

"He knows I'm going but not why."

"Is that fair?"

"Probably not. But he wasn't fair with me, either." Brenda stopped and shook her head. "That sounds terrible. But actually, I'm very concerned about Zack's future here in Ireland and that's why I want to clear things up."

"And how does his future affect you, Brenda?"

She forced a small smile. "I don't know."

"Did you listen to your heart, darlin'?"

Brenda smiled gently. "Yes. I'm still listening, Auntie Brige."

"Well, I certainly hope you hear the right things in America."

"So do I. Meantime, if Zack should come out here and visit you, please don't mention any of this to him. Just the explosion, which has been on the public news."

"Of course."

"And think about my idea for both of us to go to Baltimore. Wouldn't it be a wonderful surprise for Gran Sadie?" She smiled grandly at her aunt.

"Yes, I suppose it would," Aunt Brigid agreed.

"And it would be quite a thing for me, too. I'll think on it real hard, Brenda. You have a safe trip now. May God grant you safe passage until we're together again."

Brenda kissed her aunt's chubby cheek and dashed out in the cold, driving rain to the company car she had borrowed from Padraig.

The California sun was bright and warm and never so appreciated by Brenda before. But she was here on business, not to relish the weather, and she turned into the tall, bland building, clutching her briefcase. She checked the floor directory for the District Attorney's office and stepped into the elevator.

Brenda was ushered into a stark office decorated with several black-framed certificates signifying the credentials of the man behind the desk. He was a young, square-jawed assistant who looked as if he belonged on one of those TV shows about the trials and tribulations of up-and-coming lawyers.

He stood and shook hands with her. "Ms. O'Shea, I'm Greg Newman. Nice to meet you. Now, how can I help?"

She spread her identification on the desk between them, including an official letter from Padraig McGuinness and Sons, complete with the seal of the Republic of Ireland. "I appreciate your time, Mr. Newman. This is quite important to my company."

"I understand," he said, smiling perfunctorily. Scanning her papers, he commented, "You don't sound very Irish, Ms. O'Shea."

"Probably because I'm not Irish. I'm an American, employed by an Irish company. I work with Americans who are undertaking business endeavors in Ireland."

"Interesting concept. I've heard of several American businesses moving to Ireland."

She nodded. "They have some nice tax breaks for new enterprises. It's all a part of their efforts to rebuild the economy."

He stacked her papers together. "And we can all use a few tax breaks, can't we?"

"I'm sure," she agreed shortly.

He leaned forward. "Now, you're looking for information on James Ehrens, is that right?"

"Yes. I understand he was in prison in California. I'd like to know as much as possible about that. And anything that might be relevant for our business. You see, Mr. Newman, my company approved his entry into Ireland. But we need to know a little more about the man and what kind of risk he is."

"I see." Newman rose and took a flat manila folder from the file cabinet. "Thank God for microfilm. Without it, I probably couldn't lift this thing. As it is, his whole record fits on a few sheets of paper."

"Whole record? You mean there's more than this one time?"

"Oh, sure. This guy goes back in the criminal justice system to his juvenile delinquency days in, eh . . . let's see, Pennsylvania."

"Yes, that's where he grew up. I knew he was a rough street kid but, a criminal even then?"

"Not a criminal, Ms. O'Shea. A juvenile offender. Of course, juvenile offenses can range from a simple runaway to armed robbery. I don't have the particulars on our guy because that part of his record's been

214

closed. But I can tell you he spent some time in a juvenile detention center."

"I can't believe it—" Brenda was stunned.

Newman shrugged. "Mother was an alcoholic. That should explain a lot."

"Yes, I suppose . . ." But what about the son who made it? Or was Zack involved, too?

"Well, how's our Mr. Ehrens doing in Ireland? No major trouble, I hope."

"He's—" She halted abruptly. "This is so strange. There are two Mr. Ehrenses, you know."

"Oh yes, the older brother who's always trying to bail him out of trouble. Let's see, our man is James. And his brother is . . . ?"

"Zack. Zack Ehrens. He . . . he doesn't have a record, does he?"

"Zack? No, nothing here. He's the one with the platinum processing plant, right?" Newman scanned the second page of information. "Ah yes. Here it is. Brother Zack took responsibility for James so he could go to Ireland and assume a job awaiting him. Did he do that?"

"Yes. We've been working closely with Zack and aiding the development of his business there. And James is now gainfully employed at Ehrens Enterprises."

"So, has James sabotaged the plant yet?" Newman asked, chuckling.

"What?" She stared at the man across the desk. He couldn't possibly know about the explosion at the plant. She hadn't mentioned it in any of her information. "What do you mean by a question like that, Mr. Newman?"

215

"Sorry, it's an inside joke."

"I don't think this is a laughing matter."

He folded his arms and leaned forward on the desk. "Ms. O'Shea, James Ehrens has a record as long as my leg, dating back to his youth. Now, to expect him not to go afoul of the law again is naïve. The only possibility is that Zack is very conservative with privileges afforded James around the plant and has him immediately underfoot so that nothing gets done without direct approval."

It suddenly occurred to her that that was exactly what Zack had started out doing with James. And, at her suggestion, he began giving James more responsibility and freedom. But she still believed James to be trustworthy, especially with Zack's business. "You sound very sure of yourself, Mr. Newman."

"Cynical is the word, Ms. O'Shea. But I've been around long enough to know that some of these guys never get their lives straight. Unfortunately, I feel that James Ehrens is one of those who never will. Maybe I'm wrong. I hope so."

"Well, I hope so too. Now I want to know more about why he was in prison here."

"Okay. Our department had reason to believe James was embezzling from his brother's company here in California to finance a nasty little drug habit he had at one time. Plus he was known to have friends in the business and they all knew what he was doing and that he had access to private funds, namely his brother's. He had to get his money from somewhere, and the company where he worked was the most likely. However, our evidence was flimsy and damned if one of our witnesses didn't die before we could take it to the

Grand Jury. So that part of the investigation fell through."

Brenda looked crestfallen. "I thought he plea bargained to a lesser charge."

"Oh, he did. Bribery. He tried to buy off several witnesses."

"I can't believe it."

"He admitted it. What can I say?"

"But he was forced into an admission."

"You've been watching too many cop shows on TV, Ms. O'Shea. James Ehrens was backed into a corner and he took the easier way out. His cooperation, that is, pointing out a couple of his high-dealing cronies, netted him a light sentence. We were just glad to get him on something. He almost walked. But I understand his brother lost the business anyway. He had little brother to thank for that."

"No, it couldn't have been!"

"Come now, don't be so naïve. It's obvious. The man was stealing from his brother's business, right under his nose. Just because Zack chose not to see it doesn't mean it wasn't happening."

"No! How can you be so sure?"

"There are some things you know, even without proof." Newman leaned back in his chair and laced his fingers behind his head. "But Mr. James Ehrens had a good lawyer, probably compliments of devoted brother Zack."

"You make it sound so sordid, not fair and just."

"This is the way the justice system works sometimes, Ms. O'Shea. They struck a deal, simple as that. Believe me, the lawyer and the DA took everything into consideration, including James's past and the fact that Zack was already planning to move his business out of the country and requesting to take James with him."

"Weren't you just trying to get rid of James?"

"No, not really. But we weren't sad to see him go." Newman chuckled. "From our point of view, all James has to do now is keep his nose clean. That should be easy enough. And he can stay in Ireland forever."

"He is. I'm sure he is."

"God, I hope so. Is that why you're here? Because he's so squeaky clean?" Newman's smile was a smirk that raised Brenda's ire.

"Yes, he's doing just fine."

"Glad to hear it for your company's sake. And for his brother Zack's. I'm sure Zack's reputation and future are on the line again. I sure hate to see people's lives messed up because of a family member who can't go straight. But I see it all the time."

"But James is his brother. What else could he do?" She felt the need to defend Zack.

"Now, after all these years? He should dump him. Wash his hands of this jerk! Any other questions about our friend James Ehrens, Ms. O'Shea?"

"No. Thank you for your time, Mr. Newman. I think this is all I need to know." She stood and shook hands with him and staggered out, feeling that she had discovered more than she'd ever wanted to know about James's past. *His criminal past.* And she ached in the pit of her stomach.

She walked for hours in the afternoon sun, trying to sort everything out. She had to decide how much she would report to Padraig, how much needed to be revealed. And how damaging anything she said would be to James. How would Zack take it? Was it her place to destroy everything he was trying to build?

No, it wasn't her intent to destroy anything. Not James's efforts to go straight. Not Zack's rebuilding efforts.

Zack had a business to develop, something that was extremely important to him. She understood that, for she had been in the same sinking, bankruptcy boat. She remembered all too well finally coming to the surface, sucking for air, trying to get her financial feet on the ground. Starting from scratch was not easy. It was extremely hard and devastating to the ego.

She certainly didn't want Zack to have to endure that again. How many times could he bounce back? No, it was vitally important for her to help him retain what he had going in Ireland.

Then there was the bond between the two brothers. She couldn't deny it or destroy it. Their love had developed for years, all those many years before she entered the picture. So, where did she fit in Zack's life? Right now, she felt that Zack was telling her: love me, love my brother.

And yet, she couldn't help this deep nagging fear that James was destroying Zack.

The first thing she had to do was to be honest with Zack about her trip to America. It had concerned not her family but his. Instinctively she knew he wouldn't be terribly understanding about her reasons.

Brenda was typing her report to Padraig when she heard Zack's knock. Not an urgent pounding, but a strong, firm rap, with the indication that he wouldn't wait all day for her.

She opened the door and tried to smile. But she could tell by the way he looked at her that he could see the uneasiness through her pretense. He knew her well. There was a time when she rejoiced in that knowledge. Now she wished they were new lovers again, neither knowing much about the other. Just relying on feelings. Instinctively, she reached for his hand and drew him inside.

He closed the door behind him and stood there looking at her, questioning without asking. He knew something was wrong, but couldn't figure what. "Brenda? How was your trip?"

"Okay," she fibbed. Her smile was more of a wince. "Zack, how are you?"

"Fine. How are you? You look . . . tired."

"The time zones always tear me up. I never know when to sleep, when to eat. It always takes my body a week to catch up."

"You look beautiful to me."

She swallowed hard and lifted her gaze to his. They both spoke at the same time.

"Zack, I—"

"Brenda, I—"

"You first," she said with a little laugh.

"Bren, I'm sorry about what was said before you left. Words spoken in haste are always regretted. The whole time you were gone, I had a cold fear that you wouldn't return."

"I could never do that, Zack."

"Don't leave me, Bren. Ever." And, in a single swoop, he propelled her against him with a fervor that took her breath. His lips pressed against her, vigorous and demanding, forcing them together.

She clung to him weakly, realizing how much she'd missed him and how important he was to her. "Zack, oh, Zack," she murmured as she returned his fervent kisses, responding with fire to his quick blaze.

Finally, when both were weak and breathless, he lifted his head. "Oh God, Bren, how I missed you."

"Zack, I can't believe you thought I'd leave you."

"It's a fear I can't stop."

"Zack, I love you. Please remember that." *When I tell you what I've done.* She knew she had to admit her betrayal, her lie. It was a burden she wanted to shed. She hoped—prayed—he would understand. She kissed him again, then drew back. Love's desire was in his eyes, and she knew he wanted her. And she wanted him, too. Maybe everything else could wait a little while . . .

He framed her face with searching hands and kissed her softly this time. His lips were pliant with hers, sipping with barely suppressed hunger. He buried his hands under the weight of her hair. "Brenda, you know I want you."

"Yes, yes."

"I can't stand it here without you."

"Me too."

"Now, Brenda, now . . ."

"Yes . . ." She nodded as he continued to kiss her, on her lips, her jaw line, her neck. "Yes, Zack."

She broke away and moved back a step. Brazenly, she peeled off her sweater and slacks and underwear, dropping them sensuously on the floor between them.

She stood proudly nude before him, unashamed and glowing with desire.

He reached out and touched her, his fingertips lightly glazing her breasts. Lightly brushing. Lightly, ever so lightly caressing.

Her response to his touch was immediate and visible.

He watched her, and a spontaneous swell of passion rose within him. For a moment, he thought he might lose all control and take her right there on the spot. But he couldn't, wouldn't. He quelled a shudder.

Zack touched the quivering bloom of her rose-tipped breasts. They were like silken magic, smooth and soft and blossoming hard-tipped right before his eyes.

He swore privately, after Charmaine, that he'd never love again, never experience that pain again. But here he was, wildly in love with Brenda, anxious to spend every waking moment with her.

But this time it was different. Brenda was a special woman, one he could trust implicitly. She was a good woman to love, one who would return that love exclusively. Just for him.

His groin grew tight, and he knew he couldn't last long. He had to have her soon. His clothes joined hers on the floor between them, and he pulled her down on the sofa with him.

"I want you like this, Bren . . ."

Without hesitation, she straddled his hips. "Zack, I don't know how—"

"Sure, like this . . ."

Her voice was a raspy whisper. "Yes, oh yes. Now, that's good."

"Are you okay, Bren?"

"Wonderful. Beyond words."

"Actions speak—"

"Yeah, I know."

They rocked together, moving, merging, exploring, testing, binding their intimacy, their love, with the ultimate act of love. No more holding back. Only loving and letting go with someone they trusted completely.

When the moment of wild frenzy overwhelmed him, he began to thrust fervently, seeking the utmost depth of her inner soul. "Bren, hold me. Tighter—oh God!"

She felt him explode within her and clutched her knees tightly, accepting his deepest thrusts, relishing the friction that brought her to the brink of ecstasy. And pushed her over the edge.

Together they surged and swelled and swirled in a heaven of low moans and sweet sighs. She melted in his arms. His arms reached all around her and he held her tightly for a long time.

Finally, he stirred and wrapped her in the afghan from the back of the sofa. "Would you like a brandy?"

She nodded and watched lovingly as he slid into his jeans, sans underwear. *Damn sexy!* she thought with a warm smile.

He poured their drinks, then walked past the table where her typewriter still held the memo she was constructing to Padraig. He glanced toward it, his eyes catching a familiar word or two. Then he halted curiously. And read.

"What's this, Brenda?"

She sat upright on the sofa, the colorful afghan draping around her bare shoulders. She ran a hand through her tousled, auburn hair. "I . . . I wanted to tell you about that, Zack."

His eyes shot daggers toward her and he walked over and handed her the drink. He stood looking down at her for a moment, his dark eyes suddenly hard, his lips tight. "When?"

"Well, sit down." She gestured. "I'll tell you now."

He sat opposite her on the edge of the chair. "A memo about James? And me. What the hell, Bren?"

She took a stinging gulp of the brandy and looked up with sad, blue eyes. "I didn't go to the States to see my family. I went to California to talk to the DA's office."

"You lied to me? I thought you'd never do that! NEVER!"

CHAPTER FOURTEEN

"I didn't want to. Didn't intend to, believe me, Zack!"

"Someone forced you?"

"You were less than truthful with me, too. This was something I had to do."

"And you waited until after we made love to tell me? What kind of manipulation is that? Did you think I would be less angry? Or did you hope I wouldn't see that . . . whatever it is in your typewriter?"

"No, I intended to tell you about the memo all along. I just . . ."

"Got sidetracked?"

"You might say that." She pulled the afghan around shivering bare shoulders.

He took a gulp of the brandy and breathed out slowly, as if blowing smoke. "I thought I could trust you."

"You didn't trust me enough to tell me the whole truth."

"I've never lied to you."

"But you didn't reveal all. In fact, you didn't tell me anything about James. Padraig is the one who broke the news to me and Ehrens Enterprises is *my* account. Do you know how ignorant that made me feel?"

He ignored her question and posed one of his own. "What kind of a woman are you, Brenda? Sneaking information, then making love as if nothing at all were going on in secret." His dark eyes explored her face as if looking for an answer in her desperate, blue eyes. Then he turned away, dissatisfied with what he saw.

"What kind?" she repeated softly. "I'm a woman who cares very much about you, Zack Ehrens. And what happens to your business here in Ireland."

He chuckled derisively. "Cares so much that you're willing to go slipping around behind my back for misinformation when you could have come to me and simply asked for the truth."

"Look, Zack, you weren't completely truthful with me. It was unfair. And it's unfair now for you to make accusations that I wasn't honest when you've done the same."

"I told you all you needed to know."

"According to whom? You? Or James?"

He heaved a sigh and leaned forward, elbows on widespread knees. "Brenda, the past is gone. I didn't want any nasty secrets, skeletons in the family closet, to interfere with our relationship. You are the best thing that's happened to me in a long time, and I didn't want that messed up. Plus, James asked for a clean start when he arrived. And I was willing to give it to him. I would like to ask you do the same."

"Zack, don't you know that James doesn't figure into our relationship? It's your business that's now at risk. That's why I'm concerned."

"Oh great!" He stalked around the room, waving his arms furiously. "The DA can't give you an unbiased view. He was the prosecutor, the one on the other side. Did you expect to hear the truth from him, and not from me?"

"You must admit, Zack, your version is a little rose-tinted. Now I have both sides that can be evaluated."

He stood up and set his empty glass on the table near the typewriter. "Okay, so you're setting yourself up to decide something the jury wasn't even asked to deliberate. A man's future is at stake here, remember."

"I know." *Yours, Zack!* she wanted to cry.

His face was set in anger. "Well, what did he tell you?"

She set her glass aside and cleared her throat. "Everything. From juvenile delinquency problems in James's youth to embezzlement charges that had to be dropped due to insufficient evidence."

"That was never proven!" Zack pointed a finger accusingly at her.

She had never seen him so agitated and furious. "Zack, calm down. I know the charges were weak and obviously you don't believe them."

"Hell no! I don't believe them!"

"The thing that bothers me so much, Zack," she said, near tears, "is that the possibility existed. And the possible victim was your other company. *Yours, Zack. His own brother. How could he?"

"He didn't!" The words exploded from Zack's throat.

She raised her hands. "Okay, okay. We're speculating over something that is irrelevant now."

"You're damned right it is! This whole thing is!"

"No, it isn't, Zack. He served time for bribery. You don't offer a bribe if you're innocent."

"He only pleaded guilty to a lesser charge and was

even tricked into that. It doesn't really mean he was guilty of it."

"Zack, how can you say that?"

"It's a game, Brenda. Don't you know that by now?"

"I'm beginning to see games I can hardly believe. You are blind when it comes to James, aren't you, Zack? James has put you and your business at risk and you aren't willing to admit it."

"I don't know what you're talking about. He's done absolutely nothing over here to warrant this hysteria. Hell, he was out of town when that explosion took place."

"I know. But when you realize his past charges, his history, you have to be aware that they could be somehow related."

"What are you getting at, Brenda?" Zack stopped pacing the floor and glared at her. "Are you accusing James of anything?"

"No." She looked up at him weakly, not wanting to meet his gaze.

"Then what's in that damned report to Padraig?"

"Only the facts as they stand on public record. That James pleaded guilty to bribery and served eighteen months in a California prison, with time off for good behavior. I won't mention the embezzlement charges that were dropped because they were never proven. They may count against him."

"Am I supposed to thank you for that small favor? The embezzlement charges were false, manufactured by people trying to mess up James's life. I don't believe it for a minute. And if you do, then we'd better reexamine our relationship. I doubt if we could ever agree on anything important."

"Zack, please be reasonable. I certainly don't want any of this to come between us. I never intended for you to take it personally."

"You should have thought of that before you bought your plane ticket. And before you lied to me about it." He grabbed his clothes and stalked to the door.

Brenda ran after him, clutching the afghan to hide her nudity. "Zack, please don't leave like this. Don't you want to know why I did it?"

"Not really."

"Please listen to me."

He gazed at her coldly.

She spoke rapidly, while she still had his attention. "Padraig is planning his strategy for a presentation to the BIC regarding the progress and trouble at Ehrens Enterprises. He told me your business future here is in jeopardy. That's why I felt we should have as much knowledge about all this as possible. We need to work from strength of knowledge, not weakness due to ignorance."

"So? I have nothing to hide. Nothing to be afraid of. I'll go before the BIC myself and tell everything I know."

"You're in another country, Zack. You'll have people constantly looking over your shoulder, checking to see how things are going. You can't expect them to look the other way if you have criminal activities going on in my plant."

"I do *not* have criminal activities going on in my plant!"

"How does it look? An unexplained explosion that

229

the police are investigating. Zack, this could be serious. You—this sounds awful, but I have to say it—you brought someone into Ireland who has a criminal record. That fact cannot be ignored, and whether you or I think it's fair is irrelevant. It's what the BIC decides that counts. Your future lies in their hands. And their decisions will be based on what Padraig tells them."

"And what Padraig tells them depends on what's on that piece of paper over there?"

"In part." She nodded bleakly.

"Well, God help us! It's all up to you, Brenda!" He stormed out, slamming the door behind him.

Brenda squeezed her eyes shut but couldn't block out the sound of him thundering up the stairs. Then all was silent and a sob ripped through her. She shivered and drew the afghan tighter around her bare body. There were no sounds except for her occasional sobbing.

Well, what did she expect from Zack? She knew all along he wouldn't be pleased to hear about her trip. She knew he wouldn't accept it as an act of love. And yet, in her mind, it was. Love for Zack, for his life, his goals, his business in Ireland. What if . . . he had to leave? Tears rolled unchecked down her cheeks.

If he had to leave Ireland, he would be leaving her.

Actually, she feared James's involvement in the explosion more now than before her trip. Who were those men he was arguing with in the park that afternoon so soon after the explosion? And where did he get the money so quickly to buy the Jag?

Those incidents might be purely circumstantial. It was possible. And all the questions that plagued her probably could be answered simply. They were just suspicions going on inside her head. And James was at the top of her list of suspects because he was an ex-con. *Yes, it was unfair!*

She walked slowly across the room, her stomach knotted in agony. Maybe Zack was right. She was being unfair to James because he had a past criminal record. And she hated herself for thinking that way. But she was only human.

She gazed around the lonely, empty room. There was nothing for her except the waiting typewriter. She walked over to it and looked at the half-finished memo. It would have to be carefully constructed, not to eliminate facts, but not to include unproven accusations.

Damn it, she had to be true to her own convictions. If she listened to her heart right now, emotions would prevail and she would rip the memo to shreds. From the time she first took this job here in Ireland, Brenda had certain standards about the American businesses she assisted. She wouldn't compromise those standards, even now.

Still, she cared about what happened to Ehrens Enterprises. She loved Zack very much and didn't want to see his new business fold. She thought her heart would break if he had to leave now. Zack was foremost in her mind, not James. Regardless of Zack's denials, she would closely observe everything in the future concerning his company. She would try to protect Zack, whether he wanted her protection or not.

And she would fervently hope James wasn't involved.

By the next afternoon, her report had been filed with Padraig. She'd spent hours agonizing over it, and after she'd turned it in, she felt drained, emotionally spent. It was so vitally important to her and to Zack that she wanted to talk to him about it. How she yearned to see him again, to reassure him that she was trying very hard to make things work for him.

But he was not around for her.

As she entered her apartment alone, the empty walls echoed her every move. She changed clothes and put on a comfortable nightgown and her thick wrap-around robe. She snuggled its fuzzy collar around her neck, wishing it were Zack kissing her, holding her. It had only been one day but God, how she missed him.

A loud pounding on her door startled her out of her sentimental reverie. She knew it wasn't Zack; he was never so boldly insistent. Not surprised, she opened the door to James.

He stepped forward, entering without waiting for a civil invitation. "We have some things to discuss, Brenda."

She closed the door. "Well, come on in." She tried not to visualize him in prison garb, cuffed with a line of other convicts shuffling down a narrow hallway. She squeezed her eyes closed to shut out the awful mental image. This was the kind of prejudice Zack was trying to avoid . . . and here she was, guilty of exactly that.

Turning to face James, she forced a smile. He had stormed into the room like a bull on the rampage and her smile quickly faded. One look at his dark countenance, and she realized he knew. *Oh God, he knew.*

James was seething beneath the surface.

Brenda drew in a deep breath and followed him across the room. "What do you want to discuss, James?"

"We have a cozy little triangle here, don't we, Brenda?"

"What?" She looked startled. The man who faced her was hard-edged and had a vicious gleam in his brown eyes. Now there was nothing about this man that reminded her of Zack. This one was hostile and surly. And she was suddenly frightened.

"Don't be coy with me, Brenda. You know what I'm talking about. This—" In a quick movement, he grabbed her shoulders and hauled her into the most savage embrace she'd ever experienced.

His lips were brutal on hers, his teeth pricking her sensitive skin, his tongue forcing inside her amazed mouth. Before she could think, he was driving deep, moving in and out. She was repulsed by his violence and struggled to fight him off. Impulsively, she bit him.

He drew back quickly, uttering a string of oaths.

She clamped her teeth shut before he could kiss her again. Futilely, she pushed the heels of her palms against his shoulders, muffling objections.

But he held her firmly, her pliant breasts crushed to his unyielding chest. The lightly knotted sash on her robe unfurled, leaving her exposed as the robe fell open. She felt the heated friction of his masculine form against her silken gown.

With a super strength, he wedged her body between his sinewy thighs and she could feel the taut ridge of his manhood thrusting against their clothes. Her heart pounded wildly as his hand slid down her back and over her bottom to press her tightly to him.

She tried to push away, but her strength pitted to his was weak and futile. She felt like a rag doll, there at his masculine whim. A knot of fear clinched in her stomach. What would he do? And what would she do to stop him? At the moment, he had the power of three men. And the physical ability to assault her.

But not without a fight! Damn him, anyway! She'd fight him tooth and nail! He wouldn't take her easily.

She twisted her face back and forth, finally breaking the vicious contact with his mouth. "James! Don't . . . do this!"

His lips were close to her face, and she smelled liquor on his breath. "I like a woman with fire, Brenda."

"Let . . . me . . . go!"

His eyes were like burning black coals and his lips curled into a wicked smile. "You like it too."

"No!" She pushed at him again.

With a quick, vigorous shove, he released her.

Relieved, scared, near tears, she staggered across the room from her would-be attacker. Oh no, surely he wouldn't do such a thing! She was overreacting here! James wouldn't— "Please, leave," she muttered. Shaky fingers tenderly touched her bruised lips. She ached everywhere. Her jaws and lips were tight and hurting. She'd used every muscle in her neck and arms to resist him and now they screamed from the sudden misuse.

"Oh, you liked it, Brenda. Admit it, baby. You like a little rough stuff once in a while." His tone was derisive, so unlike the James she thought she knew.

234

"No! That's ridiculous! I . . . I want you to go now."

"Not yet. I haven't done what I came for."

She looked at him wildly. Would he come after her again? Her mind began whirling with defensive actions. He stood with his back to her, gazing out the window at the park. When he made no approach, she slumped into a chair, hugging her ribs, but keeping a wary eye on him.

His stance was wide and he stuffed his fingers into his back pockets. His large hands propped on his hips above his pockets, and she shuddered at the thoughts of those powerful, vicious hands on her.

"If you don't leave, I'll—"

"Come on, Brenda. Admit it, we've got a good thing going." He turned slowly and ambled toward her. "Don't mess it up."

"We've got nothing going, James."

He halted, looking down on her. "That's not exactly true, Brenda. I remember lonely nights, two people sharing a drink, a poem, a kiss . . . surely you remember that night."

She turned her face away. How could she deny those truths?

He continued in a low voice. "I know a beautiful woman whose lips are soft and smooth as rose petals. Her eyes are blue and sad; her hair rich red and begging to be touched. Her body craves—"

"James, don't—"

"I recall her long arms wrapping around my neck, her sensuous body rubbing against mine, so close I can still smell her scent, very faint and classy, like something taboo, something I never get to touch. But I can

235

touch her because she's a woman begging to love and be loved. Begging me with her eyes."

"James, that's enough. It isn't true! Please leave."

He walked closer and squatted near her, his large hands dangling between knees spread far apart. "Ahh yes, what we had was nice, very nice."

"There was never anything between us."

He laid a large, powerful hand on her knee. She quivered beneath the dangerous heat radiating from his touch.

"Oh, baby, don't say that. I don't think Zack would understand all this. He might think something was still lingering between us. He might be right."

"No—"

"He might even be interested in sharing his bounty with his poor blackguard of a brother. Then again, maybe not. Zack always was the selfish kind when it came to his women. He wouldn't want to share you."

"Damn it, James! Why don't you leave? What do you want?"

His face loomed close to hers and his hand tightened on her knee. "I want you to butt out of our business, baby. I want it real bad, too. And I usually get what I want."

"Don't threaten me."

"I understand you made a trip all the way to California to find out about me. Why didn't you just ask?"

"No one, not even your devoted brother, was willing to tell me everything I needed to know. Do you realize Zack's business is in jeopardy here, James? If anything else happens, he could lose his license to stay in Ireland. Or don't you care?"

"Nothing else is going to happen if you keep your

nose out of this and leave things alone. It's none of your business, Brenda."

"If Zack loses, it's my business. Then we all lose. You, too. Can't you understand that, James?"

His lips thinned. "Leave it be, Brenda. No more reports; no more trips. Or I might be forced to tell brother Zack more than you want him to know."

She drew in a sharp breath. "There's nothing to tell."

"We'd let Zack decide." He squeezed her knee and slid his hand up her thigh.

She wrenched away and flew to the door. "I'll scream if you touch me again, James."

His laugh was derisive and wicked. "Your screams don't scare me. I know how to put a stop to them. Anyway, as I said, I like a woman with fire. Now, I expect you to do as I say, or Zack'll get his ears full."

"He'll never believe you!"

"You're wrong, baby. We're brothers, remember? His blood is my blood! Our relationship comes straight from the heart, while yours is merely lust!"

She stared at the blank door long after James disappeared. Then she slumped into a heap on the sofa and buried her face in the afghan and cried. The news and events of the last few days had left her devastated. To discover that James had led a life of crime was bad enough, but to see how Zack had stood by him over the years, and how he'd used Zack's love was heartbreaking.

Then the revelation that perhaps it was happening again and she could do nothing about it, was alarming. Of course, her argument with Zack last night had been painful in itself. She could see that James was right.

The brothers' ties went back a long time; their bond was strong.

And now, James's near-assault had scared the hell out of her. What would Zack think when he heard about this? Would he even believe her? He'd said he couldn't trust her anymore.

Now, more than ever, she felt that James stood between them.

To Brenda, James's threats implicated him even more. She should warn Zack. Warn him of his own brother! Oh God, how could she convince him? Should she even try?

She just couldn't sit back and let James run rampant through everything Zack had worked for. And she couldn't bear the thoughts of losing Zack, but now, that fear was real.

Later, she gathered her wits and began to work on her plan. She had to tell Zack her suspicions, but first she had to regain his trust. She climbed into the green monster and chugged outside the city limits.

The plant hugged the hillside, dark and ominous in the twilight. One room stood out in the darkness with lights blaring. And one man hunched over a desk, working diligently on a stack of papers. He was the one man she cared about in the whole world.

She knocked lightly on his office door. "Zack?"

"Yes?" He looked red-eyed and weary. Her heart went out to him and she wanted to pull him into her arms and nestle him against her breast until he slept. Slept for hours and hours, while she soothed away his problems.

"I . . . I wanted to talk to you. It's been miserable without you."

"I've been busy."

"So I see." She looked around. "If it's an apology you want, please accept mine. I shouldn't have gone to California without your knowledge. I'm sorry."

He nodded, tight-lipped. "Me, too. I didn't mean to blow up like that. It was stupid."

She quelled the giddy desire to laugh. Both were offering ridiculous apologies, something to appease the other. "You trying to kill yourself, Zack? You have to get some rest. You can't continue at this pace."

"You don't understand the pressures I'm under."

"I'm willing to listen."

"I don't want to burden you."

"Don't you know that anything concerning you is no burden to me, Zack?"

He waggled a pencil impatiently. "Is that why you came all the way out here? I'm very busy."

"It's getting late."

"I have work to do."

"Nothing that won't wait until tomorrow? Maybe I can help."

"Nope."

"Well, actually, that's not exactly why I came all the way out here. I wanted to say that I've finished the memo to Padraig. And I . . . stuck to the facts. Didn't give him any more information than I felt I had to."

Zack listened diligently and nodded. "Thanks."

"And I talked to him about the meeting before the BIC. I felt that if you could speak on your own behalf, you might do a better job than any of us, including

Padraig. You know more about the business and James's credibility than anyone. I requested that Padraig take you along so you can make the explanation yourself. And he agreed."

Zack took a deep breath and dropped the pencil. His tired expression softened. "Brenda . . . thanks. You did this for me."

"When are you going to get it through your thick head that I really care what happens to you, Zack Ehrens?" Her voice stuck in her throat as sudden emotion took over.

He rose, looking rumpled and tired and so damned vulnerable. "Bren . . ."

She motioned with her head. "Why don't you come home with me. I made a pot of lamb stew. You need a good night's rest, Zack. You look awful."

"Is that the best compliment you can offer?"

"It's the awful truth, coming from someone who hurts when I see you looking that way."

He reached back for his jacket and, hooking it on one finger over his shoulder, he walked toward her. "You're right. I guess this stuff can wait. And lamb stew sounds great." He switched the light off.

Brenda turned to go but he touched her arm and pulled her close. "Brenda . . . wait." His lips lightly grazed hers, then paired with them for a firmer kiss.

She tried to keep from wincing as his mouth caressed her bruised lips. She couldn't let him know what had happened between her and James. Not yet. It was too soon. He might not believe her.

"Brenda, you're the best thing that's ever happened to me. Ever."

"I love you, Zack."

"Let's go home."

As soon as they stepped inside her apartment door, he pulled her into his arms and kissed her long and hard. "I hope you understand that I need you, Brenda. Now more than ever."

"Now?" She molded her body to his and wrapped her arms around his ribs. "Before dinner?"

"Yes, now . . ." He chuckled lasciviously as she began to undress him before they made it to the bedroom.

They took a shower together and made love under the warm spray. His masculine need for her was strong and demanding. And her feminine desire reached out to embrace him, to give him what he needed. All of her.

She opened to receive him as the shower spray pelted them. Soon she was only aware of the glory of uniting with Zack, of knowing his sexual power and that she could please him. He urged her closer and with strong hands under her buttocks, lifted her off her feet. He rocked, thrusting into her warmth, making sure she reached a point of ecstasy when he did. Then, he washed her with his hands, caressing every inch of her until they were completely out of hot water.

"Brr! Time for me to get out! Ready for dinner?" She stepped out and tossed him a towel.

"Starved after all this exercise."

She pinched his waist. "It'll keep you trim."

"Can't think of a better way."

"We could try to think of a better way."

"Tonight," he promised. "After dinner."

That night, she lay away in his arms long after Zack

was asleep. His regular breathing reassured her he was getting some much-needed rest. And she felt better about that. The sexual part of their relationship was blooming again and she was delighted. She didn't want to spoil either aspect.

But how was she going to tell him about James? The right time hadn't presented itself this evening, but it never did. She wasn't sure how to do it, anyway. She didn't want to destroy the fragile web they were weaving together again.

In the morning, when she awakened, Zack was already gone. On the table was a quickly scribbled note that left her smiling and hopeful.

See you tonight. Love, Zack.

CHAPTER FIFTEEN

"Just give me one hour of your time. All right, all right, forty-five minutes. Everybody has to eat, even busy executives. And you're going to." Brenda bustled into Zack's office, closed the door, and plopped a wicker basket on his desk.

"Brenda! You're a nice surprise. What is this?"

"Lunch for the workaholic. I figured if I didn't bring it out to you, you wouldn't eat. Also, I wouldn't get to see you today. So here we both are. Food and me!"

"Both sound luscious. I'm starved." Zack sat there staring at her, smiling with wonder at the red-haired whirlwind breezing into his office with lunch and a glorious smile. "You're amazing, you know."

"Save it until tonight," she advised briskly. "And come home at a decent hour. We'll discuss greatness at length."

"Don't you have to work today? It's only Thursday."

"I'm out here on official business," she said as she cleared a space on his desk and began to dig into the basket. "To inspect the plant and see how you're progressing toward first day of production."

"Does this go into another of your reports to Padraig?"

"Not our lunch, although, as I said, everyone has to eat. Padraig won't object to that. He just wants an update on things out here. And I'm only too happy to oblige." She handed Zack a sandwich on a hard roll and unwrapped one for herself. "I brought coffee, since we both have more work to do today. But the *vino* is chilling for tonight . . ."

"With an offer like that, I'll be there." Zack walked to the window that overlooked the interior of the plant and stood munching his sandwich.

"If I'd known you were that willing, I would have made you an even better offer than that," she teased, joining him beside the window. "I don't know why you didn't plan this office with an outside window that had a pretty view over the hills around here."

"This gives me the perfect opportunity to see what's going on inside the plant at all times. Anyway, if I looked over the countryside, I'd sit and daydream about you all the time and never get a thing done."

"That's why I'd want to be able to see outside, to daydream a little." She pinched his arm playfully. "But you, the consummate boss, want to see what everyone else is doing. I can see your point, though."

He gestured at the large room on the floor below them. The place was bustling with workers. "You can see for yourself that the mess from the explosion has been completely cleaned up and the damaged converter hauled away. Insurance investigators and police have finished poking around here, so we're ready to push forward again."

"Did they come up with anything conclusive about the explosion?"

"Nothing, except they still think it was set. Probably someone wanting to delay production. Hell, I could have told them that much. But, we're not going to sit around and wait for answers. The new converter is due for installation later this week. Put this in your report to Padraig: A couple of months from now, and we'll be processing platinum."

"I'll be so glad when that day comes, Zack." She gazed up at him with admiration. "We'll have a real celebration then. You know, I'm very proud of you."

"I could never have done all this without you, Brenda. If only we weren't in full view of the construction staff, I'd show you how I feel at this moment."

She smiled happily. "Save it for tonight."

"We'll have so much saved for tonight, I'll have to come home early to fit it all in."

"Fine with me. I can change my schedule to fit yours any day. Maybe we should leave now."

"I have a personnel meeting in about an hour. And before that I have to—"

"Spoilsport!"

"That's the way it is when you're the boss. As much as I'd like to ravish you this afternoon, Brenda, I can't. Too much work, too little time." He moved back to the desk and poured another cup of coffee.

Brenda stood by the window a moment longer, then leaned forward with renewed interest. "There's James. I thought he was working on a deal in Germany."

"Not yet. Something personal came up and he can't leave until tomorrow."

"Oh." It was on the tip of her tongue to ask why,

but Zack had turned his attention to the stack of papers before him, indicating it was time for her to leave. She looked down at the production room again and saw that James was talking to two men.

She pressed her nose against the glass. Two men? Were these the same two men she'd seen arguing with James in the park? Maybe . . . she couldn't quite tell. He appeared to be showing them around. But why? Was this another aspect of his job at Ehrens Enterprises?

"Zack, who are those men?"

"Which men?"

"Those two talking to James."

"Hmm?" He stretched his head in the direction she pointed. "I don't know."

"Please, come over here and look. Do you know them?"

He took one step and glanced quickly over her shoulder. "Nope."

"Then why is James showing them all over the place?"

"Don't know."

"Maybe you should ask him about them. They look—"

"Brenda, maybe you should—" He halted before he said sharply, "Look, Brenda, we seem to get along fine as long as we don't mention James or the business. Let's keep it that way."

"But Zack, I saw James with—"

He held up his hand to hush her. "Please, Brenda. I'll handle James."

She clamped her teeth together and walked over to the picnic basket on his desk. "Okay. I'll butt out. I can see you're busy." She began to gather the remains of their lunch.

He brushed her hand with his fingertips. "Thanks for lunch. You're wonderful. Let's . . . not argue over James. He's doing all right. Trust me."

She nodded. "Sure. I don't mean to meddle, Zack. I know it's your business."

He gave her a quick kiss. "See you tonight."

She blew him a kiss and hurried down the hall. Just as she was reaching the bottom of the stairs, she spotted James and the two men again. They were near the far end door leading outside, and their positioning to each other drew her curious stare. One was standing apart, looking around, from side to side. The other man stood close, facing James. Then, with a quick, covert flicker, they reached out and exchanged something.

Brenda blinked, amazed by what she was witnessing. An exchange of some kind! She was sure of it! But what? The man who appeared to be the lookout turned toward her and instinctively Brenda flattened herself against the wall so he couldn't see her. Damn! She wished she were close enough to hear what they were saying!

By the time she peeked around the corner from where she was hiding, the men were gone, and James was heading out the door. She hurried to catch up with him.

Her action was purely impulsive, because when she was close enough to touch his shoulder, she realized she had no idea what to say to him. She couldn't ask him outright what he had in his pocket, but how could she find out? Good heavens, it could have been anything from money for industrial secrets to something as simple as a cigarette lighter. But it was a small item, one that would fit into a man's hand and pocket.

James was pushing the door open when he noticed her and he paused and held it for her. "Hello, Brenda. What a surprise to see you here."

"I could say the same to you, James." She stepped beside him and halted, trying to encourage him to stop and talk. "What are you doing way out here at the plant? I thought your business kept you traveling most of the time."

"I have to report in once in a while. I'm heading for Germany tomorrow. And what brings you out to the country?"

"I came to check on the progress of the plant. And to bring Zack a bite of lunch."

"How cozy."

"What are you really doing here, James? I've been here over an hour and you didn't report to Zack."

"Since when do I have to answer to you about my job?"

"You don't, James. I was just making conversation."

He smiled sardonically. "Somehow I doubt that, Brenda. We have about as much to say to each other as a snake and a wolf in sheep's clothing."

She glared at him. "I figured we could talk in public where I could trust you."

"You've been on my case since you went to California and came back with my sordid history. I'm getting pretty tired of it, Brenda. Back off."

"Why, James, I'm just asking a simple question, and you're acting as if you have something to hide."

"Just about as much as you do, baby, and don't you forget it. You've been very smart by not mentioning anything to Zack about us. But beware, if you do. I'll counterpunch with all I've got. And we both know who he'll believe."

He strode ahead and she followed, double-stepping to keep up with his long legs. "James, listen to me a minute. I don't know what you're doing, but I feel you're up to something. Please don't hurt your brother any more than you already have. He believes in you, trusts you implicitly. He's always wanted the best in life for you and has given up everything for you. Don't make him go through that again." She sighed in frustration and slowed her step, speaking to his broad back. "Oh, James, don't you love him?"

He halted and wheeled around, heavy anger shadowing his face. "Keep your mouth shut, Brenda! About everything!"

"Zack loves you," she said fervently, her eyes imploring him to take her words to heart.

But James just glared darkly at her for a moment longer, then turned and walked away.

She stood there, seething underneath as she watched James get into his red-hot sports car and whiz down the road. What should she do? He had threatened her again. Damn it, did she have to keep quiet forever, even when she feared what would happen to Zack? To his business! James's words echoed in her head. *Keep your mouth shut!*

But, about what? If she knew, she'd be dangerous. As it was, she was ignorant but skirting on something. James, obviously, thought she knew more than she did. And he definitely had something to hide. But what?

Brenda stewed about the matter all the way home. And by the time she parked the green monster, she was convinced something was going on that Zack should know. If something bad happened, and she hadn't revealed all she knew, Brenda would never forgive herself.

Unfortunately, what she knew was purely circumstantial.

Still, she had to tell him everything. At what risk, she wasn't sure. But tonight she'd tell him. She had to.

Zack came home before eight and after they'd eaten a light supper along with a glass of wine, both were a little mellow. Brenda hated to spoil the mood, but she felt she was holding out on Zack. And she had to say something. She'd been quiet about everything in order to keep the peace for weeks now, but it wasn't right. Admittedly, she was afraid to risk tearing up the finely spun web of their relationship. Now though, she felt the risk to Zack's business was even greater.

Brenda stood at the window, gripping her empty wineglass, looking out at the black park across the street. Someone had a flashlight and it flickered along the invisible paths beneath bare branches. She watched, spellbound by the mysterious illusion of a light traveling alone. Her suspicions of James were like that light, mysteriously moving along, first one way, then another. Yet she wasn't sure what she saw. Suddenly the light in the park moved near a streetlight, and a man walking his dog was illuminated.

Mystery solved. Was James's mystery that easily resolved? Oh God, she hoped so.

Zack moved beside her. "What are you looking at? It's pitch black out there."

"Nothing. Just thinking."

"About what?"

"About something I must tell you. And I'm hesitant because I know you don't want to hear it, and I don't know how you'll react."

"Good Lord, with a setup like that, I can't resist. What in the world is troubling you, Bren?"

"Well, it's about James."

His answer was sharp. "Well, you're right about one thing. I don't want to hear it."

"But you must, Zack. I feel that something's going on, and I don't know exactly what it is, and I'm scared for you. For your business."

"You feel? Is this in the same category with your female intuition?"

"No, there are several real, concrete things you should know."

He raked his hand over his face. "I really don't want to go into this tonight, Brenda. I'm tired and—"

"You're going to hear it anyway. I can't let it drag on any longer. I have to let you know everything. My conscience won't let me keep quiet any longer." She set her glass on the table and took his hand, leading him into the living room. "Please, sit down and listen." She took a seat in the chair and motioned to the sofa. "I have to tell you that James and I . . ."

Zack sat opposite her. "What?"

"Well, it wasn't anything. Just a kiss."

He drew in a sharp breath. "You and James?"

"I said it was just a brief time that we were both, oh God, this sounds awful. Both lonely and you were away all the time and . . . it just happened. A kiss. A simple kiss! That's all, I swear. And it didn't mean anything, honest, Zack. But he . . . he intends to use it against me . . . well, he has been using it as blackmail."

"Blackmail? For what?" Zack was slumped on the sofa, as if she had knocked him back. His face was contorted with pain. As she watched at him, Brenda knew that she was placing their relationship on treacherous ground. And yet she couldn't stop. Not now.

"The only reason I'm telling you this is because he has threatened me several times to use this indiscretion against me. Now that you know, it can't be a tool."

"Brenda, you aren't making much sense here. Do you think I don't care about what happens between you two?"

"No. I'm trying to make sense, but this is extremely difficult for me, Zack."

"I'll bet. Admitting a liaison with my brother doesn't come nearly as easily as the kisses did."

"It wasn't a liaison. It was . . . oh please, Zack. Just listen to the rest."

"I think I've heard enough."

He started to rise and she stopped him with an ice-cold hand. "I've started this and you're going to listen to all of it. There's only one reason I'm telling you."

"Guilt keeping you awake nights?"

She lifted her chin. "No. Fear. Fear of what's happening, of things you should know. You have to be aware that something's going on, Zack. I think you and your business may be in danger. Otherwise I wouldn't be telling you any of this."

He stayed, but his expression was closed and angry. She'd pushed him beyond his limits of endurance and now demanded more. But, by God, she'd started this. And she would finish it, even though it might finish them.

"Directly after the explosion, I saw James talking to two strange men in the park. He was raising his arms and talking as if he were really angry."

"What was he saying?"

"I don't know. I was standing here in the window. By the time I got over there, all three were gone. And remember, James came up with some quick bucks to buy that expensive car right before the explosion."

"That's always bugged you, hasn't it? You don't know where he got the money. Maybe he came over here with a little nest egg saved up."

"The way he looked when he got off that plane— and now I know he'd just gotten out of prison—I doubt if he had a bundle of money saved."

Zack narrowed his eyes. "You're presuming a lot here, Brenda."

"I know. But when I returned from California, James came to visit me. He was furious that I'd gotten all that information on him."

"So was I. It was unnecessary."

She ignored his comment and went on. "He threatened me. Actually, he came in here and . . . forced me into a compromising position. And threatened that if I didn't butt out, he'd tell you about us."

"Was this before or after the kiss?"

"After," she admitted tightly. "But, I told you,

nothing more happened. And if he claimed otherwise, he'd be lying!"

Zack pursed his lips. His brown eyes were hard. "But probably not much."

"That's not so!" She was on her feet, frustrated, feeling she was slipping, not knowing how to make it any better. She had to go on. "So I did as James demanded and kept quiet. I was afraid of losing you, Zack. And I didn't want to do that. But I don't want to see your business destroyed, either. So I have to tell you what I know. And you must be aware that James might be working against you."

He folded his arms over his chest. "My own brother? Come on now, Brenda."

She began to pace. "Today, from your office window, I saw James with those two men again."

"Same ones in the park?"

"Well, I'm not positive that they were the same ones that argued with him in the park, but they could have been."

"You aren't even sure they were arguing in the park, but they could have been."

"Today I asked you who they were from your window, Zack, but you didn't know them."

"And that makes a difference? I don't know everyone my brother speaks to."

"I realize that. But after I left your office, I saw one of them exchange something with James while the other one watched to make sure no one came close."

"But, of course, he didn't see you." Zack's tone was derisive.

"I backed against the wall."

"You think they have a little fence operation going?"

"I . . . I don't know. I wasn't close enough to see exactly what they exchanged. But it looked suspicious because of the way they acted."

"He could have been handing over secret documents or perhaps a package of chewing gum."

"Yes, I suppose. But it looked—"

"I know, Brenda. It looked suspicious. Now, after your brilliant discovery of my brother's past, everything he does looks suspicious."

"Not so. But he threatened me again today. He keeps holding this . . . this stupid thing over my head. Why would he do that if he didn't have something to hide?"

"I don't know. Maybe because he's right. It's none of your business. Maybe he wanted to protect me from knowing the woman I was sleeping with was also putting the moves on him!"

"No! I didn't! I wasn't!"

"Oh no? Sounds like you were milking us both for your own pleasure."

"Zack! Surely you trust me more than that! I'm telling you—"

"I know what you're telling me," he said as he picked up his jacket and headed for the door. "You've enticed both brothers. And now you want to get rid of one."

"Oh God, that's not true! I love you, Zack!"

"And I love my brother. You're a fool for trying to come between us." He walked out, leaving her staring, too shocked to cry, too stunned to move.

The web was ripped to shreds. And she had done it.

Zack's words echoed in her head all night. *You're a fool for trying to come between us . . . a fool . . . a fool.* And Brenda knew she was. She'd handled it all wrong. She'd been a fool. But she loved Zack and would do anything because of that love. Even be a fool.

The next afternoon, Friday, Padraig called her in.

"Brenda, Mr. Ehrens has requested that you be removed as his liaison. He thinks you've done the bulk of the work necessary to get Ehrens Enterprises started and any future problems can be handled through me." Padraig looked at her kindly and smiled. "He complimented your efforts highly and said you did a bang-up job for him, but were no longer needed."

She felt a jab in the pit of her stomach, but sat perfectly still and watched Padraig through stricken eyes. "No longer needed? Zack said that?"

"I think he's probably right, Brenda, although I can understand your reluctance to let this novice business flounder on its own. However, there comes a time when the mother eagle must let go while the fledgling learns to fly. She hopes it will soar, but must stand back while it flaps ungracefully." He chuckled in an effort to lighten the situation, for they both knew she was being fired from Ehrens Enterprises.

"I see."

"Don't despair. I need you to take over another project. I have here a folder on a small group of investors from Connecticut who want to start an auto seat cover business here. Take it home and review it. Report to me on Monday and we'll discuss . . ."

Brenda took the folder from Padraig's hand and left his office in a daze. One thing was perfectly clear. Zack Ehrens didn't need her anymore.

CHAPTER SIXTEEN

Brenda was back to her bicycle. At this point, there was no way she would continue to drive Zack's green monster around town. Today she had slipped her key to it beneath his apartment door before she headed out to Aunt Brigid's.

It had been a rather cold ride, even though the sun was trying to filter through a layer of winter fog. She slapped her gloved hands together as she walked toward the quaint, thatch-roofed house and thought she should have brought her camera today. Oh well, they'd take a whole roll before—

"Saints preserve us, darlin'! Get yourself into this warm house! Why, it's as cold as a billy goat's horns today." Aunt Brigid ushered her grand-niece into the fragrant room and practically shoved her toward the fireplace.

Aunt Brigid bustled to get the tea kettle started. "I'll make you some tea to knock the chill from your insides, darlin'. Don't have shortbread today because I didn't know you were coming. But I have something just as good. Seedy cake." She lifted the lid from a black, cast-iron baker and a most savory vapor rose from the pan.

"Caraway-seed cake?" Brenda inhaled the marvelous aroma. "Oh, Auntie Brige, it smells delicious."

Her aunt smiled and her dancing blue eyes fairly twinkled with pride. "My Ned used to say it would cajole a dying man to eat."

"I'm sure it would." Brenda watched with curiosity as her chubby aunt slathered the cake with a dollop of pure sweet butter. It melted into luscious pools on the speckled surface of the cake. "And not a calorie in the pot!" she said, laughing. It looked delicious.

Aunt Brigid chuckled as she busily prepared them a snack of the hot tea and spicy seed cake. "Ah well, a person like me doesn't worry about calories, darlin'."

"Your food's too good to bother with calories, Auntie Brige." Brenda felt warmer and began to peel off her outer layer.

"Zack always liked my cooking. I'm sure he'd love this cake. Zack didn't come with you today?"

"No." Brenda's nose began to run and she buried it in a tissue.

"What about his brother? The prison one. He liked good cookin', too. Will he be coming out?"

"No."

"Well, maybe next week."

"No, I don't think so."

Aunt Brigid looked up curiously. "Are these men too busy to bother with an old woman, now?"

Brenda forged a stiff smile. "It has more to do with me than with you, Auntie Brige. Zack . . ." She shrugged and turned away, huddling next to the fire again as if a sudden chill ran through her.

The older woman dished up the luscious cake. "Ah, so you're telling me you're having man trouble?"

"Something like that," Brenda mumbled. She whirled around with a different expression on her face. "Auntie Brige, how would you like to go to America with me? I promised you a trip, and you've always said you wanted to go. We could be there in time to visit Gran Sadie for Christmas! Wouldn't that be a wonderful surprise?"

The knife clattered from Aunt Brigid's hand and she stared at Brenda. She fiddled with her apron and plopped down in her favorite rocking chair and pushed with her feet to rock furiously back and forth. "You mean to go now, darlin'?"

"In about a week or so. I really want you to go with me this time, Auntie Brige. Do you know how happy Gran will be to see you? How long has it been?"

Aunt Brigid shook her head slowly and mumbled to herself. Finally some words were audible. "Maybe twenty years. No, a little longer. Oh, to see Sadie again . . . what a wonder that would be. I thought . . ." She halted and tears quickly filled her blue eyes and tumbled onto her pink cheeks. "I thought we'd never get a chance to see each other again in this world. We're both getting on in years and it just seemed that we'd never get together again. I'd just about reckoned with that. But now, the thought of seeing that red-haired gal again . . ."

Brenda's blue eyes glistened. "Her hair's gray now, Auntie Brige. Gray like yours. There isn't much red left."

"Why, of course. She's near my age. I'll bet she's still a little wisp of a thing, though. She always was."

"Well, she doesn't have your wonderful seed cake and shortbread to eat. But, I'm sure she'd love to have

260

some. When you get there, you'll have to make it for her."

"I'd love to do that for my darlin' sister, Sadie."

Brenda grasped her hand. "You'll have to learn to cook on a fancy electric stove. But she'll show you all that. Oh, we're going to have such fun!"

Aunt Brigid looked up at Brenda with a teary smile and blue eyes sparkling with happiness. "You know she's still my sister, and I love her so much. Even after all these years of being thousands of miles apart, she has stayed close to my heart all this time."

"And you've stayed close to hers," Brenda said softly. "This'll be the best Christmas we've all had in a long time. Now our cake's getting cool. We can eat and make our plans at the same time. I want to bring my camera out here one day this week and take lots of pictures of everything for Gran. She'll love to see photos of where you live and of her beloved Ireland."

Aunt Brigid nodded and wiped her tears with the corner of her apron. "When do you plan to leave?"

"Soon as possible. I have some things to finish up first. I'll call the airlines and see what kind of flight I can get for us. I figure I'll be ready to go in about a week."

"So Padraig isn't in such a rush for you to go this time?"

"I'm not going on business, Auntie Brige. I'm going to stay. I'm moving back."

"I see." Aunt Brigid moved heavily to the table and quietly sipped her tea. "What about Zack? Is he going back to America too?"

"No. I don't think so. Not yet, anyway."

"Isn't he close to your heart anymore, darlin'?"

261

Brenda stiffened. "No, I guess not. We just . . . couldn't work things out, Auntie Brige. He . . . his brother is close to his heart. Not me."

"Well, I can certainly understand that," Aunt Brigid said softly. "But you'd think there was room for both of you."

"I'm afraid not."

People had been going in and out of her apartment for an hour before Zack burst through the doorway. "Brenda, what is the meaning of this?"

"Are we making too much noise for you? Sorry, I'll try to hold it down. This should be over in a few hours." Brenda turned away from him, making a great pretense of checking her clipboard.

Zack grabbed her arm. "Brenda, let's discuss this. What in the world are you up to?"

A short carrot-haired woman stepped between them. "Excuse me, miss. My brothers are here to take the table now."

"Right." Brenda nodded and directed the two burly men to the dining-room table, the one beside the window, overlooking the park.

"No!" Zack said loudly, stepping in front of one of the men who was lifting the table.

"Just ignore him. Go ahead and take your table." Brenda tried to pull Zack out of the way. "Zack, they've already paid for it. It's theirs. Move, please."

He stepped aside and looked at her wildly. "Don't you think this is a little extreme?"

"It's necessary, actually."

A skinny man with a very overweight wife stepped

between them. "Excuse me, miss. Hundred quid for the sofa?"

"Yes, that's right."

Zack jerked her elbow. "You can't sell the sofa!"

Brenda turned back to the man and accepted the cash. "Thank you, sir."

"Brenda, be reasonable. You just can't do this. Oh no!" He lunged toward a couple of elderly ladies who were taking turns sitting in the deep-cushioned chair. "Not that chair!"

"Keep it down, please, Zack." She smiled reassuringly at the ladies and pushed Zack's chest gently. "You're embarrassing me."

"Brenda, I think we should discuss this—"

A very old man with gray hair stepped between them and handed her some money. "For the bike. My granddaughter will be so happy."

"Thank you. Hope she enjoys it as much as I have."

"No! Not the bike!" Zack exploded, and everyone in the room turned and looked at him.

Brenda took his elbow and pulled him into the kitchen. "Look, Zack, either you be quiet or I'm going to have to ask you to leave."

"But you can't sell out completely!"

"Why not? I can't move all this stuff back to the States with me."

"To the States? You're leaving? What about us?"

"It won't work out, Zack. I'm sorry, but I can see where I stand with you. And James stands closer. I'm not blaming you. I understand about brothers, really I do. It's just that I can't deal with it anymore."

"We just need to talk about it."

"No. Every time we talk about your brother, the

263

past, your business, or my place in your life, we argue. We can't discuss any of that reasonably. There is little or no trust between us. I can't continue in this one-sided relationship with you. So, I'm taking the easy way out. I'm leaving. You and James can run Ehrens Enterprises to your hearts' content. Without me to interfere."

"That's quite a little speech, Brenda. Looks like you've figured this thing all out and made up your mind."

"Yes, I have."

"Well, I think you're being very narrow-minded and stubborn about this."

"Maybe. But I know where I stand. You made it clear I'm not wanted at Ehrens Enterprises and I'm not content to be the woman waiting at home for you, whenever you decide to return. I can't discuss anything personal or anything about your business with you because it's none of my business. So, my business will be in Baltimore. It's time I went back home, anyway."

A willful-looking woman stepped into the kitchen, dragging a freckle-faced, red-haired youngster with her. "The fiddle? How much?"

"The fiddle isn't for sale," Zack informed her.

"Yes, it is. Make an offer," Brenda said, stepping in front of him.

The woman looked at the kid, who was pouting his lower lip. Then she said, "I can only afford forty pounds. Then, there's his lessons." At the word "lessons," the kid groaned audibly and tried to pull away from his mother. But her grip was firm.

"Forty? Sold," Brenda pronounced.

"My God, forty pounds for that fiddle? That's preposterous, Brenda! It's worth much more. You can't sell it!"

"I just did." She took the money the woman offered and waved good-bye to them.

"Aw, Maw, I don't wanna . . ." the boy complained as they wove through the crowd in the living room.

"I . . . I can't believe you're doing this. Don't do it, Brenda."

"It's practically done." She smiled perfunctorily. "I'm taking Auntie Brige with me for a visit. She's so thrilled. It'll be the first time she's been to America. She and Gran Sadie haven't seen each other in over twenty years. Now, those two know about strong love."

"I'm sure they do." He raked his hand through his hair and watched helplessly as someone paid her for a lamp and trotted out happily.

"Much like you and James, Zack. They're close."

He looked at her distractedly. "Oh, God, I can't believe this is happening. There isn't a chance of you—"

"No, Zack. Not a chance."

He looked at her sternly for a moment, then wheeled around and stormed out of her apartment, nearly tripping over a little girl and her mother picking scarves out of a box of odds and ends.

"Dammit!"

The mother gave him a firm scolding as he tore down the stairs and outside the apartment building.

Brenda tried not to be affected by Zack's sudden

265

appearance at her sale. This had been his chance to say "I love you" and he blew it.

A young couple stood before her. "How much for the bed? We're going to get married soon and—"

"I'll give it to you as a wedding present," Brenda said with sudden tears in her eyes.

The young couple smiled gratefully and gushed their thank yous. Then they rushed to move the bed out of her apartment before she changed her mind.

"I'm as nervous as a cat scratching on a tin roof." Aunt Brigid wrung an Irish linen handkerchief between her sweaty hands.

"Don't be. Gran is probably just as excited as you are." Brenda watched the earth approach at rapid speed as they circled Baltimore.

"I should be happy. But the tears just keep coming."

"They're tears of happiness. I feel them too."

The plane jolted as the wheels touched down.

"Saints preserve us! What's that? We aren't breaking up, are we? Not when we're so close!"

"No." Brenda chuckled and patted her aunt's hand as it gripped the armrest between them. "We've landed. Won't be long now."

Aunt Brigid drew in a deep breath and muttered seriously, "Then I'd better dry up these blasted tears and get myself straight!" She dug into her purse and began to dab her nose and cheeks with a powder puff.

"You'll be seeing her in less time than it takes to tune a fiddle," Brenda said and helped her with the seat belt and to straighten her dress.

Within fifteen minutes they were meeting.

266

"My beautiful Brigid!"

"Oh, my darlin' Sadie!"

Two sets of matching Irish blue eyes met and crinkled with laughter. Two long-loving sisters embraced, squealing with delight and crying for happiness. They were a beautiful pair.

There wasn't a dry eye in the entire airline waiting area, including Brenda's. Everyone stopped for a moment to watch and share their joy. Then, it was America again and the crowds pushed past them, jostling and hurrying on their way.

Brenda wrapped an arm around each of the sisters. "I think we'd better go. We'll have plenty of time to get reacquainted at home." She steered them down the corridor.

Finally she moved behind them, listening to their animated conversation.

"I've got the evidence of all those years of shortbreads on me now, Sadie."

"Well, the gray has almost taken over my red hair, Brigid."

"Saints above, you're still beautiful to me!"

"And you're beautiful to me, too! Do you still fix shortbread like you used to?"

Brigid nodded. "I usually keep some around for company."

"Oh good. I've missed your good cooking so much . . ."

Brenda followed them, occasionally wiping a stray tear. She heard a radio blaring rock music and a teenager walked past her, carrying a large portable radio on his shoulder. Crowds of people bustled along in a steady stream, each hurrying on his or her way.

Snatches of conversation floated in and out of earshot, but of course, there wasn't an Irish brogue in the bunch.

They were in America. All sizes, colors, accents; land of the free. The melting pot. Brenda was back home.

So, I should be happy, she told herself. *I've brought these two people whom I love dearly together and wouldn't take gold for the moments we just experienced. And for the coming weeks together. I'm home.*

But she knew that wasn't true. Home was where the heart was, and her heart was still in Ireland. With Zack. She sighed and wiped another tear. She'd been a fool to get between the two brothers. Didn't James tell her blood was stronger than desire? Well, what about love? Was love stronger than anything? Apparently not for them.

Brenda knew, though, that no matter which turn her life took, Zack Ehrens would always be close to her heart. Always.

CHAPTER SEVENTEEN

Zack stood before the window in his office, his thumb and forefinger idly rubbing his chin. Lost in thought, his dark eyes reflected the deep problems he pondered. The business. His brother James. And an indescribable aching deep in his soul since Brenda left. One week, four days ago. To keep denying that he loved her was pointless. But she was gone now, and he knew that getting her back would take something spectacular. Someone else had moved into her apartment yesterday, finalizing her absence.

He hadn't seen his brother in almost three weeks, either. James had gone to Germany on business weeks ago and hadn't returned. He hadn't even called to report on progress.

Zack sighed heavily. Where the hell was James? And why had he virtually disappeared? Oh hell, knowing James, he'd show up one day and act as if nothing had happened. Nothing but the greatest loss Zack had ever experienced. The greatest heartache. But James knew nothing about that. Nor did he care, obviously.

Suddenly, Zack leaned forward and strained to see

through the window. Yes, it was James, making his way across the lower level of the plant!

He wore a hat with the brim pulled down and a leather jacket with the collar turned up, as if trying to disguise himself. He walked rapidly and looked around cautiously before ducking up the stairs. In another minute, he burst into Zack's office without knocking. He closed the door securely and with a brief nod in greeting, moved to the window and looked over the area he'd just traversed.

"Don't ask," James said. "I know what you're going to say, Zack. You want to know what's going on with me."

Zack folded his arms. "Yeah, it crossed my mind. Where the hell have you been?"

"You know me, Zack. I'm not going to tell you everything. But I'll tell you as much as I can, then I'm leaving."

"What are you talking about, James?"

James continued to stand with his back to the window, occasionally glancing over his shoulder, as if checking to see if he were being followed. "I'm leaving so I won't do it again. And so I won't drag you into it."

"Do what again? Man, talk some sense. Where have you been? And why are you acting as if the Mafia's after you?"

James chuckled bitterly. "How close you are, Zack. Hey bro, you look awful! Keeping late nights again?"

"You might say that." Zack nodded tightly. "So what are you up to?"

"First, I want you to know I talked with the German company. They're eager to do business." James

270

ran his hand nervously around the front brim of his hat, pulling it farther down over one eye. "They'll finalize the deal with you, but they want to see the operation first. I arranged for them to come tomorrow. Hope that's okay with your schedule."

"Yeah, yeah, fine."

"Here's the papers you'll need." James dug into his coat pocket for a couple of pages of scribbled notes.

"Well, that's great, James. I couldn't ask for more. I just wished you'd called and let me know how things were going. I was a little worried."

"Couldn't."

Zack frowned. "Why?"

James glanced over his shoulder again, then moved to a chair beside the desk and motioned to Zack. "Have a seat, bro. I'm going to make this quick. I don't want you involved in my dealings anymore."

"Involved in *what?*"

"I can't tell you. All I will say is that my friends, er, my associates traced me here. They started putting pressure on me again. That's why you had the explosion. It was a warning to me, not to you. But I won't stand for it. Not anymore. So I'm skipping out. I can see the trouble I've already caused. And the havoc between you and Brenda."

Zack's face tightened as he watched James's nervous actions.

"All I'll say is that Brenda was right on a lot of things. You were a damn fool not to listen to her. I guess I have to take the blame for that, though."

"You aren't to blame for anything between me and Brenda."

"Oh yes I am." James shook his head regretfully.

271

"It was a stupid thing for me to do, but she was convenient and I thought, oh hell, I don't know what I thought. If you're wondering what happened between us, nothing did. A kiss and that's it. She and I never did hit it off together. She's a damn good woman. And, if you didn't already know it, she loves you. So, when I leave, you two need to patch things up."

"She's already gone."

"Gone where?"

"Back. To Baltimore."

"Oh hell." James stood up and gazed through the window again. "Well, you know more about women than I do, bro. You know what to do to get her back. And you won't have me around to drag you down."

Zack stared dumbly at James. Hell, if he knew what would get her back, he'd already have done it! Now she was gone and James was admitting—what? Guilt? He felt as if someone were pounding his chest with a sledgehammer. He ached so bad, he wanted to yell obscenities at the top of his lungs.

He was torn between wanting to grab James and beat him senseless or boosting his morale with a strong, encouraging arm around his shoulders and the favorite cliché, *Everything's going to be all right. We're going to make it happen.* At this point, even Zack didn't believe it.

"Look, Zack, I don't want you to think I'm not grateful for everything you done for me. Not just this time, but *every* time. That's why I'm leaving. So you can get on with your life. And I can get on with mine without you. Without ruining everything for you."

"You aren't ruining everything, James." In spite of

272

the nagging reality that James needed to be in charge of his own life, Zack resisted.

"Oh yes, I am. I have in the past and I'm on my way to doing it again. If I stay around, it'll happen. It's inevitable. So, thanks for everything . . ."

"Hell man, you can't leave like this. Where will you go?"

James gave him a proud little grin. "I have a plan, bro. I know somebody who'll get me on with a small electric company in northern California. Stringing wires and putting up poles. Making repairs in remote areas. That sort of thing."

"You can't do that, James!"

"Sure I can. What do you think they taught me during this last stretch in prison? Not much money in it, but I figure that'll be in my favor, too. Plus, it'll get me out where I can do some thinking. And give me a chance to get my life straight, by myself."

"But what if—"

"What if they follow me?" He laughed dryly. "I have that figured out, too. When they see my paycheck and find that I have no access to the company's money, they'll leave me alone. There'll be no more reason to extort a poor, hard-working lineman."

"Extort!" Zack felt as if he'd been belted in the stomach. With a sudden flash of clarity the bits and pieces of James's past fell into place.

"I'm not telling you any more. I'm getting out before I reveal too much. Good luck with the business. And with Brenda."

James extended his hand, and Zack grabbed it. Then the two brothers fell together in a terrible wrenching embrace that was choked with emotion.

James tore away first. He stopped at the door. "She likes poetry and roses . . ."

"Stay in touch, James. Let me know if you need anything. Money or anything!"

"I'll write." James slammed the door and was gone.

Zack groaned low and lunged for the window to catch another—last—glimpse of James. He felt as if he'd been in an actual fistfight with his brother, and they'd both lost. In that moment, while watching James walk away, Zack thought his heart would split apart.

At the same time, he both hated and loved James. Maybe hated him more.

James had spent the last half hour admitting guilt, or at least partial responsibility for many crises in Zack's life: the bankruptcy in California which led to the dissolution of his marriage, the explosion in the converter, the near-expulsion of his business here in Ireland, the parting with Brenda. *Oh God, how could James have allowed all this to happen to his own brother? Worse yet, how could he have caused some of it?*

Zack wondered if he could ever bring himself to forgive James. His large fists knotted by his side and he flexed them, then drove his right fist into his left palm. Again and again. The sweep of confused feelings wracking his body right now was unbearable. He had lost them both. His brother. And Brenda.

His heart continued to ache for her. She was his greatest loss. Ever.

Brenda flopped wearily across her bed and buried her face in the pillow. In the blackness behind her eyes, she saw his face.

Three and a half weeks. That's how long she'd been gone, how long it had been since she had seen Zack, looked into his deep, dark eyes . . . touched him. But it had been even longer than that since he'd held her.

At least when she still lived in the apartment, they were only a staircase away, and there'd always been a brief chance of running into him in the hallway. Now, thousands of miles of ocean separated them. And there was no chance of seeing him. Ever again.

Brenda answered the soft knock on her door. "Come on in. It's open."

"I hope I'm not intruding."

"Oh Gran, you're never intruding. Come in."

Her grandmother sat on the edge of the bed. "I understand from Brigid you were offered a job today."

"Yes," Brenda said, propping up on her elbows to talk to her grandmother. "Secretary to a real estate broker at Williams and Co. The owner, Todd Williams, wants me to work for him. He was impressed with my credentials. I didn't tell him my typing stinks."

"Williams and Co.? They're pretty big in Baltimore. I'm impressed, Brenda."

"I haven't decided whether to take it. I'll call him tomorrow."

"What is there to decide? You want the job, don't you?"

"I don't know what's wrong with me, Gran. Of course I need a job, with Christmas coming and the present state of my financial affairs. I should be grateful for this job." Brenda sighed and laid her head back down on the pillow.

"Aren't they offering enough money?"

"No, that's not it. It's a good salary. I just wanted some time to think about it."

"You want to talk about it, Brenda?"

Brenda complied with her grandmother's wishes. "It seems like an interesting enough job. I'd have my own office and it's spacious and well decorated. I'd have access to a company car. Don't know what I'd do with the one I just bought."

Sadie stroked her granddaughter's auburn hair. "No, darlin'. I don't mean the job. Do you want to talk about whatever's bothering you?"

"Nothing." Brenda's words were muffled against the pillow.

"Oh, come now, darlin'. I've known you long enough to know you aren't happy. Something's bothering you. If it has to do with the job, or working here in Baltimore, don't feel that you have to stay here because of me. If you want to go off to California or somewhere exotic to find a job, that's fine with me. I'll certainly understand."

"It's not that, Gran. Honest. I don't want to go anywhere else."

"I don't know if I believe that." Gran Sadie sniffed and caressed Brenda's hair again. "I think you'd like to be somewhere else. According to Brigid . . ."

"Well, ignore Auntie Brige. She doesn't know everything!"

"Brenda!"

"Oh, I didn't mean it to sound that way." Brenda turned over on her back and stretched. "She's just a little overly romantic, and you know it."

"Who mentioned romance?"

Brenda started giggling. "Me! That's who! All right, you got me. So just forget it! And help me forget him . . ."

Gran walked over to the second-story window and peered out. "A cab? Now who would be coming here in a cab? Maybe your parents decided to surprise us. No, your father would never pay for a cab to drive him here." She held her finger up, telling Brenda to listen. "Whoever it is, Brigid is talking to them."

Then they heard a sound. A squeaking, screeching noise. A noise drifting upstairs, turning into music. A song, familiar, yet foreign. Then, they recognized it. "My Wild Irish Rose."

"Oh! Oh-oh-oh!" Brenda bolted off the bed and uttered the only words she could think of as she passed Gran and ran down the stairs. On the bottom step, she halted, holding her wildly pitching stomach.

There, in her grandmother's living room, stood a stranger playing "My Wild Irish Rose" on a fiddle— *her* fiddle!

And Zack.

He stood there, straight and tall, dark eyes glowing with emotion. He walked over and handed her a single, long-stemmed red rose which, by now, looked fuzzy to Brenda. So did Zack, for her tears were impossible to stop.

"May I have this dance?"

"Yes." She could barely choke it out. She moved into his waiting arms.

He held her close and she could feel his heart beating close to hers. And hers literally pounded in unison with his! He felt so good she just wanted to press him into her, body and soul. God, how she loved him!

"What are you doing here, Zack?"

"I missed you."

"I missed you, too, but—"

"Sh, we'll talk later. Just hold me now."

And they waltzed around the living room while Aunt Brigid and Gran Sadie watched, smiles etched upon their beautifully lined faces, hands clutched to bosoms, remembering.

As the last strains were playing, Zack cleared his throat and said, so all could hear, "I love you, Brenda O'Shea."

The sisters applauded and melted into awed exclamations while the fiddler launched into "When Irish Eyes Are Smiling." Halfway through the classic Irish tune, Zack left Brenda by the staircase and reached for a startled Aunt Brigid and whirled her around the floor.

When the song was over, the musician walked over and gave the fiddle to Brenda. She murmured a barely audible, "Thank you, it was beautiful," as he bade them all good luck and went back out to the waiting cab. She raised the instrument to Zack. "My fiddle? This is my fiddle? But how—" Her eyes searched Zack's.

"I bought it back from the woman before she could get away." His eyes twinkled. "Saved the kid from hours of torture, I'm sure. I would have bought everything back if I could have found all those people who came to your sale."

"But why?"

"Because I love you, Brenda. And I want you and all your stuff back."

"But Zack, I—" She stared at him, shaking her head. "Don't understand all this."

"I'll explain later. Now, would you introduce me to your grandmother?"

She obliged. "Gran, this is Zack Ehrens. Zack, my grandmother."

"Zack, please call me Gran. I have a feeling we're going to be friends."

He took her frail hand. "I hope we'll be in the same family soon, Gran."

"Zack!" Brenda said. "Until this moment, I've never even heard you say you loved me!"

"I meant it all along. I just didn't say it."

"And there's been no proposal."

He dropped Gran's hand and reached for Brenda's. "Will you marry me, Brenda?"

"I . . . I don't know. I have to think. This is too much, too fast for me."

Aunt Brigid spoke up. "Saints above, it's not too much for me. I'd say it's about time, young man!"

They all laughed, and Brenda looked at him with wonder and curiosity. And undeniable love.

"As you can plainly see," Zack explained to the sisters, "Brenda and I have a lot to discuss. So, if you'll excuse us, I'd like to take her out to dinner."

"Of course," Gran said, patting Brenda on the shoulder. "I think we understand more than she does."

"Uh, I need to, uh, get my shoes," Brenda stammered.

"And I'll call a cab," Zack said.

"We can just take my car," she said automatically.

"You have a car? Already?"

"Over here, you have to have a car. I thought I was staying."

"I hope not."

"Zack, I—" She looked down at the beautiful crimson rose in one hand. And the fiddle in the other. "I don't know what to do."

"Get your shoes."

She handed the rose to Gran and the fiddle to Aunt Brigid. "Would you find a vase for this? And a place for this instrument?"

"Of course." Gran Sadie smiled graciously at Zack. "It's a beautiful rose, Zack."

"For the most beautiful woman in Baltimore."

Zack took Brenda to his hotel.

"Dinner?" she questioned with a knowing smile.

"So we can talk privately." He unlocked the door and she walked into a gorgeous suite, complete with a dozen crimson roses on the dresser, soft music, and chilled champagne.

"Zack . . ."

"Yes, I want to love you, Brenda. I want to show you how much I love you." He gestured to the champagne in the cooler. "I was hoping we could toast our reunion. I've been sick without you, Brenda. I've never known this kind of pain."

"Zack, the last time we talked . . ."

"I've never been so miserable in my life. I was a fool to let you get away. I realize it now. Even James said so." He uncorked the bottle and poured them each a glass. "To us, Bren."

She toasted his glass and sipped. "Zack, this is all

very nice, but I don't think it can work. What about—"

"James?"

She nodded silently.

"You were right all along. It's been damn hard for me to see it. And to admit it."

"Right about what?"

"About James. And his shady involvement in my businesses."

"How do you know for sure?"

"He told me."

"Oh, Zack . . ." She looked at him with sympathy, knowing it must have hurt like hell to hear such a painful admission from James.

"I realize that all along you were trying to warn me out of love and nothing else."

"And you resisted believing anything bad about your brother for the same reason. I understand that."

He set his glass of champagne down and took hers. With slow, secure hands, he framed her face, caressing her cheeks with his thumbs. "Do you understand that I love you? Do you believe me? I love you more than anything. More than any*one*. And I need you with me, Bren."

"I love you, too, Zack," she whispered as his lips came down to claim hers.

Soon they were on the huge, king-sized bed, kissing and touching each other. His hands fumbled for the buttons on her blouse and she helped discard it. Then the skirt. Then her underwear and pantyhose.

She was beautiful, a pale, red-haired beauty waiting for him on the flowered bedspread. Crimson-tipped breasts, thrusting upward and eager. Silky skin, unmarred by tan lines or freckles. A triangle of strawberry hair at the juncture of her long, shapely legs. He couldn't undress fast enough.

They came together in a rapid heat, each exclaiming words of passion and love and unsatisfied longing. And separation that was unbearable. "Never again," he muffled against her heated skin. "We'll never be apart again. Not if I can help it."

"I've missed you so. Missed your touch, your arms around me."

His moist kisses left her weak and wanting more. His hands caressed gently, his lips brushed her with velvet, his tongue stroked sensitive areas. "Brenda, my beautiful Bren, I can't believe we're together at last."

"Oh, Zack, touch me there again." She writhed in pleasure and took his hand and moved it erotically over her. "And here. Ohh . . ."

He obeyed and found himself wrapped in her exquisite warmth from which he never wanted to escape. "Hold me, Bren."

Her hands stroked his back, moving sensuously all the way down to his buttocks. Continuing to stroke over the slight curve of his hips and to the intimate parts of his thighs. "Oh God, Bren—"

He rolled her to her back and thrust against the soft pliancy of her femininity.

Almost immediately he was inside her, stroking her most sensitive areas with his unrestrained strength, plunging deeper each time. Together they rocked, reaching a breathless rhythm of love and keeping the beat hard and hot until she cried out in ecstasy, "Zack! Zack!"

He urged harder, faster, then with a low moan, joined her frenzy, burning his love deep into her soul.

Slowly the wildness subsided, and they relaxed and curled together, two lovers finding each other again.

"Did you really mean it, Zack?"

"What, my love?"

"That we'd never part again?"

"Absolutely. I came to take you back. And I won't go until I can."

"Zack?" She sat up suddenly. "Who's minding the store back in Ireland? James?"

"No. Padraig helped me hire a plant manager. James has gone back to California."

"What's he doing there?"

"Finding work by himself. And possibly finding himself. I hope so." Zack stretched on his back, locking his hands behind his head.

He was a gorgeous masculine creature, and Brenda gazed at him in frank admiration. He was the man she loved, the man who loved her. And he was here. She never wanted to let him go.

"I hope so, too. I honestly do. Zack, I want you to know that I do care for James. He is an appealing man. After all he looks a lot like you, yet he's vulnerable. I think what actually developed between us was a sort of strange love-hate relationship. I loved him because he was your brother and similar to you. Yet I hated him for what he was doing to you."

He reached up and touched her lips with gentle, caressing fingers. "You don't have to say those things. I never really believed what I accused you of."

"I just wanted you to know."

"I know." He kissed her again. "Before he left, James spoke very highly of you."

She raised her eyebrows. "He did?" She flashed back to that last, awful conversation she had had with James in the parking lot when she implored him, *Don't you love Zack?*

"Yes. And he said you liked roses and poetry. That's why I brought roses. But poetry . . ." He leaned back on the bed laughing. "I'm afraid I'm not much of a poet."

She hovered over him, letting her nudity tantalize him sensuously. "I love you just the way you are."

He reached for her but she slipped out of his hands and grabbed their champagne. "I'm thirsty. How about you?"

Laughing at her antics, he agreed. "Yes, I want anything you want. Do you know how long it's been since I've laughed?"

"Weeks? Months?"

"Eons! There had been no laughter in my life, Brenda. Now, there is you!"

They entwined their arms and gave each other a drink, spilled it on nude bodies, then laughingly licked it up. "Oh, Zack, I love you so!" She started giggling. "Wouldn't Auntie Brige be shocked if she could see us now! We're supposed to be out to dinner. But here we sit in the nude, sipping champagne!"

"Thank God she won't have to. But we can call for room service when you're hungry."

"Sounds great. Suddenly, I'm starved."

"How do you like your steak?" he asked as he picked up the phone.

"Medium rare!" She sighed, gulping the rest of her champagne while he ordered.

He replaced the receiver and refilled their glasses. Then, with a folded hand towel over his arm, he stood stiffly beside the bed, extending the glass of bubbly. "I salute the most beautiful eyes in all of Ireland and Baltimore. I've come here as an envoy from the Republic of Ireland to offer you your old job back. Padraig said something about seat covers."

She grinned at him, standing there so formally in the nude. "I appreciate the offer, but I have a job offer here. Anyway I've already bought a car."

"Sell the thing. The green monster will be at your disposal, m'lady."

"But where would I live? I've sold all my furniture and my apartment has already been rented."

"You would live with me. In a little house by the Irish Sea."

"Is this a proposal or a poem?"

"It's the closest I'll ever come to a poem. But I'd say or do anything to persuade you to marry me, Bren."

"Zack," she said softly. "Do you know how absolutely silly you look? Proposing to me in the nude with a towel over your arm and holding a glass of champagne!"

"This is not the story one passes down to the grandchildren—or to grandmother and great-aunt, for that matter. But I've never been more serious in my life. Brenda O'Shea, I love you with all my heart, and I want you to marry me and come live with me in Ireland."

"Yes."

"Did I hear that correctly—yes?" He discarded the towel and set his champagne on the table and grabbed her up in his arms and whirled her around and around the room. "I have never been so happy in my life!"

"Me, either!" She shrieked and clung to him. "I'm dizzy!"

Finally, they fell breathlessly onto the bed.

"I don't know if I'm drunk or dizzy," she said, laughing, laying her head on his chest.

"Both!" He kissed her fervently.

"Zack," she murmured between kisses. "Could we get married in Ireland? In the little church in Rathcoole where Gran Sadie married Grandpa Walt?"

"Of course. Wherever you want."

"And could we honeymoon in the little house by the sea?"

"Anything your heart desires."

"My heart desires you for the rest of my life."

"You've got it. And me." He kissed her again, and she melted against him, pressing their hearts together. "This is where I want you forever, Brenda. Close to my heart."